Challenge
in Mobile

A Dave and
Katie Adventure

Kit and Drew Coons

Challenge Series Book Three

Challenge *in* Mobile

A Dave and Katie Adventure

Kit and Drew Coons

Challenge in Mobile

© 2018 Kit and Drew Coons

ISBN: 978-0-9995689-9-6

Library of Congress Control Number: 2018907832

Scripture quotations marked (NIV) are taken from the Holy Bible, New International Version®, NIV®. Copyright © 1973, 1978, 1984, 2011 by Biblica, Inc.™ Used by permission of Zondervan. All rights reserved worldwide.

Illustrations by Julie Sullivan (MerakiLifeDesigns.com)
Design: Julie Sullivan (MerakiLifeDesigns.com)

First Edition

Printed in the United States

23 22 21 20 19   1 2 3 4 5

To all who persevere in difficult circumstances
for the good of others.

Not only so, but we also glory in our sufferings,
because we know that suffering produces perseverance;
perseverance, character; and character, hope.

Romans 5:3–4 (NIV)

Acknowledgments

———•———

This novel would not be possible without professional editing and proofreading by Jayna Richardson. All the artwork and formatting are by our graphic designer, Julie Sullivan. We also thank our reviewers, Leslie Mercer and Marnie Rasche, who read the manuscript and made valuable corrections and suggestions. CPA Kevin Freier helped us to understand some accounting terms and provided a tour of the firm at which he is a partner. Walter and Rita Bryant, former residents of the Gulf Coast, provided color and details into that wonderful region.

Mobile, Alabama

Spanish Fort

Tunnels, Bridges, Causeway

Eastern Shore

O Fair Hope

➡ **Pensacola**

Mobile Bay

Fort Gaines

Dauphin Island

Fort Morgan

Gulf Shores

Gulf of Mexico

Artificial Reefs

 Mobile Bay

Principal Characters

Dave and Katie (Grandkate) Parker

Jeremy and Denyse Parker • son and daughter-in-law of Dave and Katie

Katelyn • two years old, daughter of Jeremy and Denyse

Dingo and Beatrice Larkin • Denyse's parents

Caleb and Jordan Fogle • Dave and Katie's neighbor and Denyse's principal

Herschel and Candace Johnson • accountant and homemaker

Dorothy Goldsmith • secretary/receptionist

Tom and Randy • Dave's former partners

Buddy (Thunder) and Mary Oleson • former police chief from Washita, Minnesota

John and Ellie Foster • pastor from Washita, Minnesota

Jeremiah Wallace • bombastic political leader

Lightning • Captain Stewart in the militia

Mr. Timothy Jackson • one of Herschel's clients

Anthony Marshall • one of Denyse's students

Harmon Floyd • Mobile's chief of police

Dan Hunt • Mobile's mayor

Mark Whitten • FBI agent

Old Yeller • cat from Minnesota

Ripper • Labrador retriever

Dave and Katie's House

Chapter One

Dave Parker stared intently at the computer screen that displayed a spreadsheet of numbers and cryptic descriptions. Beside the computer a pad of handwritten notes to himself recorded his observations. An orange striped short-haired cat slept on a nearby easy chair.

Katie, his wife of thirty-eight years, came into the bedroom he had converted into a makeshift office. She sat down at a table strewn with documents and references. When Dave didn't acknowledge her, she asked, "What are you working on?"

Without glancing away from the screen, Dave answered, "This is the embezzlement case I've been consulting on in Charlotte."

"Oh." Katie waited another minute. "I think there's something you'll want to know."

"I doubt that," Dave answered while remaining fixated on the numbers.

Katie gestured toward the sleeping feline. "Old Yeller threw up on the new carpet."

"Then I was right. I didn't want to know."

"Alright then, I'll leave you to your electronic mistress," returned Katie with some malice as she rose to leave.

Dave realized that the interruption signaled that Katie needed some attention. His concentration broken, he turned away from the screen and his notes for the first time in hours.

"Wait. Wait. I'll clean up after the cat."

"I've already cleaned up the mess."

This confirmed what Dave had anticipated about Katie needing attention. "So how are you doing today, love of my life?" he asked.

Katie turned around and returned to sit on the lap Dave had offered. "I'm not doing very well." Her lower lip protruded a bit.

"What's the matter, sweetheart?"

"If I knew that, I'd take care of it myself."

"Then what were you doing just before you came in here?"

"I was looking at the photos and video Denyse sent of little Katelyn. She's walking now and starting to use a few words. I just wish Jeremy and his family weren't so far away."

"I know what you mean. Australia could hardly be any farther away from Mobile."

"Do you think we could go there for Christmas?"

"Probably. Except when a trial is scheduled requiring one of my clients, I have to be available to testify."

Katie rolled her eyes. "I know."

"Let's you and I have an early dinner out this evening. You pick the restaurant," Dave offered.

Katie brightened. "A good idea. I'll get ready."

Dave suspected that the theme of their only son, Jeremy, his Australian wife, Denyse, and their daughter, Katelyn, would be part of their dinner conversation. Rather than return to his work, he turned on the news while Katie showered in preparation to go out. A national TV network featured crowds of African Americans marching and singing. A few whites sullenly watched from curbside. "Eyewitness reports dispute the policeman's account that he fired in self-defense. The citizen died on the way to the hospital," a broadcaster reported. The screen showed a picture of a young African American man followed by a photo of a Caucasian police officer. "The mayor and police chief of Mobile, Alabama, have appealed for calm."

Mobile, Alabama? Dave wondered.

The TV screen showed a late-middle-aged and harried-looking Caucasian man speaking into several microphones. A tall and burly African American in a dark blue police uniform stood behind him. Network technicians had superimposed *Mobile Mayor Dan Hunt* at the bottom of the picture. "Nobody should rush to judgment," the mayor warned. "I'm asking everybody to go home and await the results of an official inquiry." The mayor looked behind him. "Now I'd like to introduce Mobile's police chief, Harmon Floyd."

3

Dave could remember Harmon Floyd when he played defensive lineman for the University of Alabama. Harmon had then been drafted by the Green Bay Packers. A pre-season knee injury had ended his professional football chances. Every time he saw the chief, Dave recalled Harmon's dominance of the annual Auburn-Bama game with regret.

Chief Harmon stepped forward. Before he could speak, a reporter yelled, "Is it true that the body cam recorder is missing?"

The chief took a deep breath before speaking. "Somehow in the confusion the recorder has been misplaced. We're doing all we can to recover it." He looked directly into the cameras. "To those demonstrating in concern, I pledge to make a just evaluation of the facts. Please make certain that all public displays are orderly and law abiding."

"Katie, come look at this," Dave called.

She came into the den in a bathrobe with her salt-and-pepper shoulder-length hair wrapped in a towel. "What's so urgent?"

"Look what's happening in Mobile."

Katie stared at the TV in disbelief. "I thought things like this happened other places."

—◦◦◦—

The Mobile area offered a plethora of wonderful seafood restaurants. Katie selected her favorite at the marina where they kept their boat on the eastern shore of Mobile Bay. A summer breeze brought muggy air containing the odors of salt grass and exposed mud flats. Because of the early

4

hour, plenty of empty tables offered splendid views of the bay. After ordering a flounder entree, Katie chatted about the possibility of going to Australia for Christmas. "Maybe we could stay from mid-December until mid-January."

"That would be summertime Down Under and miserably hot," Dave warned. "The season wouldn't feel like our Christmas. And we'd miss our Cajun traditions like we did during our time in Minnesota."

"I don't care about the weather or any traditions as long as I get to see my granddaughter."

Dave gazed out the restaurant's shaded picture windows at Mobile Bay. Boats seemed motionless on the smooth brown surface. Various water birds patrolled the hazy blue sky. A seagull suddenly folded its wings to dive onto a school of mullet. "I'm glad we drove to the restaurant rather than walking. This June has been the hottest I can remember."

"Maybe we should take a day to go fishing," Katie proposed. "The ocean will have a nice breeze off the water. You've been working on consulting cases without interruption for more than a week. Even forensic accountants deserve a break."

"I did hear that the snappers are biting."

◄◆►

The phone ringing greeted the couple when they came home after dinner. Dave answered, "Hello."

"G'day, Dad!" The voice identified Jeremy.

"Hi, Jeremy." Dave waved for Katie to pick up the extension. "How are things in Sydney?"

"Denyse is a bit harried right now. Her students have exams coming again."

Katie broke in to ask about her granddaughter. "Have you and Denyse finished Katelyn's potty training?"

"We're trying. But Katelyn forgets to tell us when she needs to go sometimes. She *is* adding new words to her vocabulary nearly every day, though. Denyse manages to do more in any twenty-four hours than anybody else I know. Still, being a mother to Katelyn, taking care of me, and teaching is stretching her pretty thin."

Katie followed up with, "Do Denyse's parents visit often?"

"Occasionally. Beatrice and Dingo are on the road a lot speaking and promoting their book. They visit us whenever they're in Sydney."

Dave asked about Denyse's younger brother and Ukrainian wife. "What about Trevor and Lena?"

"They're fine and always ask about you. They'll never forget all you did to rescue them in New Zealand two years ago. Trevor is restricted to Melbourne due to the plea bargain you arranged. But his first novel is selling well. Lena opened a daycare center with her mother and younger sisters. She hasn't been to Sydney since not long after Katelyn was born. We haven't been to Melbourne, either," Jeremy admitted.

"Life fills up," Dave spoke from experience.

Jeremy's voice became more business-like. "Listen, Dad. The reason I called is that my company is closing their office in Australia. They're going to call me back to Atlanta."

"Will you look for another job Down Under?" asked Dave.

Jeremy's sigh could be heard over the phone. "I could. But there are plenty of Aussie accountants looking for work. They all know their tax codes better than me. And the entry salaries offered by Australian firms are significantly less than I made before."

"Then you're coming home?" Katie could not disguise the hope in her voice. "How does Denyse feel about living in America?"

"She's lived her whole life in Australia and is positively eager to experience life in the US. She only regrets leaving her students. But here's the thing. I've had enough of living in big cities. I'd rather not move back to Atlanta. That's why I was hoping you might inquire around for me about a position in south Alabama. I looked online but didn't see anything."

"What does Denyse think about living in a small city like Mobile compared to Sydney?" Katie asked.

Jeremy laughed. "I've filled her head up with so many stories about the bay and south Alabama that Denyse is the one who insisted that I call you."

Katie put down her phone, joined Dave, and demanded with exaggerated nodding for him to answer affirmatively.

"Sure, Son. I can ask around. But I can't promise anything. When would you be available?"

"The job here ends in mid-November. So about five months from now. I don't want to quit my current job until I have something else lined up. We could move to Atlanta for a while, if we had to."

Prudent and responsible. Just like his father, thought Katie.

"Email me your resume. I'll see what I can do," Dave promised.

Dave and Katie chatted a few more minutes with their son. Then Denyse came onto the phone. She and Katie talked about Katelyn and the possibilities of living in Mobile. Dave could hear female laughter from both ends of the line. He excused himself and turned on the TV.

After saying goodbye to Denyse, Katie found Dave watching a televised fishing show. She turned off the TV and stood in front of him with her arms crossed. "Why aren't you looking for a job for our son?" she demanded.

Dave looked at her with surprise. "He just called. And I need to think. Finding a job for him won't be so easy. Lots of young accountants are looking for work. They usually need to know somebody or move to a big city firm to get started."

"Fortunately for Jeremy, he does know somebody. He knows you! Can't you try your old firm, Bayside Accounting? You founded the firm and built the business. That has to count for something."

Dave shook his head. "Do I need to remind you that my partners and I had some major disagreements? That's why they bought me out four years ago."

"Okay. But aren't you still on friendly terms with Tom and Randy?"

"Sure, on a personal basis. But I hate to impose on our friendship to ask such a big favor."

Katie stepped closer to Dave. "Maybe they're looking for someone to hire."

"I really doubt that. I heard that they've lost some major clients in the last year."

Katie's voice became uncharacteristically authoritative. "Listen, Dave. I want my son, and my daughter-in-law, and my granddaughter living here. You need to find Jeremy a job in Mobile. I don't care what favors you must ask or what friendships you have to possibly jeopardize. Is that clear?"

Chapter Two

———•———

Dave knew better than to argue when Katie felt so strongly. "Very clear."

Katie turned the TV fishing show on again and went to peruse the internet herself looking for employment opportunities for Jeremy. She found nothing available locally for a young CPA.

Pondering the options to find a job for Jeremy troubled Dave. Lack of available jobs in the Mobile area had motivated him to found Bayside Accounting with two college classmates nearly forty years earlier. Employment opportunities hadn't changed much during those years except maybe more young CPAs looking for work. But he certainly couldn't blame Jeremy for preferring laid-back Mobile on the water over an inland metropolis like Atlanta.

The fishing show ended without Dave noticing. Once he did notice, he switched to a national news network still covering the racial unrest following the police shooting in Mobile. Fortunately, no reactionary violence had yet occurred. But a local activist had stirred up additional tension. A clip showed a gaunt middle-aged white man speaking into several microphones. Younger white men stood behind him with their arms folded. "I'm calling on the governor of Alabama to send in the National Guard to restore order in our streets."

A network reporter protested, "But the marchers have been peaceful."

"Crowds of people like these can turn violent in an instant. Should we wait until our homes and businesses are burning? If the state authorities won't act, then I call on the federal government. If they don't act, then patriotic Americans will be forced to intervene to protect their homes and families."

"That was Jeremiah Wallace, leader of White America, a political action group reputed to have links to white supremacists," the news anchor explained to his listeners.

—◆—

Anthony Marshall walked with throngs of fellow protesters. Barely sixteen, he had never felt so important, so noble. Stories about the heroes of the 1960s civil rights movement whirled in his mind. Now he, Anthony, walked where heroes had marched, standing up for justice not only for African Americans, but for all people. He could almost feel the heroes' presence with him. Somebody started an a cappella hymn, "Onward Christian soldiers." Anthony knew the words from church. He sang along with all his heart and lungs in the warm summer night. Blue flashing lights marked police squad cars monitoring the demonstration.

The next morning Dave phoned his previous accounting firm. One of his former partners surprised him by personally answering the phone. "Tom, this is Dave Parker."

"Dave!" Tom responded. "Randy and I were talking about you just the other day."

"Reviewing my mule-headed personality no doubt."

"No, no. Nothing like that. We reminisced about the good times we had starting the firm together."

"Yeah, those were pretty challenging years. Really tough but exciting all the same."

"So, what can I do for you this morning?" Tom offered.

"Well Tom, I'm calling to ask a big favor. Do you remember my boy Jeremy? He got his accounting degree from Auburn, like we all did."

"Of course, I remember Jeremy. Susan and I had always hoped he and our daughter might get together."

"Too late for that, I'm afraid. Jeremy took a job with an Atlanta company who sent him to Australia. He married a girl from Down Under. They have a little girl almost two years old."

"Congratulations. It's too late for our Gayle, too. She married a lawyer from the University of Alabama. They live in Birmingham."

"Sorry, Tom." Dave sympathized about Gayle's choice of a husband.

"Oh, he's not a bad kid, actually. Except during football season, he's insufferable."

Dave forced himself to laugh and took a deep breath.

"Anyway, Jeremy is coming home from Australia and hopes to find a job in the Mobile area. He's passed the CPA exam and has experience working with international trade. Is there any chance you could find an entry-level position for him?"

Dave held his breath waiting. Silence returned from the other end. Dave tried not to listen to Katie's grandfather clock ticking from their living room. *Tick, tick, tick . . .*

Finally, Tom spoke, "Uh, could I put you on hold for a minute, Dave?"

"Of course."

Canned music came over the phone as Dave waited. He could also still hear the clock ticking. After waiting awhile, he started counting, *one, two, three . . .* While he counted he thought, *It's not an outright rejection. Twenty-three, twenty-four, twenty-five . . .* He gave up counting as the seconds stretched into minutes. Dave envisioned a dial tone abruptly ending the music. *Would I call back?* he wondered.

Randy, his other former partner, suddenly came onto the line. "Dave, glad to hear from you."

Dave's stomach lurched. *This has to be bad news.* Randy had always been the most forceful of the three partners.

"Let's you, Tom, and I have lunch together," Randy continued. "Could you meet us at Luchino's? Say at one o'clock today?"

"Why sure. I can be there." The invitation perplexed Dave. Tom and Randy had always enjoyed taking clients to Luchino's Italian restaurant in downtown Mobile. But he wasn't a client.

"Great! Bring Katie along if she can make it."

"Got it. See you at one." Dave hung up. *What is that all about?*

Katie noticed a quizzical expression on Dave's face as he walked into the kitchen. "Any luck?"

"I don't know. They acted strangely. They invited me to lunch this afternoon at Luchino's. That's where Tom and Randy take clients to schmooze or to give them bad news. But I'm certainly not a client. They could simply have told me if there weren't any positions available. They even invited you to attend. I can't guess what that might mean."

"They invited me along too?"

Dave shrugged his shoulders. "I told you they acted a bit strange."

Katie put her arms around her husband and looked up into his face. "Dave, I know that calling them was difficult for you after Tom and Randy basically pushed you out of the firm. But I do appreciate your effort. And so will Jeremy whether a job with them works out or not."

"Anything for our son," he said out loud.

Katie squeezed Dave tightly. "And for me."

Dave acknowledged that by returning his wife's hug. "Especially for you."

—◆—

Katie and Dave arrived at the restaurant early to get a table. To their surprise, Tom and Randy had arrived even earlier and had a table waiting. They indicated to Dave and Katie the seats facing the restaurant's dimly lit interior, usually reserved for the most important clients.

They all made polite small talk after the waiter brought drinks and took their orders. Katie asked questions about the men's families. They in turn asked about Katie's cancer. She reported no reoccurrence. Tom and Randy queried Dave about his forensic accounting consulting business.

"The worst part is hanging around a trial venue waiting to testify or in case I'm recalled to the witness stand. In St. Louis, we had to stay for fifteen days," he told them.

"Both of you stayed?" Tom asked.

"I got so bored waiting in the hotel that Dave let me fly home after a week," answered Katie.

"How did the case turn out?" Tom and Randy leaned forward.

"The jury believed me rather than the defendant. They convicted him of a Ponzi scheme involving a barge-leasing operation," explained Dave.

Tom and Randy leaned back, happy to hear about one of their profession winning. The lunches arrived. Dave started eating, leaving the initiative to his former partners.

"You had called about a position for Jeremy," Randy began.

Katie felt her stomach tighten. The hope of having Jeremy, Denyse, and Katelyn in Mobile would not allow her to chew the pasta in her mouth, let alone swallow. She saw Dave nod casually.

"The truth is, Dave, that Bayside Accounting isn't doing very well. We've lost a lot of clients and had to let nearly everyone go."

Kate felt like her heart would break. *They won't have a position for Jeremy.*

"Who do you have left?" asked Dave.

"Just us and Dorothy that you know. And she only works three days a week." Neither Tom nor Randy could look Dave directly in the eye. Dorothy was a late-middle-aged receptionist and secretary who had been with the firm for more than three decades. Dave knew that the business could hardly operate without her.

"Didn't you have about twenty associates at one point?"

"Yeah," Tom admitted. "But we couldn't keep them on when we started losing clients."

"Their inexperience and sloppiness were the primary reasons we lost so many clients," Randy admitted with grimness. "Maybe Tom and I didn't check their work as thoroughly as you would have done."

"We still have one associate CPA," Tom offered. "A black kid from Auburn. We had given him all the African American bookkeeping accounts. None of them have dropped us."

They probably would have dropped you if the young man had been laid off, Katie thought. *That's why you kept him.*

In a level tone of voice, Dave clarified. "Then you don't have any place for Jeremy?"

Both of his previous partners shook their heads.

Katie looked down at her plate. Her disappointment felt overwhelming. The three men didn't seem to notice her despair.

"But telling you that is not why we invited the two of you to lunch." Tom tried to appear friendly and professional at the same time.

Dave waited without speaking or eating. Katie looked up from staring at her plate. Tom made eye contact with Randy and nodded imperceptibly.

"Dave," Randy began, "what would you think about buying out Tom and me? You would own the entire firm. Jeremy could be your first hire."

Katie looked up. *What?* she thought. She looked over at her husband, who appeared totally un-phased by the unexpected offer. *And I thought I was a poker player.*

Dave resumed eating. "That's flattering, Randy. But my forensic consulting has me pretty busy already. And I've been enjoying semi-retirement."

17

'Enjoying semi-retirement' is an odd description for the adventures *we've had the last few years,* Katie thought. She doubted Dave would be able to settle back into an office routine. Still, the thought of the calm years she and Dave had enjoyed before retirement intrigued her.

Tom spoke hopefully. "As sole owner, you could have complete control of Bayside Accounting. Run it the way you always wanted. Hire who you choose." He paused. "The truth is that you were always the heart of the firm, Dave. Randy and I are competent CPAs, but not brilliant like you."

Dave showed no reaction to the compliment or offer. "I don't think I could afford to buy both of you out."

Tom looked at Randy and tilted his head slightly toward Dave. Randy grimaced slightly and sighed deeply. "Dave, we would let you have the entire firm for three million dollars."

Dave maintained his expressionless posture. "That's what you promised me for my third. The end result would be the same as me having bought you both out for zero dollars."

Katie sat frozen in attention. *This could bring Jeremy, Denyse, and Katelyn to Mobile.* She realized that her mouth had gaped open and forced herself to shut it.

When Randy looked down at his plate, Tom resumed the offer. "We know that, Dave. But Randy and I each made a lot of money by using the associates during the last few years. Now we want to travel, visit our grandkids, and play golf." Randy looked up and nodded.

Chapter Three

Dave looked at Katie and saw hope in her eyes. "Does the firm have any legal liens or liabilities?" he asked his former partners.

"No, we settled those. But not many major clients are remaining either."

Dave used his napkin on his mouth before speaking. "We had amortized your buyout settlement to me into annual payments. I've only received about one million dollars so far. I assume the two million you still owe me would come off the three million?" Dave's former partners nodded again.

Dave sat thinking, *Since the revenue generated by the firm has dried up, they won't be able to continue making the annual payments to me. But because Tom and Randy owe that debt personally rather than the firm owing me, I could sue them and take their personal assets. They're trying to avoid bankruptcy and walk away with their retirement savings intact. I'm in a strong bargaining position.*

Then Dave remembered the friendship the trio had shared all the way back to their university days. He saw defeat in his friends' eyes and decided to not take advantage of them. "I'd need to look at your books and accounts before even considering the offer," said Dave. "I'd like to talk to Dorothy too. And after that I'd need a few days for Katie and me to consider the implications."

"Of course," both of his former partners agreed.

"Maybe I could start looking at your books this afternoon. Is Dorothy available today?"

"Today is one of her days off."

"Then tomorrow morning."

"Alright," Randy agreed.

—◆—

Dave walked around Bayside Accounting the next day. Photos and awards displayed remained as he remembered them. Large prints of sailing ships and English foxhunts decorated the walls. He thought the arrangement of artificial flowers on the mahogany conference room table could stand updating, or maybe just a little dusting. In the library, Dave felt soothed by the sight of orderly bound sets of regulations and file cabinets for the records of major clients. In the break room, he remembered celebrating Auburn's wins on the gridiron along with Tom and Randy.

The grim feeling of his last day working at the firm came back vividly. He had boxed his personal possessions and said farewells. Returning to his empty office, Dave had realized that there was nothing left to do but go home. *I do miss this place*, he thought. *My life's work is here.* The thought of Jeremy carrying on what he had begun made him feel hopeful.

Unlike the old days, the firm's offices did not overflow with the quiet energy of professional work. A young, slightly built African American man seemed lonely as he issued paychecks, reported sales taxes, and paid bills for about a dozen retail establishments from his cubicle. *Bringing the firm back to prosperity will be a big job. I can do it*, Dave assured himself.

—◦—

Katie met Dave at their front door on his return from Bayside Accounting. "So, what did you find out?"

Dave couldn't disguise his disdain about how Tom and Randy had ruined the business built over a lifetime. He shook his head in disgust. "I warned them that the relatives of friends and recent graduates of accounting school couldn't handle the complex accounts by themselves. The IRS found errors in the returns of some big clients, which severely damaged the firm's reputation. One audit as part of a lawsuit failed to discover several of the defendant's resources. All the major clients are gone.

"Tom and Randy are mostly back to filling out individual income tax returns the way the three of us started. In non-tax season, there's not enough net revenue to pay Dorothy's salary, the cleaning service, and utilities. Most of the current income is generated through bookkeeping by one associate, Herschel. It barely covers his and part of Dorothy's salary. There are no reserve funds. Tom and Randy already used them to pay the liabilities."

"Is the firm even worth three million dollars right now?" Katie asked.

Dave poured himself a glass of iced tea from the refrigerator and leaned back against the kitchen counter.

"No, it's not worth that right now. But the offices, the computers, and records are all intact. There are no debts. The tax and audit software only need the routine yearly updates. Rebuilding the client base and reestablishing the firm's reputation would take some time. The revenue justified a value of nine million before I left and received my third. With a few years of diligence and professional work, the business could be worth nine million again."

Katie followed Dave to the living room couch. "How many years is a few?"

Dave shook his head in uncertainty. "How soon we could even become self-sustaining would depend on a lot of factors—return of some of my old clients, Jeremy's ability, and some dumb luck."

Katie bit her lip. "Can you and I afford to buy out Tom and Randy?"

"We had to pay taxes on the buyout payments they gave us. Then we spent nearly two hundred thousand dollars Down Under a couple of years ago. That means we have about $700,000 remaining of the million Tom and Randy have paid us. In addition to the two million dollars they already owe us, we'd need to contribute $300,000 from our personal retirement accounts. And since Tom and Randy spent the firm's reserve, you and I would also need to front some operating money to keep Bayside Accounting in business until our revenue increased. Then first-quality work is the long-term way to bring in clients and build a business."

"How much operating money would you and I need to front?"

Dave shrugged slightly. "A few hundred thousand dollars

in addition to the purchase price. All that would take the biggest part of our savings."

"You've always insisted that we not risk our 401k and IRA money," Katie reminded Dave.

Dave agreed, "Yes, I have. That makes this a big moment for us. We need to make a good choice. So just how badly do you want to have Jeremy and his family here in Mobile?"

Katie thought to herself, *We could ruin ourselves financially.* But she answered, "Pretty badly."

"Enough to take a risk?"

Katie felt torn. "How much of a risk?"

Dave reassured her somewhat, "Not a total risk. We'll both still be eligible for Social Security and Medicare in a few years. And we have no debts. If the business totally collapsed and we lost all our money, we could still survive. I'd catch enough fish to feed us and Old Yeller. Or better yet, he could catch his own food." Hearing his name, the cat looked up from where he had been relaxing on a chair. *Rrrow.*

"You would like fishing full time for food, wouldn't you?" Katie teased. "But do you remember when we figured that with the cost and upkeep of the boat, marina fees, fuel, tackle, and licenses, the fish you brought home had cost us over two hundred dollars a dressed pound? You'd fish us into the poorhouse."

Dave chuckled. "Yes, I do remember figuring that." Old Yeller jumped up onto the couch between them. Dave reached out and rubbed him behind the ears. The cat rolled over for a belly rub. "Old Yeller is pretty spoiled, too. I can't see him eating a mouse or even fish scraps. I'd have to make the business a success to keep fishing and feeding this cat."

Katie smiled at Dave's acknowledgment of her objection and scratched Old Yeller's stomach. "But would you want to go back to working full time?"

"No. I like concentrating on something difficult and important. But I've grown accustomed to the freedom of working independently. It's just that Jeremy and Herschel aren't experienced enough to establish the quality of work needed to expand the business. We'd need to set some limits on my working hours."

Dave and Katie looked into each other's eyes for a long moment. Then she nodded. Dave in turn nodded himself. The decision made, Katie moved on to other issues. "I think I'll have Katelyn call me 'Grandkate.' "

"Oh, then what should she call me?"

Katie grinned with mischievousness. "How do you like 'Old Man'?"

—◆—

In their Sydney apartment, Denyse answered the phone to hear, "Hi Denyse. This is Dave."

"G'day, Dave." Denyse could not hide the hope she felt. "Jeremy's excited about the conversation he had with you a few days ago. Do you have any good news for us?"

"Maybe. Could you get Jeremy and put us on speaker phone? Katie is with me on this end."

"Hi, Denyse," said Katie.

"Good morning, Katie. I guess it's evening for you in Mobile. Jeremy just woke up here."

Dave and Katie heard their daughter-in-law shout, "Jeremy, your mum and dad are on the phone. They want to talk to both of us."

Denyse talked again while Jeremy came. "Katelyn called me 'Mum' again yesterday," she reported.

"You'll have trouble getting her to stop talking soon," suggested Katie.

"Hi, Mom and Dad. What's up?" Jeremy asked.

Dave outlined Bayside Accounting's dire financial position and the proposal he had received to become the sole owner.

"But the firm thrived before you left," Jeremy objected.

Dave explained, "Tom and Randy were good at socially networking and bringing in clients when we worked together. But after I left, they hired people fun to be around—like picking fraternity brothers—rather than the most capable accountants. And they especially looked for recent graduates whom they wouldn't need to pay a high salary. The difference between the cost of low salaries and the billing rate made plenty of fast money for my old partners. But the strategy caught up with them when the likeable young associates did sloppy work, which Tom and Randy didn't check thoroughly. If you want to join me, we'll need to do first-class work to regain the firm's reputation."

"Sure, Dad. I'd love to join you. But have you forgotten that my personality is a lot like Mom's? I'm a competent accountant, but not first class like you. I'd do better meeting clients like your old partners did."

"You're more conscientious than Tom or Randy. And we'd need you to handle some complex accounts. But as soon as our business increased, I could hire very detail-oriented associates to work for you. You'd become the firm's business manager."

"I could do that."

Dave added, "When I went into the office yesterday, they only had one associate remaining, Herschel Johnson. He says you and he went to Auburn together."

"Herschel Johnson is working at your firm? He's a genius. I hated having him in my classes because he raised the grading curve. I'd probably have made more As if he hadn't been at Auburn. Herschel is quiet and shy, but he was a lot more lucid than some of the professors. Some guys graduated because of Herschel's coaching."

"That's great. He's the only one bringing in any revenue to the firm right now. And if Herschel is as competent as you say, he can do a lot more difficult work than bookkeeping. We'll need to find new clients and serve them with excellence to return the firm to prosperity."

"Dad, what would you think about changing the firm's name from 'Bayside Accounting' to 'Golden Rule Accounting'? You know, 'Do for others as you would have them do for you.' That might attract clients."

"I'm okay with that as our goal, Son. But that standard might be too high for our name. People would judge us according to their expectations. A few might expect us to work for free. What we'll promise is consistent professional service and 'do for others' as a fringe benefit."

◄◆►

After the phone call, Dave and Katie tuned in to the evening news. "Racial tensions in south Alabama eased after Mobile's mayor and police chief personally promised a full inquiry into last week's shooting of an African American

26

juvenile by a white police officer," the national network's news anchor reported. "This followed several additional days of public demonstrations. The officer in question has been placed on desk duty pending the results of the inquiry."

Chapter Four

—•—

Five months later, Dave and Katie waited at Mobile's airport. Katie talked almost constantly to cover her excitement. "Our meeting Jeremy and Denyse at an airport rather than them always meeting us in Sydney feels funny."

Dave smiled inwardly at his wife's joy. As Jeremy and Denyse exited, Katie waved and uncharacteristically hopped in place. Jeremy carried Katelyn, who somewhat apprehensively surveyed the unfamiliar surroundings. Tear trails marked the child's little cheeks. Denyse pushed a cart with six large pieces of luggage.

Jeremy put down Katelyn while he and Denyse hugged Dave and Katie. After the hugs, Katie immediately knelt before her granddaughter. "Katelyn, you can't remember me. But I'm your grandmother. You can call me Grandkate."

The little girl recoiled from the stranger she perceived and took refuge behind her mother. "She's a bit out of sorts," Denyse explained. "Her ears started hurting when the plane began its descent. And everything is new to her."

"We're all pretty tired," Jeremy added. "That's a long trip, especially with a two-year-old."

"Your dad and I remember traveling with you as a two-year-old," Katie responded. "Every trip seemed to take forever."

"We rented an apartment for you as you had asked. And we've rustled up some furniture," said Dave. "Let us take you straight there to get some rest. Katie will drive you in the car. She's already purchased a car seat for Katelyn. And she's stocked your cabinets and refrigerator with things you might need. I'll bring your luggage in the truck. We've already put the boxes you had shipped in the apartment."

"Dad, I'll come with you and help with the luggage. The girls can all ride together," suggested Jeremy.

❦

"Spanish Fort is convenient to Mobile, where the office is located, and also close to our house near Fairhope," Katie explained in the car. "That's why we selected an apartment for you there. You can relocate when you find an area you like better."

"I think Jeremy has his heart set on buying a house," Denyse responded. "We've diligently saved for the down payment."

That's a good sign, thought Katie. *They're planning on setting down roots here.*

"You'll need to buy a car first," Katie said. "You can use

our car for a couple weeks until you find one you want."

"What will you drive, if we're using your car?" asked Denyse.

"We'll do fine with Dave's truck."

"You mean like a ute?"

"Yes, we say pickup rather than ute." Katie continued, "You'll need a couple of days to settle in. Jeremy knows the area. We'll let him show you around. Then Thursday, three days from now, is Thanksgiving. We would like to invite you for Thanksgiving dinner at our house."

"You mean a traditional American Thanksgiving, with the turkey and everything? I've always wanted to experience one. I served Jeremy pizza once for his Thanksgiving dinner in Australia."

"Yes, we'll have turkey and all the trimmings. If you could come about ten in the morning, you could help me with the preparations. We'll actually eat about three."

"I'd love that, Katie!"

"Of course, Dave and Jeremy will be watching football."

―◦―

"How's Auburn doing this season, Dad?" asked Jeremy in the pickup.

"Eight and three. About normal."

"Any chance against Alabama next Saturday?"

"Pretty good this year, I think."

"You always say that."

―◦―

After Dave and Katie had left them at the apartment, Denyse put Katelyn to bed. Curious to see American TV, she turned on the set Katie had furnished then joined Jeremy

31

unpacking the boxes of clothes and household items they had pre-shipped.

"Last night several establishments flying confederate flags were defaced with spray paint. The Daughters of the Confederacy monument was likewise defaced. This followed last week's appearance of nooses in areas frequented by African Americans, especially around Central High School. Tensions have remained high since last summer's yet unresolved shooting of a local African American by a white police officer," a local TV anchor reported.

"What does this mean?" she asked Jeremy.

"Probably nothing. Racial tension like this isn't normal in Mobile. I'm sure it'll blow over."

—◦—

Jeremy and Denyse arrived with Katelyn at Dave and Katie's house just after ten a.m. on Thanksgiving morning. Both senior Parkers met them in the driveway. Denyse brought Katie a gorgeous arrangement of white and yellow fall mums. "These will be perfect for the table," Katie thanked them both.

"What a lovely place. Everything is so lush and green," said Denyse. "And these trees with the branches spreading low. I've seen them in movies that take place in the American South. But they're much more majestic in real life. Their branches sometimes spread horizontally across a street. What are they?"

"These are called 'live oaks' because they don't shed their leaves in the winter like other oaks," answered Dave.

"What's the gray stuff hanging from the branches?"

"That's Spanish moss," Katie answered. "It's an epiphyte,

a type of plant that grows without roots by absorbing water and nutrients from the air."

"Is that how Spanish Fort got its name?"

"No, during the initial settlement of the Americas, men from Spain built a stockade on the high ground to protect themselves from Native Americans and soldiers from other countries."

Denyse noticed that Katie's eyes remained on Katelyn while she spoke. She nudged her daughter from behind. The little girl took a couple of hesitant steps toward her grandmother. Katie knelt. "And how are you today, honey?"

Katelyn retreated to her mother. Katie could not hide her disappointment. "She's acting shy in a new environment," said Denyse. "She'll get to know you very quickly."

"So, what have you done for the last few days?" asked Dave as they went into the house.

"Jeremy took us everywhere," responded Denyse. "We saw the bay and walked on a sandy ocean beach. We went on the World War II battleship named for Alabama and saw a lot of military equipment. Mobile has even had several battles nearby. America is more martial than Australia, I think." Without waiting for a response, she continued, "Jeremy had me try a delicious spicy Cajun food called jambalaya. People are so friendly. Even strangers say hello to us. Jeremy drove me by the big house where he grew up near downtown Mobile. It's in a neighborhood with *Gone with the Wind* mansions."

Katie smiled. "Hardly that. And that old house required a lot of upkeep. But it was convenient to Jeremy's schools and Dave's downtown office. We downsized to this house on the eastern shore when Dave retired."

"When would you like to start at the office, Son?" Dave asked Jeremy.

"He'd like to start next week, if that's alright," Denyse answered for her husband.

"Sure. We'll have a lot to do. I'm the legal owner starting Monday." The two men went into the den where they turned on pre-game football commentators while talking about the accounting firm.

Katie's eyes remained on her granddaughter. "I've got something for you, honey." Katie produced a stuffed toy in the form of an alligator. Katie reached out to hand Katelyn the gift.

"We saw a real one of these yesterday, didn't we Katelyn?" Denyse prompted. Katelyn stretched out both hands to take the toy and hugged it to herself.

In the kitchen, a high chair Katie had purchased waited. Denyse put Katelyn into the chair and then sprinkled a few pieces of cereal on the tray. Katelyn started reaching out to pick them up and put them into her mouth. Her eyes explored Katie's kitchen. "So where do we begin?" asked Denyse.

"You can help me bag the turkey before we put it in the oven."

"You cook the turkey in a bag?"

"The bag helps keep the bird moist during roasting," Katie explained. After bagging, she put the turkey in a roasting pan and opened the preheated oven. "Would you put the bird in here?"

Denyse placed the pan inside. Katie closed the door. "Next we'll make the oyster dressing. First, I'll need to make cornbread to soak up the oyster stock. You could peel some sweet potatoes for us to make candied yams." She pointed to a sack containing rust-colored tubers.

"Candied yams? How do they need potatoes?"

"Sweet potatoes are a type of yam. When we fix them for Thanksgiving, we add lots of butter, brown sugar, and a little cinnamon. After baking, we call them 'candied yams.' "

"This is fun, Katie. Mum never taught me much about cooking."

Katelyn became restless in her high chair. Denyse put her on the floor where she toddled around while Katie and Denyse chatted as they prepared the dinner.

A large orange cat sauntered in. Katelyn noticed Old Yeller first and approached him. The cat lay down for her to grab double fists full of warm skin and fur.

"Oh, is this the cat we heard about?" Denyse asked.

"Yes, this is Old Yeller. We brought him home from Minnesota. He's been around lots of children and never scratched one." Just then Katelyn poked one of the cat's yellow eyes with her finger. Old Yeller shook his head and moved a couple of feet away before he lay down again.

"We want her to love animals like Mum does," said Denyse. "Don't touch his eyes, darling," she told Katelyn. The child moved closer and resumed grabbing at the living stuffed animal.

—◆—

At three, Katie interrupted the men's football game. Dave and Jeremy came to the dinner table where Katie had asked Denyse to set out her fine china. "We use the china mostly at Thanksgiving and Christmas," she told Denyse. Jeremy moved the high chair near the dining room table and put Katelyn in it.

"Let me say grace," Dave offered.

Katie stood up immediately after Dave's prayer. "I forgot the cranberry sauce." She hurried to the kitchen, from where the others heard an electric can opener followed by a *plop* sound. Katie returned with a cylindrical burgundy-colored gel in a saucer.

"That's American cranberry sauce?" Denyse reacted. "It comes out of a can?"

Katie shrugged. "Not always. But most families use canned cranberry sauce."

During dinner Denyse placed some bits of food on Katelyn's tray. Her daughter enjoyed picking them up, looking at them, and putting most into her mouth. Old Yeller came to demand a serving. Katie placed some turkey on a saucer for him in the kitchen. After a wonderful meal, the men returned to the TV.

"Pecan pie later," Katie announced as Dave and Jeremy left the room. "I invited the Fogles over for dessert. They're serving dinner right now at a homeless shelter," she explained to Denyse. "Leave the dishes. Dave will clean them up later. Let's watch part of the game."

In the den, Denyse got her first introduction to American football. She saw padded groups of men smashing into each other. At least the oblong ball resembled a rugby ball. After observing several tackles, she asked, "They didn't hold the runner down. Why doesn't he pick up the ball and run again?"

"Once a man is tackled the ball is dead," Jeremy explained.

"Dead? You mean the ball comes back to life after the teams line up?"

"That's correct. Then it's considered a live ball again."

Two men then forced a ball carrier out of bounds. "That means the other team gets the ball, right?" Denyse questioned as she tried to follow the game.

"No, forcing a ball carrier across the sideline is the same as a tackle."

"Then the ball dies?"

"Right."

Denyse waved at the TV screen. "Now why are they stopping the game?"

"The referees called a time out so that the TV network could show a commercial."

"I thought maybe they were having a funeral for the dead ball," commented Denyse with a smile.

Chapter Five

———•———

Jeremy couldn't help but laugh at Denyse's observations of American football. Then he pointed to where Katelyn had fallen asleep on the couch. Denyse gently picked up their daughter and placed her on Katie, who sat in a rocker. Katelyn stirred slightly and then fell back to sleep content in her grandmother's arms. Old Yeller went over to Katie, found his favorite spot filled with the newcomer, and retreated to his heated box.

An hour later the front doorbell rang. "That's probably the Fogles. I'll get it," said Dave as he got up.

Denyse heard voices exchanging Thanksgiving greetings in the foyer. A late-middle-aged couple with dark skin entered. "These are our friends and neighbors, Caleb and Jordan Fogle. They took care of Old Yeller while we were Down Under." Dave then introduced Denyse and Jeremy, who had risen to meet them. "They're different from the rest of us." Dave let his words hang for a moment. "Caleb and Jordan are from the University of Alabama."

Jeremy groaned appropriately for an Auburn grad.

"Roll Tide," responded Caleb.

"Hey, we're all Alabama fans when they play out of conference," Katie contributed without getting up. To Denyse, Katie said, "Would you mind serving the pecan pie?"

While Denyse went to the kitchen, Jordan leaned over sleeping Katelyn. "This is your granddaughter? Isn't she pretty?"

All the men talked about football until Denyse returned with the pecan pie cut into six portions. "Whoa, honey! Half of that will be fine for me," said Jordan. The others agreed. Denyse returned to the kitchen. While she was gone, Katelyn woke to see strangers admiring her. She then looked up to see Katie's smiling face and snuggled more deeply into her grandmother's arms.

Soon Denyse returned with smaller portions of pie. She served them on Katie's china dessert plates. Katie took a little bit of the soft filling and offered it on a spoon to Katelyn. The toddler tasted the pecan pie and made a face. "She isn't used to something so sweet," explained Denyse.

"Caleb is the principal of Central High School in Mobile," Dave told Denyse. "While Jeremy grew up, Katie did a lot of volunteer work for Mobile's public schools. We found this house through the Fogles."

"I taught college—you say high school—maths in Sydney," Denyse responded. "I loved teaching. Most of my students came from disadvantaged backgrounds, like me. But with the right encouragement and some discipline they did well on their exams. Maths opened a lot of opportunities for them."

Caleb spoke earnestly to Denyse, "I desperately need a substitute math teacher next week. Our regular teacher is having unexpected surgery and will miss several weeks. I've called our regular substitutes but none of them are available so near the holidays. This is a bit unusual, but do you think you could help us out for a couple days at least? Substitute teachers aren't required to have a teacher's certificate from the state of Alabama."

"I'd love that. But I have a daughter to care for and Jeremy will be starting work on Monday."

"I could take care of Katelyn," Katie volunteered.

Denyse's face lit up with hope. "I'd love to teach some American teenagers."

"Most of them are African American kids. I need to warn you that some of them come from pretty rough home situations," said Caleb.

"You're African American too, aren't you?" asked Denyse.

"Yes, but I had more opportunities than most of these kids."

"Maths can make opportunities for anyone."

Caleb laughed. "Where did you get her?" he asked Dave.

Dave smiled at Denyse. "Jeremy had to go a long way to be so lucky."

Not deterred, Denyse asked, "In Australia, we're always seeing news items about American racism. Not saying that we

Aussies don't have our own issues of racial strife. But if I'm going to teach African American kids, I need to understand a little about the situation."

"That's a complicated issue, Denyse," answered Dave. "Modern-day racism probably has roots in our Civil War."

"That was about slavery, right?" Denyse persisted.

"Partly," Caleb answered. "Certainly, it was for all of the people of African descent. But there were also issues of tariffs and state sovereignty left vague by the original US Constitution. Actually, only a small percentage of southerners owned any slaves. Most southern men who fought did so because they saw armies invading from the North. Most northerners fought to preserve the concept of the United States as President Lincoln laid out in the famous Gettysburg Address. And few people know that slaves in some Union states weren't freed until two years after the war had ended. But the most important result of the war was the end of slavery."

"Our racial problems persist because prejudice had become part of the culture during slavery. And many whites blamed the former slaves for the suffering the war brought," Dave added. "Maybe the biggest reason today is that a lot of people simply mistrust and dislike people different from themselves."

Caleb sighed. "I'm afraid things are about to get worse."

"What do you mean?" asked Jeremy.

"At the shelter today, we heard that a young African American police officer shot and killed an older white man last night. I'm sure the news media is covering the story nonstop. We just haven't been watching."

On Monday morning, Denyse saw a huge, somewhat dilapidated school building. Groups of mostly African American students congregated outside the front doors and on the grounds. "This is Central High School," Katie told Denyse from the driver's seat. "I'll be back to pick you up at three."

"I'll be able to drive myself soon," Denyse said to Katie. "My Australian driver's license is good for several months. I just need to get used to driving on the wrong side."

Katie smiled. "You mean on the right side?"

"Of course. Goodbye, darling," Denyse said to Katelyn in her car seat. "Mum will see you in a few hours."

Katelyn, used to being left at childcare, answered, "Bye, bye." That her mother was the one being left this time didn't seem to faze her.

Denyse took a deep breath and entered Central High School. An hour later Caleb ushered her into a classroom of tenth graders. The activity and noise stopped as the kids saw a tall, striking young woman with a bushy chocolate-brown ponytail standing before them. He introduced her. "This is Ms. Parker. We're fortunate to have her in Mr. Busby's absence." To Denyse he whispered, "Remember, you can always call in the football coach if you have trouble." Caleb left the room.

"Dorothy, do you remember my son, Jeremy?" Dave asked the receptionist at Bayside Accounting.

A well-dressed lady wearing wide glasses with lanyards and a string of pearls smiled. "Of course. Jeremy, I remember you from when you were just a baby. Your father vacillated between being proud and insecure at the same time."

"Dad acted insecure?"

Never reluctant to evaluate a situation, Dorothy explained, "The responsibility scared him. Your mother had quit teaching to take care of you. Your dad had always been a hard worker. Once you were born, he doubled his efforts."

"Who would have anticipated that I'd be here working with you one day?" Jeremy said.

Dorothy laughed. "Me. When your father told me you had started studying to be an accountant, I hoped you'd work here someday. You remind me of your father thirty years ago."

"Thanks, Mrs. Goldsmith."

"Oh, you're all grown up now, Jeremy. Please call me Dorothy. Makes me feel younger."

Dave led Jeremy down the hall and into one of the former partner's enclosed offices. A slightly built man Jeremy's age stared intently at a computer screen. So intent was he that he didn't notice their entry. Dave waited a few moments and then cleared his throat. Herschel looked around and recognized Jeremy. His face broke into a big smile. "Jeremy! A long time since Professor Maples' accrual class." Herschel stood to warmly shake Jeremy's hand.

"I'll leave you two to catch up," said Dave. "Jeremy, your office will be right next to Herschel's. We'll have a staff meeting at one o'clock."

The two young men sat down. "How did you end up here, Herschel? I expected some big prestigious accounting firm to snap you up," Jeremy said.

"My fiancée's parents were elderly. She didn't want to leave them alone in the Mobile area. I had to find a job here."

"You had a fiancée while still at Auburn?"

"Sure. Why did you think I traveled home every weekend? We got married my senior year."

"Everybody thought you had holed up somewhere studying."

"Not hardly. Certainly not our senior year. I hear you're married too. And have a baby."

"I met Denyse in Australia. We have a two-year-old little girl, Katelyn. You and . . ." Jeremy didn't know Herschel's wife's name.

"Candace. She's named after the Ethiopian queen mentioned in the Bible."

"Do you and Candace have children?"

"Two, both boys, aged four and two."

"Congratulations."

The two young fathers sat in silence a minute. "Your father and you are going to be great to work for," ventured Herschel.

"Actually, we're both working for Dad. Even if I'm to eventually be the firm's business manager, I know you're a better accountant than me. I won't interfere with your work."

"Didn't you graduate from Auburn with honors?"

"Yeah, but you graduated with highest honors."

◄◆►

45

As soon as the classroom door closed behind Principal Fogle, bird whistles came from some of the boys among Denyse's first American pupils.

"Whichever ones of you galahs brought your myna birds to school can leave them home tomorrow," said Denyse in a rich Aussie accent. "Otherwise they might defecate on your dipstick work."

The boys, mesmerized by the strange and bold voice, quieted. They thought they might have been insulted but weren't certain.

Denyse handed a pad of paper to the student in the first row. "You'll expect me to call roll and try to remember your names. Then you'd have fun mixing up your names for the rest of the period. Let's try something different. Each of you sign your name, so we'll know who is present. If your American George Washington signs, he'll get credit for being here, but you won't."

"But I am George Washington," a voice came from the back.

"Fair dinkum, George. If you're sitting in the seat of a chap who is supposed to be here, better sign that student's name, or he'll get detention."

The students laughed. They had no idea how to react to such an unusual teacher. Denyse went on, "I grew up in a dysfunctional family with a mostly absentee father. Most of you have a better lot than I did. Maths gave me a decent chance in life. It can for you too. You can drop this class if you don't want to learn maths."

"This basic math course is required for everybody," a girl protested.

"Then you'll bloody well learn your maths, or you won't graduate." Denyse stood defiantly before the class. "George Washington, what page are we on in your textbook?"

"Uh, page sixty-two."

Denyse opened the textbook she had been given, glanced at the page, and went to the blackboard. "Today we'll be learning about adding and subtracting fractions. Those of you who might become chefs or master carpenters will need this. The secret is creating common denominators . . ."

Chapter Six

Katie played with her granddaughter at Jeremy and Denyse's apartment. Katelyn laughed and giggled as she tottered around the room. She spoke a series of disconnected words to Katie as they played. Eventually, Katelyn tired. Katie brought out a series of children's picture books. On the couch they sat together turning the pages. Katie read the words and asked the names of various items depicted in the pictures. Katelyn snuggled up against her grandmother and fell asleep. Katie felt her heart pounding from pure joy.

Dave, Jeremy, Herschel, and Dorothy met at one o'clock in the firm's conference room. Dave started by putting a handwritten page of notes in front of himself. Consulting the notes, he reviewed their working arrangements. "I own Bayside Accounting. The rest of you are technically employees. But all of us know that the business isn't healthy. We'll all need to do top-quality work to restore the firm's reputation. I'm starting the CPAs at eighty thousand dollars a year. Dorothy will return to a five-day work week with a salary raised to sixty-five thousand."

Herschel audibly gasped. The salary Dave offered represented a big raise for him. Jeremy likewise felt stunned. That salary would be about the same as he had received in Australian dollars, equivalent to only 75 cents in American currency. Dorothy had received a larger raise than the previous ten years combined.

Jeremy spoke up, "Dad, are you sure? I'm guessing that buying out your former partners was a financial stretch for you and Mom. I can work for less." Herschel and Dorothy nodded willingness to take less.

"Thanks to each of you. But I want you to have a stake in making Bayside Accounting successful again. I calculate that at an average of a hundred dollars an hour charge rate, we'll need to bill 4,800 hours a year just to break even. Right now, we're billing less than a quarter of that. The CPAs will eventually need to average billing thirty-one hours a week. That should allow us to usually put in a forty-hour week and then go home to our families. Of course, during tax season we'll all need to work more hours taking care of tax returns. We'll make up some of those hours by extra time off during our slack times."

After consulting his notes again, Dave then explained Jeremy's idea about their motto being the Golden Rule. "Dorothy, do you have any problems with our using a Christian theme?"

"No, certainly not that one. Jesus was teaching a key principle of modern Judaism."

"How about you, Herschel?"

"I'm fine with that."

"Thanks." Dave then continued, "Now, responsibilities. Jeremy, because you're very personable, you'll be the face of the firm. Plus you'll be our business manager. When I'm not here, you're responsible. You'll meet with prospective clients and hopefully get their business. You'll pick up the tax return clients Tom and Randy had remaining and handle any new accounts involving international reporting." Jeremy took notes and nodded assent.

"Herschel, you'll continue with the accounts you already have. Mostly I think that's simple cash-basis bookkeeping, paying bills, and issuing paychecks for some local business establishments. How well do you know GAAP, general accepted accounting principles?"

"I know the textbooks," Herschel answered.

"He knows them backwards and forwards," Jeremy offered.

"Good. Then whenever you get any slack time, study even more and email me reports of what you're learning. When we can get some new clients who need audits, I'd like for you to take over those accounts. Doing audits would give us more year-around work. Also, Tom and Randy laid off the former IT guy. We can't afford a new one. You're obviously excellent with computers. Would you be willing to double as our IT guy?"

"Yes, sir."

"You don't have to say 'sir' to me."

"Today I feel like you deserve a 'sir.' Starting tomorrow I'll call you Dave."

Dave smiled acceptance before continuing, "Dorothy, you'll continue as receptionist, handle all the mail in and out, keep the books for our firm, and do the firm's billing. You'll be our Human Resources department and supervise future clerical staff we might hire." Dorothy nodded.

Dave looked each of his team in their eyes one by one. He saw their unreserved support. "Okay, then. Starting right now, this firm will issue *no more documents with errors.*" He paused between each of those words to add emphasis. "Because any of us can make occasional mistakes, I'll personally check every financial statement we send out. Statements I create will be checked by Herschel or Jeremy. Until we improve our revenue, I'll also continue forensic consulting. Unfortunately, all those accounts are currently out of state. Therefore, if I'm out of town or otherwise occupied, Herschel, I want you to check Jeremy's work and vice-versa. I'll also start contacting the major clients I had before retirement. Maybe I can get some of them back. As soon as our business warrants it, I'll hire more help."

⸺◦◦◦⸺

"Dave Parker is treating me like he treats his own son!" Herschel told his wife Candace over the phone. "I got a big raise. And I'll get to conduct audits when we have those clients."

"He'll probably want you to be at work all the time," she warned.

"No, he wants us to go home after forty hours, except during tax season."

"This can't be true," Candace still worried. "But you do the best you can to make it come true."

"You can count on that."

—•◆•—

"I'm worried about Mom and Dad," Jeremy commented to Denyse that night. "I think they've sunk most of their savings into buying the firm. And the firm isn't generating nearly enough revenue right now to cover the salaries he promised and the overhead."

"How will your father pay the salaries, then?"

"I presume he and Mom will be subsidizing from their personal retirement accounts."

"Listen, Jeremy. Your father is rather sharp. He thinks things through and believes he can make this work."

Jeremy nodded his head. "I hope he's right."

"You can help him to make the firm successful. It's our future too, you know."

"Yeah, I do. I'm still worried, though."

"You know that your mum is watching Katelyn while I'm teaching."

"Mom loves taking care of her granddaughter."

"Well, it isn't fair she should do that while I'm making money. I offered to give Katie half of the salary I get paid for teaching. She just told me to save the money toward buying a house."

"Okay. We'll save the money like she says. But we'll have it ready in case Mom and Dad get into financial trouble. No house for us until the firm starts making a profit."

—•◆•—

"All the boys are crushing on Denyse," Caleb Fogle told Dave at the neighborhood's Christmas party two weeks later. "She's attractive and unique, of course. But she's got a firm mothering quality that a lot of the boys crave. They want to please her. She keeps them busy, which makes her classes seem short. And she gives praise that few of them receive otherwise. Some of the girls reacted in jealousy at first. Then Denyse had Katie bring in your granddaughter, Katelyn. Denyse let the girls hold her and play with her. That won them over."

"Denyse has empathy for kids who, like herself, come from difficult circumstances," Dave explained. "She feels passionately about mathematics helping them."

"She got all of her students involved when she divided the classes into teams for math competitions. Kids that age love to compete. I never thought I'd see students at Central High cheering and doing high fives over basic math scores." Caleb shook his head in wonder. "One of the other teachers told me that Denyse has been telling the girls, 'Make something of yourself so that you can have a successful life.' And then she tells the boys, 'You'd better make something of yourself if you want to marry one of my girls.' Some of the female students have started calling themselves 'Denyse's girls.' I've never seen a set of classes change so quickly."

Dave chuckled. "Down Under, I saw Denyse whip a group of drunken men into order during a fight. Her father calls her 'a corker.' "

Caleb switched topics. "How are things at the firm?"

"Hopefully moving toward breaking even; that is, without paying me any salary," Dave admitted. "We'll make up ground during tax season. Jeremy and Herschel are working like it was their business. They try to get everything done by five o'clock because they know I'll send them home whether they're finished or not."

Caleb laughed. "I appreciated you giving Herschel that day to address each of Denyse's classes about the importance of mathematics. I'm thinking about having a general assembly for him to talk to the entire student body. He's an alumnus of Central High School, you know?"

"No, I didn't know that. Just tell us when you're ready for Herschel. Even if it's during tax season."

—◄◆►—

"Isn't it strange that only a few months after a white policeman was accused of killing a black perpetrator, a black policeman killed a white man?" Jeremiah Wallace said to a local TV interviewer.

"Are you suggesting some sort of payback?" the young woman reporter asked.

"That's for the authorities to determine with a thorough investigation," retorted Jeremiah.

The reporter persisted, "Hasn't the body cam worn by the African American policeman clearly shown that the man he shot brandished a gun and made threats?"

"I still think the timing is strange. If not a deliberate shooting, why didn't he use an electric Taser? Finally, the white policeman is still on a desk assignment while the African has been exonerated and returned to duty. I might add by a black chief of police."

"Are you alleging some sort of favoritism by the chief?"

"I'll let the patriotic citizens of south Alabama decide for themselves."

—◆—

Katie sat down next to Dave as he read a news magazine after dinner. "Dave, I need to talk to you."

He didn't look up. "What is it, sweetheart? Something cute that Katelyn did today?"

"No, I've found something in my other breast."

Dave laid down the magazine. "You mean like another lump?"

"Maybe."

"Is it like the first one?"

"Not exactly. Certainly not as big. Maybe because I've been more attentive and caught it earlier this time."

"When did you find it?"

"Three days ago."

"Have you made an appointment for a mammogram?"

"Not yet."

Dave's voice raised a little. "Why not?"

"I don't know. I just didn't want to believe it was happening all over again. And I've been so happy taking care of Katelyn. What if I can't continue taking care of her?"

Tears started to roll down Katie's cheeks. "Denyse is making a major difference in her students' lives. You and Jeremy are trying to rebuild the firm. We used nearly all our money buying the firm from your former partners. All our futures depend on your success!" Katie stared at the floor. "I just couldn't let my health interfere with everybody's future."

Chapter Seven

———·•·——

"Come over here," Dave told Katie and indicated his lap.

She came to sit on his lap and put her head on his shoulder. Dave could hear her sniffling. He put his arms around her. "You know that you *are* my future, sweetheart. Nothing is more important to me than you."

"I knew you would say that. But maybe you'd be better off without me."

"My, aren't you in a funk? You know that's not true. You've been thinking about this too long just on your own. I'd be lost without you."

"Well, wouldn't you be upset in my position?"

"No, I'd be a complete basket case, if I'd endured what you have and then faced the prospect of having the same suffering again."

Katie looked up at her husband. "Well then, what are we going to do?"

"As soon as the clinic opens tomorrow, I'll call and schedule an emergency mammogram for you. I'll tell them that you've found a lump and that you had cancer four years ago."

"Almost five years," she corrected. "Thanks, but I'll call the clinic. The scheduler knows me."

"I'll go with you for the appointment," Dave offered.

Katie leaned back to look into Dave's face. "No, they need you at the firm. And I'd rather not get everybody worried until we know something."

"Then I'm glad Jeremy and Denyse bought their own car last week. She drops him at the firm before going to school," said Dave.

"I know that. I'm with Katelyn all day. I usually cook dinner for them before coming home to meet you. I take Katelyn grocery shopping for them too."

"We're all pretty loaded down," Dave admitted.

Katie shed some more tears. "See what I mean? My problem will mess everybody up."

"It's not your fault, Katie."

"I know." She rested her head on his shoulder again. "Dave?"

"Yes, sweetheart?"

"What if it *is* cancer again?"

"Then we'll deal with it like before. Remember how well you did? Better than me. I was proud of you then and will be this time too."

"Somehow I'm more scared this time."

"My father never talked much about WWII. But he did

58

tell me that young men first going into combat often had a feeling of invulnerability. They always thought someone else would be the one hurt or killed. But once a man had been wounded, controlling his fear in combat became much more difficult. Maybe that's why on D-Day, General Eisenhower used nearly all troops without combat experience. You're like that wounded soldier, sweetheart. This time you know what could be ahead."

Katie put her arms around Dave's neck and held him tightly.

＊＊＊

"Dave, Katie is calling on line one," Dorothy announced shortly after he had arrived at the office the next day.

He punched the appropriate button. "Hello, sweetheart."

"They can get me in for a mammogram at one o'clock today," Katie told him.

"Wow, that's quick and good."

"I know. But what about Katelyn?"

"I'll take care of her," Dave offered. "Where are you now?"

"I'm at Jeremy and Denyse's apartment."

"Okay, I'll be there at noon."

At 11:30, Dave told Dorothy, "I'll be taking a half day off this afternoon."

"Remember that you have the phone conference with the DA in Charlotte about that embezzlement case scheduled at three."

Dave grimaced. "I had forgotten that. Would you reschedule it, please? Tomorrow, if possible."

"Got it!" Dorothy said. Dave knew his actions would seem out of character to Dorothy, but she didn't ask any questions.

Katie opened the door to Jeremy and Denyse's apartment to admit Dave. "Thanks for coming. Katelyn's lunch is ready for you to feed her. Mostly she uses her hands when you put the food on her tray. Then she'll enjoy you reading to her." Katie pointed to a stack of children's books. "Afterwards she'll take a nap for an hour or more."

"You go on and don't worry. I can handle this."

"I'll take the pickup in case you need the car and car seat," Katie suggested before she hurried out the door.

Fortunately for Dave, Katelyn did know the routine. An hour later she had fallen fast asleep next to him on the couch.

At two thirty, the little girl woke up. Dave changed his granddaughter's diaper. Afterwards, he gave her a little apple juice and let her play with her stuffed animals. Dave laughed when Katelyn tried on his work shoes and clopped around the apartment in them proudly. "You like my shoes?" he asked.

"My shoes," Katelyn echoed. "Like my shoes."

"But they're too big for your tiny feet," Dave said. "Want me to help you put on your shoes?" He held up her little pink sneakers. Katelyn grabbed them eagerly and attempted to fit them onto Dave's feet. She managed to hook one onto his big toe then stood back and announced, "All done!"

At three thirty, the phone rang. Katie's voice sounded flat. "The mammogram is conclusive. The doctor is sure the lump is cancer again. It doesn't seem as advanced this time. They're offering a lumpectomy rather than a mastectomy like last time. But they'll do the mastectomy if we want. I think that's the best course, if you don't mind. You know my mother . . ." Katie trailed off.

"Yes, of course. I'm so sorry, sweetheart."

"I know you are. The surgery has been scheduled for early Friday, two days from now."

"Okay, I'll stay with Katelyn until Jeremy and Denyse come home. Why don't you meet me at the marina and we'll have dinner?"

"No, I'll go home and fix dinner. I need something to do. Grilled salmon, okay? Maybe some asparagus?"

"That sounds fine. I'll talk to Jeremy and Denyse about this. You relax. After dinner, we can take a long walk together. We'll look at some of the Christmas lights."

"Good idea."

—◆—

Finding Dave with Katelyn surprised Jeremy and Denyse. "Ah, this is where you've been all afternoon," Jeremy commented. "Where's Mom?"

Dave thought it best to be direct. "Your mother has had a recurrence of breast cancer. She's scheduled for a second mastectomy the day after tomorrow."

"Oh my gosh!" responded Denyse. "I'll go with her on Friday."

"No, that's my job. I went with her last time and I'll go with her this time. She'll be put under general anesthetic. You can probably see her Saturday morning if all goes well."

Jeremy stood stunned. "How bad is it?"

"We don't know yet. Maybe not as bad as last time. She caught the cancer earlier."

"What can Denyse and I do, Dad?"

"Just keep up what you're doing. Your mother is very proud of both of you. The thought of possibly disrupting your lives upset her more than anything."

"Well, I think some prayers would be in order," suggested Jeremy.

"Yes, that's a good idea. But your mother won't be here to take care of Katelyn on Friday."

"I can stay home with her," Jeremy offered.

"No, I'll ask Jordan Fogle to take care of Katelyn," said Denyse. "You need to go to work."

—◦—

Katie was working on dinner and waiting for Dave to get home when her phone rang. "Mom, we're so sorry," started Jeremy. "We'll pray for you and we'll call Lena to pray too. Judging by what we saw happen Down Under two years ago, I think God listens closely to her prayers."

"Thank you, Jeremy. Tell Denyse that I'll be there to stay with Katelyn tomorrow morning as usual. But I can't come on Friday."

"You don't have to come tomorrow either, Mom."

"Jeremy, if I knew I had only one day remaining on earth, I'd want to spend it taking care of that child."

—◦—

Being at the hospital at five a.m. unnerved Dave just as it had before Katie's previous surgery. Patients, mostly elderly, scheduled for surgery reported to the front desk, signed a sheet attached to a clipboard, and found seats in the quiet lobby as far as possible from the others waiting.

Like Dave, a loved one or two accompanied most of the patients. Some of these tried to put on a cheerful demeanor. Dave heard one speak in a hushed tone, "You'll be back to normal in a few days. We'll make that trip to Cancun we had always dreamed about."

But all present knew that life would not return to normal for everybody sitting in that lobby. So many things could go wrong in surgery. The doctors might find the condition to be worse than they had expected. Every patient faced the ever-present possibility of a life-changing stroke or a blood clot during surgery. The patients looked around at each other without speaking in the tense atmosphere. Some of them possibly would not survive. Those accompanying them simply tried to hold back their fear.

Eventually, a door opened. A nurse in green hospital garb appeared, glanced at a paper in her hands, and called somebody's name. Dave and Katie held hands, not certain whether to hope Katie would be called first or last. As they waited they whispered remembrances and expressed gratitude for the happy and meaningful years lived together.

Dave's heart jumped when he heard, "Katherine Parker."

She stood resolute. "I'll see you in a few hours. Why don't you go out and enjoy a nice breakfast?" she reassured him. They embraced for a long moment. The nurse waited patiently with the door held open. Dave saw Katie turn back and smile at him before she disappeared.

Chapter Eight

Denyse hardly realized that attendance at Central High School had noticeably diminished that Friday afternoon. She mechanically conducted her classes while praying for Katie.

At the beginning of her last class of the day, one of her students approached Denyse at the front of the classroom. "Ms. Parker, you live in Spanish Fort, don't you?" a girl of sixteen spoke quietly. "And your little girl, Katelyn, is there?"

Denyse turned to look at her. "Yes, Sherri. Why?"

"You should go home now. Get through the tunnel and across the bridge."

For the first time, Denyse noticed that almost half the seats in her classroom sat empty. "What's happening?"

"Some people are coming in from out of town."

Denyse stood perplexed. "Who's coming into Mobile?" The girl merely shrugged and looked at the seated students for support.

"You don't need to stay here any longer, Ms. Parker," said Anthony, a male student. "We promise to behave and stay in this room until the final bell rings." Most of Denyse's students nodded or waved for her to leave.

Denyse gathered the few things she had brought with her to the classroom. She found Principal Fogle patrolling the hallway. "What's going on, Caleb?"

"I don't know for certain. Some sort of mass demonstration, I think. You can go on home, Denyse. I'll look in on your class."

Coaches routinely scheduled high school athletes for gym class the last period of the day. As she passed the gym, Denyse noticed the school's various coaches talking to over a hundred students who knelt on one knee. She caught the head football coach's words, ". . . stay out of trouble. Any of you who gets arrested will be in bigger trouble with me."

◄◆►

Katie slowly realized she had woken. The last thing she could remember was the anesthesiologist telling her to count backwards from five. She couldn't remember reaching two.

A nurse immediately appeared at her side. "Oh, you're awake." The nurse pushed a button to raise Katie's head and upper body from lying prone to a leaning position. "Could you sip a little ice water?" She placed a covered cup with a straw in Katie's hand.

Katie sipped a little water and semi-dozed as the anesthetic wore off. Vaguely she felt the gurney rolling through hospitals halls. Finally, it stopped. Strong arms transferred her to a hospital bed. Katie opened her eyes again. She saw Dave's smiling face. "How are you, sweetheart?" he asked.

"Okay." Katie closed her eyes again.

Dave picked up her hand that didn't have an IV tube attached. "The surgeon said that the surgery went very well. They're pretty sure they got all of the cancer."

A floor nurse appeared. "Are you doing alright?" she asked. Katie nodded. "Wonderful. Here are a couple of pills to help you sleep some more." She handed Katie two pills in a paper cup. "If you wake up and need pain medication, just punch the call button."

"I'll be here with her," explained Dave.

"Good. Just come to the desk if you need anything, Mr. Parker."

━━◆━━

Jeremiah Wallace's cell phone rang. "Hello."

"Colonel, the Africans are planning a major demonstration in Mobile tonight. The marchers will assemble at Mardi Gras Park. At eight p.m., they'll start down Government Street. The route will take them to Broad Street then James Seals Community Center for a rally."

"Good work. Maintain your cover. Act to support us as the situation warrants. This will be a Code Red. Repeat, Code Red."

"Yes, sir!"

Without putting down the cell phone, Jeremiah thumbed in characters, "Code Red in downtown Mobile. Government Street. All available patriots respond immediately. Defend liberty as planned."

━━◆━━

Denyse dialed the firm on her cell phone as soon as she reached the car. She was surprised when Dorothy didn't answer. She heard Jeremy's voice. "Hi, Denyse. We're closing the offices early today. Come pick me up as soon as your last class finishes."

"I'm on my way already. Why are you closing the office?"

"Candace called Herschel and asked him to come home. A friend had called to warn her about something happening. I sent him and Dorothy home a half hour ago. I'll lock up tight here and walk down to meet you on Government Street. We'll take the Bankhead Tunnel and causeway home."

Heavy traffic slowed Denyse's progress. She saw groups of policemen mustering at strategic intersections. Jeremy waited on the curbside. Denyse stopped in the slowly moving traffic, opened the driver's side door, and hurried to the passenger side. Jeremy walked between cars then slipped in behind the steering wheel. Car horns from behind urged him to get moving.

Both Jeremy and Denyse breathed easier as traffic speeded up slightly driving east through the tunnel under Mobile River toward Spanish Fort. Exiting the tunnel, they saw hundreds of vans and cars, even a few buses, full of people waiting their turn to enter downtown Mobile.

"How's Katie doing?" Denyse asked as soon as the traffic congestion diminished.

"Dad said that the surgery went well. She's out of the recovery room and sleeping. We'll need to wait on the biopsy of the removed lymph nodes."

—◄◆►—

"Did you see Caleb?" Jordan Fogle asked when Jeremy and Denyse arrived at their apartment where Jordan had been caring for Katelyn. The TV tuned to a local station showed crowds of African Americans converging on downtown Mobile. "He's not answering his phone."

"I saw him at the school," Denyse told her. "He excused me early."

Jeremy looked at the TV and saw crowds of people blocking the entrance to the Highway 98 tunnel and cars and buses gridlocking the access to the interstate highway. "I'm afraid he can't get home right now. I'm sure he'll come as soon as the way is clear."

Jordan shook her head. "I don't think so. He won't leave."

"Why not?"

"He and a few other men have started calling themselves the Can't-Get-Away Club after that nineteenth century group."

The odd name puzzled Denyse. *I'll need to ask about that later.* "Why don't you stay and have supper with us then?" she invited Jordan. "We can keep trying all his numbers until we find him."

"No, I'll go home in case he calls there on our landline."

◄►

Denyse and Jeremy sat watching the TV showing crowds of mostly African Americans gathering in downtown Mobile and receiving instructions in Mardi Gras Park. A TV reporter interviewed one of the men organizing the march. "What is this demonstration about?"

"We mean to express support for the police officer who has been receiving racist death threats after being exonerated for shooting a man who was at that time threatening others with a gun. We also want to demand the completion of the inquiry promised after the shooting of an unarmed young man last summer. That policeman in question is still employed by the police department."

The reporter then asked, "This demonstration wasn't publicized openly in Mobile. Why didn't you reveal your plans beforehand?"

"We did notify Mobile's police chief. We avoided publicity to prevent the possibility of confrontation with counter-demonstrators."

"Wouldn't you have gotten a larger turnout by announcing this in advance?" the reporter persisted.

"I think we'll have as much turnout as Mobile can handle. These are just the marchers," the organizer gestured toward those behind him. "Most of the people are meeting us at James Seals Park."

Behind them various signs waved and proclaimed, "No to Racism" and "Freedom for All." Other bouncing signs showed pictures of a rebel flag with a big red X across the image.

"I'm so glad you could pick me up early," said Jeremy. "The way home is completely blocked now. How did you know something was happening?"

"A few of my students tipped me off. They didn't tell me what would happen. Only to go home early." Denyse then commented, "I hope your mom is doing okay."

"Dad promised to call after she was fully awake."

—◦—

Anthony marched again in support of justice and equality. Unfortunately, he had somehow become separated from his friends and classmates. That hardly mattered. Being a participant was what counted.

The crowd moved slowly in the early December darkness along the route designated by rough maps distributed by the organizers. Young white men and a few women lining

Government Street, jeering at the protesters and shouting racial slurs, surprised Anthony. "Ignore the hecklers," one of the march organizers ordered through a megaphone.

The demonstrators inched along. More counter-protesters appeared on the sidewalks. A rock came from somewhere to hit a woman walking near Anthony under her eye. She cried out in pain and held her hand over the bleeding wound. A marcher, decades older than Anthony and apparently the woman's husband, picked up the rock and hurled it back in anger. More rocks came through the night toward the demonstrators. Someone from among the marchers picked up a thrown rock and in anger used it to break a store window.

Some younger African American men started to push through the crowd. They stood confronting and insulting the white counter-demonstrators. Another store window shattered. Anthony saw a few from the crowd step past the broken glass to grab items from the store. Turning his head, he saw a white man tackle one of the looters. A black man came to aid his companion. More white counter-protesters rushed in. Soon a melee of black and white men cursing and punching at each other caused the peaceful marchers to recoil at the violence.

Uniformed policemen trying to reach the fight forced their way through the demonstrators. One policeman accidently knocked down a young woman carrying a baby. Misunderstanding, several demonstrators pushed that policeman to the ground. A whistle blew. A loud explosion sounded like a gunshot. Anthony felt himself crushed body to body in a mass of frightened people. The megaphone instructed, "Everybody stay calm. Withdraw carefully the way we came."

But the masses of marchers still coming blocked any retreat. Another explosion startled everyone. An African American voice shouted above the confusion, "Fight! Fight! This is our home. Show the racists they can't intimidate us." Anthony recognized the voice as belonging to Tyrone, a large, rough man in his twenties from a downtown neighborhood. Young men rallied to Tyrone. Others—male and female—joined the looting. Anthony stood wide eyed as eight men turned over a car and set it on fire. The yellow flames reflecting off the live oak trees and buildings gave an unworldly orange effect.

The crowd of marchers started to panic. Those attempting to escape accidently knocked others down in their fear. A voice inside Anthony said, *You can fight. Don't let the racists get away with this.* He clenched his fists and started edging toward the group of brawling blacks, whites, and police. Suddenly Anthony felt someone strong grab him by the collar and jerk him backwards. Anthony spun around to find himself face-to-face with his high school principal.

"Don't you get involved in this, son!" Mr. Fogle shouted into his face from three inches. "Run like hell and don't stop until you're home." A dull thump sounded nearby. Anthony felt his eyes start to burn from tear gas.

Mr. Fogle released Anthony's collar and roughly shoved him in the direction that most of the crowd had started to flee. Anthony saw his principal turn into the fighting to look for other Central High students.

Anthony dodged through the marchers to a side street and ran like he had never run before. Lights-flashing police cars passed him followed by a shrieking fire engine. Behind him Anthony heard screams, shouting, and gunshots.

Chapter Nine

———•———

Jeremy met Denyse when she emerged from the bathroom after helping Katelyn to her morning potty. "Dad called again," he told her. "He's taking Mom home from the hospital this morning. I'll go see her at their house this afternoon."

"I'll go too, of course," said Denyse. "And bring Katelyn."

"Mom will be happy to see you both."

"I've never visited anybody with cancer," Denyse confessed.

Jeremy looked nervous. "Me neither."

"But didn't your mother have cancer before?"

"I had just gotten to Australia when Mom was diagnosed with her first cancer," Jeremy told Denyse. "My work visa would have been invalidated if I left the country during the first six months. Dad told me to stay put, that he would take care of Mom."

"That must have been terrible," his wife sympathized.

"Actually, I felt sort of relieved. Watching someone you

love suffering would be awful. And it can affect you for your entire life."

"How do you mean?"

"Do you remember when I told you how Uncle Chuck's trauma over Vietnam affected him and Dad?"

Denyse nodded. "Yes."

"Mom's got her own nightmare. Her mother died of breast cancer. Mom spent several months caring for her and watching her gradually deteriorate. I think Mom is more concerned about not putting Dad and us through that than she is of herself dying."

Denyse got some cereal out of a kitchen cabinet for Katelyn. "Then breast cancer runs in your family?"

"From Mom's side, yes."

Jeremy saw Denyse glance at Katelyn, who sat watching *Sesame Street* on TV. "But Mom only got half of her genes from her mother," he reassured her. "And Katelyn only has a quarter of her genes from Mom."

Denyse bit her lip. "That's not much comfort to a fearful mum."

—◆—

"Mayor Hunt, do you have any comment on last night's riot in downtown Mobile?" a reporter asked outside City Hall and thrust a microphone forward. A cameraman hovered nearby recording.

The mayor stopped and turned to the reporter. "I deplore and condemn the violence between blacks and whites in our community. We need to come together as a community to ensure the safety and welfare of all. To prevent future episodes of violence, I'm bringing a measure before the city council that would require scheduling public demonstrations a month in advance."

"Wouldn't that constrain free speech in violation of the First Amendment?"

Looking directly into the camera the mayor responded, "Public safety is my first responsibility."

"Couldn't prior notice give counter-demonstrators more time to organize and thereby make confrontation more likely?"

"Now who is constraining free speech?" The mayor hurried away.

━◆━

Caleb returned home the next morning. "What did you think you were doing?" Jordan shouted at her husband. She stood glaring at him with her hands on her hips.

Maybe I made a mistake phoning her late last night, Caleb thought. *If I hadn't, she'd be relieved to see me now. Instead, she's had all night to get mad.*

He sat down in exhaustion. "These kids, a lot of them don't have anybody to look out for them."

Jordan smelled the tear gas on his clothes. She saw his red-rimmed eyes from the tear gas and a sleepless night. Still her emotions controlled her. "How could you expect to find any of them in the dark and that crowd?" Without waiting for an answer, she asked, "How many *did* you find?"

"About two dozen."

Still, she didn't relent. "Why did it have to be you, Caleb?

75

Just because we don't have any kids of our own, you don't have to look out for all of them."

"Oh, it wasn't just me. I saw a lot of adults looking for kids, in some cases their own kids. Others were like me. I saw a couple of white policemen grabbing kids, yelling at them, and sending them home. One policeman recognized me. He asked me to talk to some kids he had caught before he released them."

Jordan sighed. "Have you had anything to eat?"

Caleb rubbed his eyes. "No."

"Then you go shower the stink off of you. I'll have breakfast ready when you come out."

Over breakfast Jordan softened her tone. "Twenty-four kids kept out of trouble. Not a bad night, really." After Caleb's acknowledging nod, she asked, "Honey, what went wrong last night?"

"Some white supremacists showed up and goaded young hotheads into a fight. But it wasn't just the racists. Some among our African Americans came looking for trouble or an opportunity to loot. They don't realize they're hurting our cause. Or maybe they've become so disaffected that they don't care anymore. What I can't figure out is how the counter-demonstrators got organized so quickly. If they hadn't shown up, probably nothing would have happened."

————◆————

"Didn't I warn you?" Jeremiah Wallace asserted in front of several TV cameras. He stood outside of a White America rally at their sprawling headquarters in an old shopping center on the outskirts of Mobile. In the background,

76

strident tones of an angry voice could be heard shouting into a microphone. Jeremiah continued, "Riots and looting are happening right here in the streets of Mobile. If the police can't control the criminals, American patriots need to protect our city."

"Mr. Wallace, the police reports indicate that the demonstration remained peaceful until hecklers provoked a reaction," returned a reporter.

"Oh, so you're saying that looting is a peaceful demonstration?" sneered Jeremiah.

"No, but the looting—"

"Let me ask you," Jeremiah interrupted. "Of those arrested for looting, were any white Americans?"

—◆—

Sitting in his living room and watching the news report on TV, Caleb Fogle shook his head. "See what I meant?" he asked Jordan. "A few troublemakers mixed in with the peaceful demonstrators reacted to the racists. Others used the opportunity to steal. They discredited our entire movement." Caleb thought for a minute. "The same is probably true on the White America side too. You have young white men who want a cause to believe in, to feel part of something. They've glamorized their heritage and consider themselves marginalized. Then you mix in some thugs, and you've got a racist mob."

"Mobile's police made fifty-nine arrests," the local anchorwoman reported. "Local hospitals admitted thirty-seven, mostly for abrasions and broken bones. Four have been treated for gunshots. One is in critical condition but expected to survive."

Jordan tried to be positive. "At least none of your students were hurt or arrested."

—◆—

Dave came home early from the office a few days later. "How are you feeling today, sweetheart?"

"Physically, I'm okay," answered Katie.

"Didn't finding out that your lymph nodes had no sign of the cancer cheer you up?"

"I'm relieved that the cancer hadn't metastasized like last time," Katie admitted.

"So, non-invasive so far?"

"So far."

"Then what's keeping you down?"

"While you were at the office, a young pastor from our church came to visit. She meant to cheer me up by quoting Romans 8:28, 'And we know that in all things God works for the good of those who love him, who have been called according to his purpose.' But I just don't see the good in my having cancer, especially not right now. Remember the emotional trauma my cancer caused you last time? The whole family needs you in first-class condition right now." Katie paused, then spoke more softly. "I've also been thinking about Katelyn. What if I've passed on a cancer gene to her?"

Dave sat down. Although a believer in Christ and faithful in church attendance, theology had never been his expertise. As a history hobbyist, he knew that many Christians had died miserable deaths or had seen their loved ones experience horrible suffering. The circumstances did not always seem to work out for the good of those individuals in this life. "Those are valid questions, Katie. Struggling for answers caused part of my funk the last time you had cancer. I simply don't know why these things happen."

"I don't expect you to know everything."

Dave's love for Katie prompted him to promise, "I'll get some answers for you, though."

"How can you do that?"

"I don't know. But I'll make a deal with you. If you'll try to stop worrying and enjoy the holidays, I'll promise to get some meaningful answers for you."

Katie brightened. "Alright."

"You understand that this may take me a while, weeks or even months."

"You always keep your word. Just knowing answers are coming makes me feel better. Let's start putting up our Christmas decorations tonight."

―•―

Dorothy, Jeremy, and Herschel sat waiting at the firm's conference table three days before Christmas. Dave came in and joined them. *He looks wasted*, thought Dorothy.

Unlike their first meeting, Dave sat and spoke without notes. "I'd like to thank each of you for the effort you've demonstrated during our first month. I've been pretty busy with Katie, so I haven't managed to attract any new business yet. Therefore, I won't be able to give Christmas bonuses this year."

"We never got any Christmas bonuses at Bayside Accounting," interrupted Dorothy.

Dave smiled, "That's true. But—"

"The reason was that Tom and Randy were too stingy," Dorothy told the others. To answer Dave's surprised look, she added, "We could all hear through the walls whenever you three partners started arguing about employee compensation." To Jeremy and Herschel, she continued, "I know everything that's happened here for the last thirty years." They both laughed.

Dave struggled to maintain professional dignity and not laugh himself. "Well, okay. In lieu of the bonus you wouldn't have received anyway, I propose we close the office starting tonight until after New Year's Day. All of you will receive your full salaries for the month." Everybody brightened.

"What about the office Christmas party?" Herschel asked.

"With all that's been going on, I just forgot. There's only the few of us. Unless someone feels strongly otherwise, let's just skip the party this year." When no one objected, Dave concluded the meeting, "Then let's wrap up what we're doing, and all start the holidays at five."

◄─◆─►

"You gave everybody ten days off for Christmas with pay?" Katie wondered when Dave came home.

He put down his briefcase and hugged her. "We didn't have enough work to keep them busy anyway. How did you know?"

"Jeremy told me when he and Denyse came home. Does 'with pay' include us?"

"Not yet. I couldn't bill much on my forensic consulting jobs this month either. Don't tell Jeremy, but I'll be trying to catch up on those accounts over the holidays. That should lessen our losses."

To Katie, Dave looked tired and discouraged. "What's going to happen?"

"You and I can subsidize the firm for a while, but not indefinitely. I just need to find more clients. We're fortunate that tax season is close. We'll need to do well on tax returns this year or be out of business by next summer."

"Didn't Tom and Randy do tax returns?"

"Yes, but not enough to keep us afloat. And nearly all those jobs are on a year-by-year basis. Those who had a personal relationship with Tom or Randy won't necessarily continue with us."

"My medical bills aren't helping any either," Katie volunteered. "I knew my cancer would complicate everything."

"That's not your fault, sweetheart." Dave thought another minute. "Let's just enjoy Christmas and not worry about all this. Okay?"

"Okay," Katie answered. Then she thought, *Not worrying doesn't mean I can't think and do something, though.*

Ripper

Chapter Ten

"Merry Christmas," Katie greeted Jeremy and Denyse as they arrived with Katelyn on Christmas Eve. She held open the front door for them to enter. "Your bedroom is ready. We're so happy to have you spend Christmas with us."

Jeremy carried in something furry and black. "Look what Santa brought early to Katelyn." He set down a ten-week-old Labrador retriever puppy.

"Santa brought him, alright," whispered Denyse. "But I'm not sure Santa brought him for Katelyn."

The puppy started to ramble around Katie's living room. Katie envisioned an accident on her light cream Saxony carpet. "What's his name?"

Jeremy, obviously excited, responded, "We call him Ripper because he ripped apart Katelyn's favorite alligator toy we had left on the floor."

"Katelyn doesn't know yet," Denyse confided in Katie. "Do you remember where you bought it?"

"Sure, we'll get her another," answered Katie. To Jeremy she suggested, "Maybe you should take Ripper into the backyard. I'll tell your father you're here."

Dave found Jeremy happily watching Ripper use his sharp puppy teeth on an old shoe. "Nice dog." He bent over to pet the boisterous puppy.

Jeremy stared at his puppy with pride. "Isn't he great? He'll be perfect for Katelyn."

"Uh-huh. For Katelyn."

Suddenly the puppy saw something new and inviting to play with. Old Yeller had heard human voices and came to have his tummy rubbed. Ripper approached the cat, wagging his tail. Roughly the same height, neither Ripper nor Old Yeller had ever seen anything like the other. *Hsss.* The cat arched his back and burred up. Ripper backed away.

"I'm sure they'll be friends," predicted Jeremy.

Dave and Jeremy watched the cat relax and warily approach the young dog. Without warning Ripper lunged forward to initiate wrestle play. *Eeow.* The puppy retreated with a drop of red blood on his damp, black nose. "I have no doubt they'll become friends . . ." Dave suggested, ". . . on Old Yeller's terms."

◄─◆─►

Inside, Katie talked to Denyse as she made an étouffée. "As I explained to you, the Parker family celebrates a Cajun Christmas." She placed a bowl of raw shrimp and a pair of kitchen scissors on the kitchen bar where Denyse sat on a stool. "Could you peel these, please?"

Denyse looked over to where Katelyn stood mesmerized by the lighted Christmas tree. "What is Cajun?" She started struggling to peel a shrimp while keeping an eye on her daughter.

"In what Americans call the 'French and Indian War,' the English and their colonists fought the French for control of North America. That was in the middle seventeen hundreds before the American Revolution. Dave could tell you the dates. At the time, a lot of French had settled in what is now Canada, especially in the eastern provinces called Acadia. After the English army and navy defeated the French at Fort Louisbourg in what is now Nova Scotia, they forcibly relocated the French settlers and dumped them in the swamps near the mouth of the Mississippi River. The Acadians' descendants became the Cajuns." Seeing Denyse struggling with a shrimp, Katie took the kitchen scissors and cut the shell along the shrimp's back then easily pulled the shell away and broke off the head. She handed the scissors back to her daughter-in-law. "Leave the tail on."

"This doesn't look like we're making a French dish," Denyse waved at the étouffée ingredients.

"The Cajun people had to learn how to live on the food they could catch—things like crayfish and even alligators— in the low country of what is now Louisiana. They developed a unique and spicy cuisine including a lot of red peppers. Etouffée is a Cajun seafood stew which we serve over rice."

"Are the Parkers Cajuns?"

Katie opened the kitchen door to let in Old Yeller. The cat immediately plopped down to let Katelyn grab fists full of his fur. "Partly Cajun. Some people call part-Cajuns

'Creoles.' Dave's grandfather was an eighteen-year-old from south Alabama put into a regiment with mostly Louisianans during World War I. After the war, Grandfather Parker visited his best army buddy in Louisiana. Both had come from families of fishermen. Grandfather Parker's friend had a seventeen-year-old spunky, dark-haired sister. Evangeline had been named after Longfellow's epic poem and tragic love story about the Acadians. Grandfather Parker fell in love and convinced Evangeline to join him in Mobile as his wife. She made the Parker family Christmas forever Cajun."

"What a marvelous story. What else do the Parkers do Cajun?"

"Dave and Jeremy are probably preparing a bonfire now. An outdoor fire on Christmas Eve is part of Cajun tradition. After it burns down, Dave will light a fire in the fireplace. We'll eat the étouffée by candlelight. The Fogles are coming. They're Creoles too."

Cajun Bonfire

Denyse held Katelyn in the cold Christmas Eve twilight. "This feels strange, being so cold at Christmas. Do you think we'll have snow?" she asked Katie.

With a leash, Katie constrained Ripper to keep him from possibly being burned by the fire. "Occasionally we do have snow in Mobile. Not tonight, though. The sky is clear."

Jeremy stepped back from lighting the small pyramidal bonfire built in a fire pit behind Dave and Katie's house. He approached his daughter. "This fire will show the way for Papa Noël and his flying sleigh to find the homes of good girls and boys. If you've been good, you'll find presents tomorrow morning. This present came early." He picked up the puppy, Ripper, for Katelyn to grab an ear. The wiggling puppy licked her hands and tried for her face.

The group traded stories and memories of Christmases past as the evening grew colder. "Come on inside and get warm," Katie told her guests as the fire died down.

Dave had already kindled a blaze inside the fireplace. Evergreen magnolia branches and fresh holly with red berries decorated the fireplace mantle. The Fogles stood next to Denyse before the fire warming their hands. "I hear you're part Cajun too," she said.

"Jordan is," answered Caleb.

"And so you could be related to the Parkers?"

Jordan laughed. "Honey, nearly all of us Creoles are related to each other somehow."

"Y'all get a bowl from the dining room table and bring it to the kitchen to be served," called Katie.

Denyse found the dining room lit by candles. Lights from a cedar Christmas tree glowed in the semi-darkness. The scents of hot candle wax and rosin permeated the air. In the kitchen, Katie put a scoop of jasmine rice in each bowl then ladled on the étouffée. Jeremy attended to Katelyn in her high chair.

After leading a prayer, Dave added another bowl to the table. "These are for those who want them."

Peering into the bowl, Denyse saw tiny lobsters turned red after having been boiled. "You eat yabbies?"

Dave laughed. "Cajuns call them 'crawfish.' A lot of people consider them a delicacy. Have you noticed some men with one fingernail grown very long?"

Denyse admitted that she had wondered about that Gulf Coast oddity.

"That fingernail is to scoop the meat out of the crawfish heads. Try one. The best meat is in the tail."

Denyse took a crawfish and put it on the edge of her bowl. Everybody pretended not to watch as the Australian wrestled to split open the tail. She finally held the split tail to her mouth and sucked. The crustacean's tail meat had a shrimp-like texture, only tasted fishier. She decided to not attempt eating the creature's head. "That was good," she announced after realizing that all had watched her.

Katie pointed toward the fireplace where coals glowed red. "Look at that." Soaking up the warmth, Old Yeller stretched out on the hearth rug. Two feet away a black puppy, exhausted from the day of new experiences, curled up asleep.

"I told you they'd be friends," said Jeremy.

After everyone had enjoyed the étouffée, Katie turned up the lights and served coffee and tea with pecan pralines in the living room. Katelyn, as exhausted as the puppy, nodded off to sleep almost as soon as Jeremy took her from the high chair. Denyse and Jeremy together took her to the guest bedroom and tucked her into a baby bed Katie had borrowed.

Returning to the living room, Denyse found the Parkers and Fogles talking about the downtown riot that had occurred a week earlier. Caleb described the horror of the situation from his eyewitness experience. "Hotheads and provocateurs on both sides made a crisis where none was needed." He told about pulling out and chasing home Central High students. Then he praised the actions of the policemen who had helped him keep inexperienced and impressionable kids out of trouble.

"Jordan said something about you being part of the Can't-Get-Away Club? Why couldn't you get away?" Denyse asked Caleb.

"I'm not really part of that club," he answered. "The Can't-Get-Away Club started in the yellow fever epidemic of 1839. When most people left Mobile to escape, a few men and women stayed behind to care for the afflicted. Most of the caregivers died themselves. The point was that they could have gotten away, but their love of God and their neighbors wouldn't allow them to leave. The club lasted up until 1897. A lot more men and women gave their lives helping others in subsequent plagues until science discovered the causes, primarily mosquitos."

"He deserves the title, though," Jordan insisted. "Caleb has been offered big, important jobs up at the state capital in Montgomery. But he stays here in Mobile taking care of his students."

Dave went to his bookshelves, selected a reference volume, found a place, and started to read:

Let none suppose that by thus anticipating death I would, in the smallest degree, distrust the power of the Almighty God to preserve me. That God will give me protection, I have not the shadow of a doubt. But I thus calmly anticipate death in recognition of the truth that God in His wisdom may see that the enclosure of the coffin and the grave is the very best protection that He can furnish for my body, and the bosom of my blessed Savior the very best protection for my immortal soul and spirit. I do not doubt the power of God. He will keep me in being as long as His glory demands it. And the very moment His glory will be more promoted by my death than by my life, then that moment I shall die.

I do not say that I expect to live or die. With me this is not the question. I have asked God to work in me His own will, having I trust, no other motive than the glory of God. If I am submissive to His will He will show forth in me His glory and thus will He fulfill in me the Scripture which teacheth us that the "joy of the Lord shall be our strength."

Nothing but the confidence which I have in the special providence of God could have enabled me to resist your pressing solicitations to fly from the danger. I felt that the danger was in flying. In the midst of destruction I feel that I am in safety, because I am in the place, and surrounded by the circumstances which God ordered for me. Already, however, do I sympathize with you in your sorrowings, as by anticipation I view my death.

"That was part of the last letter from a Methodist minister, John Wesley Starr, to his family and friends. He stayed in Mobile as part of the Can't-Get-Away Club and died here at age twenty-three," Dave concluded.

The group became silent at the solemn, reverent words. Dave looked lovingly at his wife. Katie exchanged a glance with her husband and wiped away a couple of tears.

Jeremy spoke first, "Christmas is about the joyous birth of a child." He gestured in the direction where Katelyn slept. "The man Jesus that child grew up to be would have said the very same thing as the Can't-Get-Away Club."

Chapter Eleven

———•———

Little joy accompanied Dave's first workday of the new year at Bayside Accounting. The coming year had the potential for financial disaster for everyone involved. He started going through lists of departed clients, pondering whom to solicit.

"Dad, could I talk to you for a few minutes?"

Dave tore his eyes away from the computer screen he studied. "Of course, Jeremy. What's on your mind?"

Jeremy sat down. "We all know that we need more clients. The coming tax season could be the best time to find new clients. When we do their taxes well, some could become year-around clients."

"You're right. As you know, I've been very busy. I'll get us some new clients. You don't need to worry."

Jeremy tilted his head in acquiescence. "I'm not worried," he lied. "But you don't have to carry the load all by yourself. We're all in this."

"You sound like you're leading up to something."

Jeremy gave the winsome smile he had used as a teenager when scheming. "As the firm's business manager, I've taken on a marketing consultant."

"You've taken on a consultant without my approval?" Anger tinged Dave's voice. "Who is this consultant?"

"She's in the conference room."

Dave stood up and without another word stalked to the conference room. Inside he found Katie entertaining Katelyn. "What are you doing here? Where's Jeremy's consultant?"

"I'm Jeremy's consultant. Have you forgotten what a marketer I can be? Remember the big campaigns I led to get parents involved and raise funds for the public schools?"

Jeremy had followed his father into the conference room. "I got her services for a good price, Dad."

Despite himself, Dave had to grin. "You two . . ." He couldn't find the appropriate words. "Katie, you're supposed to be recovering."

"I needed a diversion. And I hardly saw you most days during the holidays."

Jeremy spoke again, "Just hear us out, please, Dad. Remember that you appointed me the business manager. Part of my job is to help find new clients."

Dave regretted wasting time but decided to humor them. "Okay, what have you got?"

Jeremy continued, "First, we need to have a good tax season. We have an online publicity campaign designed to attract tax filers."

"Advertising is undignified for accountants."

"Maybe we can afford dignity next year," answered Katie. "I've got thousands of addresses. Mostly electronic."

Dave remained standing. "Where did you get the addresses?"

"Old Bayside Accounting clients, everybody's personal address books, the networks I used in public service. Since we have prior relationships with these people, contacting them is legal." Katie went on to outline other social media strategies. "Dorothy helped me with the firm's database. She thinks late January to mid-February would be the optimum time to start online publicity."

"Dorothy was supposed to be on vacation over Christmas," Dave complained.

Dorothy's voice came through the open door. "I did what I wanted to do during the holidays."

"Next, we've got new promotional graphics." Jeremy opened his laptop and started clicking through new graphics all proclaiming the advantages of allowing Bayside Accounting's CPAs to prepare IRS and state tax returns. Each graphic had been designed to fit a niche market. One showed a picture of Herschel and explained his qualifications. Several featured Dave using a responsible-looking photo of him supplied by Katie.

Dave pointed at the screen. "How did you generate these?"

Jeremy stopped clicking up graphics after a dozen. "Candace studied graphic arts in college."

"Candace was involved?"

"Sure, everybody helped," answered Jeremy.

Dave had remained standing. "Weren't you all supposed to be enjoying the holidays?"

"We did enjoy the holidays. Didn't you work nearly every day on your forensic consulting accounts?"

Honesty prevented Dave from pursuing that argument.

"Have you got anything else?" he demanded instead.

Jeremy and Katie looked at each other. "Only one more major thing," began Jeremy with a little trepidation. "And we all agree."

"Who is all?" Dave demanded.

"Everybody associated with the firm and their spouses."

"Especially *your* spouse," Katie inserted.

Jeremy brought a newly created website up on the laptop. The screen showed a photo of Dave and Katie smiling. "Bayside Accounting" had been replaced with "Parker and Company—Certified Public Accountants."

"No, you can't change the firm's name," Dave reacted.

"Why not? Because of the poor decisions by Tom and Randy, the name 'Bayside Accounting' carries negative baggage. Your name inspires confidence from everybody who knows you."

Dave sat stunned. He stared at the photo. "Why does the picture include Katie? She's not a CPA."

"That was my idea," Jeremy conceded. "Even if Mom isn't doing the accounting, you're great as a team. More importantly, many people in the community know and respect her."

Dave crossed his arms in frustration. A tone of contempt tinged his voice. "We're an accounting firm, not a public relations company. An accounting firm builds a clientele based on the excellence of their work. I appreciate what you've tried to do. I can get the clients we need for us. You just need to give me some time." He stalked out of the conference room to his office and closed the door behind him.

—◄●►—

Denyse stood before her first class of the new year. "Your former teacher, Mr. Busby, will need longer than anticipated for his recovery from surgery. I'll be your teacher for the remainder of the school year." A smattering of applause demonstrated approval. "Thank you," she acknowledged. "First, I've got some practice problems from the materials we studied before Christmas."

A girl raised her hand. "Yes, Charlene?" said Denyse.

"Ms. Parker, we've already covered those chapters. We know how to do those problems."

"Let me answer you with a question, Charlene. I've heard you play the piano beautifully. Did knowing where the keys are and learning how to read music make you a piano player?" Charlene didn't know how to answer. "I'll bet playing well took a lot of practice, didn't it?" Charlene nodded. "How about you basketball players?" Denyse continued. "Don't you practice what you already know, to get better? Maths is the same as playing a piano or basketball. You have to practice to be good."

Although they wanted to, none of her students could argue with that. Denyse started passing out the exercise sheets. "It's red team against blue team today. Oh, one more thing, Charlene. All of you did improve your maths before Christmas. That's why I've made these problems harder." A collective groan answered her.

—◆—

Dave sat in front of his computer. But he couldn't concentrate. *Nobody here but me has ever run an accounting firm. Jeremy and Herschel are inexperienced. None of the others are even CPAs.*

Turning our business around is up to me. He looked at the diploma and certificates mounted on his office wall.

His desk phone buzzed. "You have a call on line one, Mr. Parker," said Dorothy.

Mr. Parker? Dave thought. *Dorothy must be irritated.* He remembered that Dorothy had always gotten annoyed when people acted stupidly.

"Dave Parker here," he said into the receiver.

"Are you over your snit fit yet?" asked Katie.

"Where are you? And I'm not having a snit fit."

"I'm back at Jeremy and Denyse's taking care of Katelyn. If walking out on your son—who spent the holidays trying to help you—isn't a snit fit, then I don't know what would be. Jeremy knows how much you hate soliciting business. All the others contributed to the ideas too. They just wanted to help."

"I didn't ask them to give up their holidays!"

"And they didn't ask you to give up your holiday by working nearly every day to bring money into the firm."

"I'm the one who's responsible."

Katie's voice softened. "Yes, you are responsible. I love that quality about you. That doesn't mean you have to save the firm all alone. Now hear me, Dave. Bayside Accounting became so successful because of the combination of Tom and Randy's social skills with your genius for accounting details. Now, listen to your son. He has an ability for dealing with people that you—most probably the best pure accountant anywhere—don't have." Katie let that soak into her husband. "Sweetheart, you should be really proud of Jeremy, the way he led everybody to work together, the way he brought the best out of each person."

"Let's not argue," Dave insisted.

"We're not arguing. You men think every discussion is an argument. Just realize that Jeremy has some good ideas."

"I'll think about them," Dave told Katie and said goodbye. After hanging up, he looked at the photos on his desk of Jeremy as a little boy. *Do I still think of Jeremy as a little boy? Are his skills as necessary as my own for a successful business?* He quietly opened his office door and stepped softly until he could peek into Jeremy's office. There Jeremy sat reviewing files of tax returns done by Tom and Randy the previous year. Dave tapped on the door frame.

Jeremy looked around and saw Dave. "Oh, Dad. Listen, I'm sorry for—"

"No, I'm the one who should be sorry." Dave sat down in a chair. "I shouldn't have been so abrupt, even if you had been wrong. And you aren't wrong. Your approach is just . . . different than my own expectations. I guess that I . . . maybe I should . . . I'm . . ."

"Old school?" suggested Jeremy.

"Yeah. And overly self-reliant, I think. Could I have a look at your ideas again? I think maybe we do need to think more creatively." Dave raised his voice a little, "Did you hear that, Dorothy?"

"Smart man," came back from her.

Jeremy's face broke into a big smile. "You haven't even looked through our new website design. Can I invite Dorothy and Herschel to meet with us in the conference room? They proposed some of the best ideas. I'd like you to hear directly from them."

"Of course. And get Katie on the speaker phone."

"Got it! Just one more thing before we leave my office." Jeremy pointed to the IRS form he had been reviewing. "This former client of Randy's could have paid fewer taxes by writing off depreciation over the last couple of years. He's not our client anymore, but I'd like to put together an amended return for him. It's the right thing to do."

"Fine. Don't bill them extra charges, though."

To himself Dave thought, *The quality of our services isn't going to suffer through Jeremy. He also adds an element of caring we didn't have before.*

Chapter Twelve

—•—

The first week of February, Dorothy walked into Dave's office and stood in front of his desk. "We're going to need some seasonal help. Jeremy has the lobby full of new tax clients. He meets with each one, takes their documentation, then promises their completed return in a week. For basic 1040 tax filing, he's charging $100 for each simple W-2 return, and $150 if a 1099 or capital gains are involved. The same for state returns. Beyond that he bills by the hour. Herschel can't keep up with the new tax clients even with the updated software. Jeremy himself is working on returns late every night after office hours."

Dave rubbed his face. "You don't need to tell me about it." He pointed to the floor where Herschel and Jeremy had stacked about sixty completed returns for Dave to check over. "I don't have time to interview and hire anyone right now, though."

"Would you trust me to bring in some temporary help?" asked Dorothy.

He looked sideways at her. "Where would you get them?"

"We had a lot of associates here under Tom and Randy. You wouldn't want most of them. But one older man, Mr. Henry, is a CPA. He did multiple state business returns you'd appreciate—that is, if you can put up with his grouchiness and borderline obsessive-compulsive tendencies. I saw him sitting at a tax service booth in a discount store waiting for walk-up W2 customers. Then we had a girl, Beverly, studying accounting at the University of South Alabama. She drops out of school whenever she runs out of money. She's working at McDonald's right now. She could easily handle the simpler individual returns. One of you CPAs could check her work."

"And you'll vouch for both of them?"

"For their work, not their personalities."

Dave wasn't certain what Dorothy had meant by personalities. Herschel brought in another pile of completed IRS returns and added them to the stack waiting for review before hurrying back to his computer. Dave noticed among them several more lucrative business returns which would be billed by the hour. "Bring in your candidates for an interview," Dave told Dorothy.

She held her ground. "I could use a part-time mail clerk and office gopher too."

Dave opened another file. "Why not?"

━◆━

The bell rang ending the last class of the day. "Could you stay behind a few minutes, please, Anthony?" asked Denyse.

102

Hoots came from the other boys as they filed out, each wishing he had been the one invited to stay.

Anthony remained seated at his desk. He wondered, *Did somebody report me from the riot?*

"The accounting firm Parker and Company where my husband works needs an office helper for a couple of hours a day and maybe on Saturdays. The job would pay above minimum wage and last until about May. Are you interested?"

"Why me? I'm not even your best math student."

"You've improved the most, though. Maths is about more than numbers. It also develops a skill to do things carefully and precisely. You may not be the best at solving the problems yet. But you're solving the problems you do understand without many mistakes."

Anthony stood up. "I could be interested."

Denyse smiled. "Okay, then you'll need to go to meet the firm's owner tomorrow at ten a.m. It's like a job interview, so dress a little nice like you would for church."

"I'm in school at ten o'clock tomorrow."

"I've already talked to Principal Fogle. He'll take you to the interview. You'll still be legally in school while you're with him."

"Thank you, Ms. Parker."

—◆—

Dorothy had asked Dave to come to the conference room. There he found a scowling man of about seventy years, a purple-haired young woman with a lip ring and one heavily tattooed arm, and a scrawny, frightened-looking African American teenager.

103

Dave forced himself to show no adverse reaction as he shook hands with each one. Starting with the older man, he asked questions about business taxes. Obviously, the candidate would never win any congeniality awards, but he knew the tax code. The girl didn't understand the nuances of business taxation but seemed familiar enough with individual taxes. The young man, noticeably nervous, appeared willing and teachable.

Dorothy had watched quietly while Dave met her prospective temps. Dave made eye contact with her and nodded before thanking the candidates and saying, "Mrs. Goldstein will talk to you about temporary employment."

Leaving the conference room, Dave saw Caleb Fogle sitting in the firm's lobby. "Caleb, you don't need to wait here. If you want us to do your taxes, I'll take your information."

Caleb stood up. "Actually, Jeremy already did. I'm waiting for Anthony."

Dave shook his hand. "You mean the high school student I just met, Anthony Marshall? How well do you know this kid?"

Caleb answered evasively. "I've spoken to him outside of school hours."

"Will he do dependable work?"

"I think he's worth taking a chance on."

Dave smiled. "You say that about all of your students."

—◆—

Working part time at the accounting firm transported Anthony into a different world. Hope and promise filled that world. Dorothy kept him busy running errands for the accountants, making copies, and sealing envelopes. On a Saturday morning, Dorothy directed him to the small mail room in the back of the building. There he found more than two hundred completed tax returns with invoices for their preparation and a neat stack of preprinted manila envelopes. "Look at both addresses. Put each form and invoice into the corresponding envelope, seal it up, weigh the envelope, print the metered postage strip, and apply it," Dorothy instructed him. She demonstrated on the first. "Come to me if you have any questions."

Anthony started checking each envelope versus the name on the return. The first six envelopes corresponded with the first six returns. *This is easy*, he realized. His thoughts turned to his co-workers. Mr. Henry had been gruff and demanding. But he treated everybody the same way, even the senior Mr. Parker. Jeremy—whom he knew to be his math teacher's husband—always had encouraging words for Anthony. The girl, Beverly, only a few years older than himself, had talked about meditation and the power of crystals. She seemed a bit scatterbrained until she sat down in front of a computer. Then she became a perfectionist. Just then Beverly came into the mail room. "Here's one back, Anthony. I pulled it out of the stack to recheck a deduction." She handed him a tax return before returning to her cubicle.

Anthony looked at the name on the form. *Where in the order does this go?* he wondered. He could not find an empty envelope with that name. To his horror, he found a sealed envelope bearing that name. *This means the envelopes and returns are out of order. I've sealed who knows how many in the wrong envelopes.*

Anthony felt like his world of hope and promise had ended. *Just mail out the envelopes*, a voice whispered in his head. *Maybe someone else, like Beverly, will get blamed.* His own thoughts made him ashamed. He remembered Mr. Parker talking about doing everything exactly right. *These people tried to give you a chance. You have to tell them your mistake*, another voice in his head answered. *They'll fire you*, the first voice argued. *You were supposed to check each address*, replied the second.

Anthony went to stand by Dorothy as she prepared invoices. "Yes, Anthony?" she asked without glancing away from her computer monitor.

"I've made a mistake."

She stopped and looked at him over her close-up glasses. "What's that?"

"I think I put some returns in the wrong envelopes."

"How many?"

"I don't know," Anthony confessed.

"Anthony . . ."

"I know. I'm fired."

Anthony heard a male voice behind him. "We don't fire people for making a mistake," said Jeremy. "We do fire people for keeping a mistake hidden. Mind if I fix this, Dorothy?" asked Jeremy.

"Be my guest." Dorothy looked severely at Anthony. "Don't you make any more mistakes. Being fired will be the last of your worries if I catch you being careless again."

"Yes, ma'am."

In the mail room, Jeremy looked at the pile of sealed envelopes. "We'll need to open every envelope."

"But I've already stuck on the postage," Anthony reminded him.

"Look, here's what we'll do." Jeremy took one of the sealed envelopes and tapped it on the counter to force the contents to one end. Then he took a paper cutter and sliced off a minuscule sliver of the envelope. He pulled out the tax return. The return did not match the client's name printed on the outside of the envelope. Jeremy searched for the return and invoice to match the envelope, inserted it, and applied a strip of clear tape to reseal the edge. He re-weighed the envelope to check the postage. When the envelope needed a little more postage, he subtracted the affixed amount then metered the difference and applied it under the first sticker.

"Anthony, we all check each other's work. But you're the last one of us to see these returns. That's why you need to be extra careful. Check each one over twice to make certain everything is right."

"You're going to leave me to finish them?" wondered Anthony.

"Are you going to make any more mistakes?"

"No, sir."

"Well, alright then."

◄••►

Colorful floats passed in front of Jeremy, Denyse, and Katelyn. Costumed revelers threw candy and strings of beads from the floats to those lining Mobile's streets. "Mardi Gras started in Mobile over three hundred years ago, you know?" explained Jeremy. "Originally it was a Catholic religious event marking the beginning of Lent. Over the years, the celebration evolved into a series of parties or balls, many of them private."

Denyse picked up Katelyn. The little girl put her arms around her mother's neck but continued to stare at the floats and costumed people. "And this is the parade?" asked Denyse.

"Actually, one parade of several parades. Some of the events are during the daytime and family-friendly. Other activities involve a lot of drinking and are rowdier. There are any number of cliquish social clubs and mystic societies that associate with Mardi Gras. Dad's old partners, Tom and Randy, were both part of a crew, one of the social groups that might sponsor a float or a party. Mom and Dad never had much interest in Mardi Gras. Both would rather go fishing."

A masked reveler walked alongside one of the gaudier floats. Suddenly he lunged close to the spectators, shouting "Aaaugh!" close to Katelyn's face.

Startled, the little girl started to cry as the masked one proceeded on down the street periodically trying to frighten others watching. "I don't think I like Mardi Gras either," said Denyse as she comforted her daughter. "Not this part, anyway."

◄━◆━►

Three weeks later, Dave had to admit that Jeremy's strategy to generate business doing tax returns had paid off. He looked at a stack of more than fifty business returns and two hundred individual returns waiting for his final approval. Seeing everyone busily engaged felt good.

This is how a first-class accounting firm is supposed to operate, he thought. *Even the temporary employees hired by Dorothy are working out well.* He smiled when he thought about the young African

American kid, Anthony. *Jeremy should have told me right away about the near screw-up of the mailing. But I did make Jeremy the business manager. And that young man is trying hard. Caleb will be proud. Anthony was worth a chance.*

Something left undone nagged at Dave's subconscious. *What have I forgotten? Have I made any unkept promises?* Dave's mind shuffled through his employees. *Nothing there. Katie?* Immediately he remembered, *I promised her I'd find out about suffering.*

His eyes returned to the pile of tax documents awaiting his attention. *After tax season,* he told himself.

Dave's Boat

Chapter Thirteen

———•———

Jeremy entered the bathroom where Denyse was bathing Katelyn in about three inches of warm water in the tub. "The weather forecast predicts Saturday will be warm, sunny, and nearly windless," he told Denyse as Katelyn giggled and splashed.

Denyse didn't look up. "Isn't March still part of your North American winter?"

"Yeah, officially. They're still having frigid weather up North. But some beautiful spring days start coming to the Gulf Coast about now. You've already seen the azaleas blooming."

Denyse lifted Katelyn out of the tub. "You mean the banks of white, pink, and red flowering bushes in the parks and around people's houses? They're magnificent. We didn't have anything to compare to that in Australia."

Jeremy handed Denyse a towel. "The crepe myrtles will flower soon. Those are bigger trees full of pink or white flowers."

"What's all this got to do with Saturday?" Denyse used the towel to dry her daughter.

"Everybody at the firm has been working long hours on the tax returns. Dad insisted that all of us take this weekend off. Low tide is near noon on Saturday. If we want to go along, he's offered to take you, me, and Katelyn collecting oysters and crabbing. We might get a few shrimp too."

Denyse looked at her husband and smiled. "Catching oysters, crabs, and shrimps? That sounds like a lot of fun."

—◆—

A bright sun above a clear blue sky warmed the air on Saturday morning. Jeremy led his family down the marina dock to where Dave and Katie readied their twenty-four-foot cabin cruiser for a day on the water. Many other boats had already gone out. Denyse saw on the side of the boat the name "Audit."

"Jeremy didn't say anything about you being here," Denyse said to Katie.

"Oh, I nearly always go along. I'm just glad we're going after oysters today, not fish."

"Why's that?"

"The fish must wake up early because avid fishermen want to be on the water by five a.m. Oysters like to sleep in. We can collect them anytime. I'm glad you brought Ripper too."

Denyse looked at the dog. "He's another one Jeremy didn't mention."

"We invited Old Yeller. But he gets seasick," Katie joked. "Labradors bring joy and energy to any outdoor activity. Ripper will be good company as long as we can keep him dry."

"Ripper loves water. How would being wet hurt him?"

"It wouldn't hurt *him*. But a wet dog in the boat would shake sand and water all over us." Katie opened the built-in seats. Then she put a small life preserver onto Katelyn. "This was Jeremy's jacket until he learned to swim like a river otter." Katie passed out hats and sunglasses from a small storage compartment. "We're ready, Dave," she called. "There's a small toilet in the cabin, when you or Katelyn need it," she told Denyse.

A few minutes later, Denyse could feel the cool air blowing her hair as Dave backed the boat from the slip and guided it into Mobile Bay's calm waters. Both Katelyn and Ripper reacted to their first boat ride with uncertainty. Katelyn looked more relaxed when Denyse took her into her lap. "You're on your own," Denyse said to the growing puppy.

Jeremy fussed with two long-handled hinged rakes. Then he put a piece of raw fish into an open-sided wire box attached to a nylon rope. He placed the box by Denyse's feet. "This trap is for you and Katelyn," he explained.

Before Denyse could inquire how to use the trap, she heard Dave cutting the engine. As the boat coasted to a standstill, she saw Jeremy test the bottom with the long rakes. "About six feet, Dad," he reported.

Dave took a pole and pushed the boat further toward an unseen objective. "See anything yet?"

"Not yet," Jeremy answered. Then he shouted, "Now. I can see bottom at about three feet. Should be less when the tide is fully out."

"Okay." Dave threw out an anchor.

Jeremy scrambled to the bow of the boat with the hinged rakes. Dave followed him with several shallow trays. Together they stood staring down into the water. "Go ahead," said Dave. Jeremy started grappling with something under the water using the rakes like tongs.

"Those rakes are called nippers," Katie explained to Denyse. "Jeremy is trying to detach the oysters from the bottom. Let's put out your trap now." Katie pointed to the wire box Jeremy had baited.

"Oh. Will the oysters come to the trap?"

"No. Oysters grow stuck to the bottom, sucking in murky water to filter for food. This is for crabs." Katie dropped the trap into the brown water and handed Denyse the rope. Katelyn and Ripper watched everything happening with interest.

Denyse saw Jeremy grunt and pull. Then using the nippers like tongs, he hauled a black and gray encrusted mass up and dropped it into the shallow tray. "Are those oysters?" she asked.

Katie pulled on a pair of heavy gloves. "Well, some of that cluster of stuff is oysters. Mostly it's old shells and debris the spats attached to." To Denyse's puzzled look she added, "Spats are the fertilized larva of oysters. Barnacles also attach to the shells and the oysters. All together they make a clump with a few live oysters included."

Dave had brought the first tray with clusters of Jeremy's haul to set down on the boat's stern deck. It smelled like mud mixed with seaweed. He hurried back to the bow to help Jeremy. Katie started using a hammer and a short crow bar to separate the living oysters from the cluster. A moment later she held up an irregular flat shell that looked like a dirty rock to Denyse. "See, this is a live oyster," said Katie. She then dropped the oyster into a burlap bag and threw the other debris from the cluster back into the water. "Separating the oyster from the junk is what we call 'culling.' "

Dave returned with another tray of oyster clusters and started culling with Katie. Katelyn wriggled down from her mother's lap to get closer. Ripper came to sniff the bag with the oysters. "Is this how they harvest the oysters we see in a store?" asked Denyse.

"This is how generations of Parkers commercially collected oysters, even up into my grandparents' lives," answered Dave. "But nowadays commercial operations use a dredge. Locals can use a residential license to harvest oysters by hand for personal use."

Jeremy joined them dragging another tray of clusters. He looked bushed. "This is hard work."

"I'm up, then." Dave took the tray Katie had emptied and took Jeremy's place on the bow.

Denyse looked around at the huge bay. "How do you know where to find the oysters in all this water?"

Jeremy started culling before he spoke, "Granddad started this reef on a shallow mud flat in the early 1950s. He sank some old junk and threw in shells he had collected behind a restaurant. The oysters just came to where they could attach to something solid. We don't legally own the bed. But we don't tell anyone where it is either. Dad is willing to give away the oysters, but not reveal their source."

"Let me help culling," suggested Denyse and put down Katelyn.

Jeremy smiled. "Sure. But maybe you should check your crab trap first."

"Already?"

"Maybe. Katelyn, can you see anything coming up from the water?"

Katelyn peered over the boat's side. Ripper joined her with his big feet rested against the gunnel. Denyse started pulling up the trap with the nylon rope. To her surprise, two hand-sized crabs clung to the chunk of fish inside the trap. She swung the trap onto the boat's deck where it dripped. Ripper, perceiving living creatures inside the trap, started to bark. Katelyn stared with fascination at the two blue shell crabs. She said, "Big bug," and started to extend a little hand.

Katie laughed and reached out to pull her hand back. "No, honey. That's a blue crab, not a bug. Don't touch it." Katie used her gloved hand to reach inside and pull out one of the crabs. She placed it on the deck for Katelyn to see, then put her gloved hand where the crab immediately pinched her. Lifting her arm, Katie let the crab dangle in the air. "See? A crab can hurt you." Then Katie dropped both crabs into a five-gallon plastic bucket. "We'll need a few more," she said and threw the trap into the water again.

Dave returned with another tray of clustered oysters.

"Wow, that gets harder every year. I'm getting too old to hoist oysters."

"I don't remember your father complaining," Katie teased him.

"Could I try pulling the oysters up?" asked Denyse.

Jeremy waved her toward the bow. "Come on." Up front he handed her the nippers. "Try to use them like chopsticks to pinch the oysters and pull them up."

Denyse could feel the nippers touching the reef below the boat and hear clicking of the tines against the hard shells. But unlike Chinese food on a plate, the oysters remained attached to the bottom. Eventually, she felt something loosen. She scooped it between the rakes and brought it toward the surface. When she tried to lower her grip to pull the handles higher, the oyster slipped away and sank.

Jeremy knew better than to laugh. "You're doing fine. Try again."

On her next attempt, she got a small piece to the surface and proudly deposited it into the waiting tray. Jeremy picked it up, looked, and then tossed it back into the water. "Sorry. Just a shell." To Denyse's look of dismay, he suggested, "It takes upper body strength. Let me break off a bigger cluster for you. They're easier to grip."

A minute later he rested the nippers on a basketball-sized cluster still under the water. "Feel that hunk?" he asked. "Grab it then haul it onboard."

Denyse could feel that piece through the nippers. She pinched the detached cluster and lifted it toward the surface. But once her burden cleared the water and lost buoyancy, it became impossibly heavy. She could not raise it all the way onboard while keeping the nippers tight. Her arms ached. She sensed Dave come up behind them and hand something to Jeremy. Her husband extended a fishing net to scoop up the cluster she had raised to the surface. "Nice one. Probably four, maybe five oysters in that cluster."

"Four or five? No wonder oysters cost so much. I'll be better at culling," Denyse promised.

"You did better at this part than Katie could have," Dave answered.

In the boat's stern, Denyse found Katie helping Katelyn to pull in another crab. The bucket now held four. "We hope for at least one for each of us," said Katie. "Even if we don't get more, that'll be enough to taste their sweet flavor. Dave took me crabbing with a dip net on our first married Valentine's Day. I had dolled up for his 'surprise.' It was a surprise, alright. After we started crabbing, I thought that my new dress had been ruined."

Denyse laughed, sat down, and started culling. In the cluster she had brought up, she found five live oysters. Dave took one of her oysters and with a knife-like tool and a flick of his wrist popped it open. He extended the shellfish to her on a half shell and said, "This is one you collected."

"Alive? Raw? Are you sure it's safe to eat?"

"Oh, sure. The state tests the water quality constantly. Only occasionally do they have to close an area for hepatitis or pollution. You'll be fine."

She held the oyster on its shell in both hands and watched while Dave shucked another. He leaned back his head and let it slide from the shell into his open mouth. Dave chewed the shellfish with relish. Denyse tilted back her head and held up the oyster shell. Suddenly, a soft lubricious mass filled her mouth from her teeth to her tonsils. She tasted brine and muddy water. Without room in her mouth to properly chew, she simply swallowed. As quickly as it had come, the oyster disappeared.

"Now wasn't that good?" Dave shucked another oyster and to Denyse's relief didn't offer it to her. He headed forward to share the delicacy with Jeremy. "Help yourself to more," he told her over his shoulder.

Denyse noticed Katie watching her with amusement. "Raw oysters make me want to gag," Katie confided. "You did well to just swallow that one. From now on, you can say 'I'm not hungry,' if you want to."

The two women laughed. "I love coming out here, though," Katie continued. "Just look at Dave and Jeremy. See how happy they are? Watching them spending joyful time together is the best part for me."

Denyse nodded in agreement. "Living here is a wonderful adventure. The type I had never expected to experience. I can see why Jeremy wanted to move back to Mobile. Life is somehow more real . . . simpler here, day by day."

"In bad weather on the water, life can seem like minute to minute," Katie replied. "Even inside the cabin can get hot and stuffy."

"What happens next?" asked Denyse.

Katie looked at the burlap bag nearly full of oysters. "Dave and Jeremy are almost halfway finished collecting oysters. Afterwards, they'll be starving. Dave will beach the boat somewhere secluded and build a fire with driftwood. He and Jeremy will use the throw net trying to catch shrimp and more crabs while jibing each other about who catches the most and the biggest. You'll probably want to try throwing the net yourself. I'll boil the crabs on the fire and hopefully a few shrimp you'll catch. Plus, I brought plenty of hot dogs, chips, and cold drinks. Katelyn can play in the sand at the water's edge and get dirty. Ripper will get wet and then come close to us to shake off. We'll all go home tired and smelling of wood smoke, brackish water, and oysters."

Denyse sighed, "This is really a wonderful life."

"Yes, it is."

—◦—

On Monday morning, Dave set aside checking one of the multiple state tax returns Mr. Henry had completed to answer the phone. "Mr. Parker, this is Harry Collins at Bank of Alabama. You may remember me as the investment advisor who set up the fiduciary accounts for you."

"Of course. What can I do for you, Harry?"

"Our records show that you've depleted the individual brokerage account and that you are withdrawing heavily from your and Mrs. Parker's IRAs. I'm checking to determine if Bank of Alabama or I myself have done anything that would cause you to take your personal banking business elsewhere."

"No, my accounts are still at Bank of Alabama. And because we're both over fifty-nine and a half years old, we can withdraw from our IRAs without penalty." Mr. Collins remained silent on the other end, the obvious question unverbalized. Dave tried to explain, "I've repurchased the accounting firm I had founded from my former partners. I'm trying to make it profitable again. And we had my wife's

120

medical bills to pay as well." Realizing that clarity would require time he couldn't spare, Dave concluded, "We're having a good tax season. The firm's revenue should improve as our clients pay for the services in thirty to ninety days."

"I hope so, Mr. Parker. A few months ago, you looked financially secure for life. At the current rate of withdrawals, you'll have depleted your funds before the end of the year. In addition, I'm required to inform you that your assets have fallen below the threshold that qualifies you for a personal investment advisor."

"Thank you for calling, Harry."

"Good luck, Mr. Parker."

Chapter Fourteen

The culmination of tax season in April relieved everybody. Parker and Company had completed 1,748 returns. Mr. Henry expressed eagerness to resume full-time retirement. "Until next year," he hinted. Beverly had re-enrolled in classes at the university. A few new clients—more than enough to stretch Herschel—had retained their services as bookkeepers, plus three had requested simple audits for businesses being sold. Jeremy took responsibility for all the tax returns on which they had filed for extensions due to incomplete documentation. At Dorothy's request, Anthony continued working Monday, Wednesday, and Friday afternoons.

"We had a good tax season," Dave told Katie over their private celebration dinner at the marina. "It felt wonderful to be busy again. But the hard part will be turning this surge into year-around clients." He told her about the phone call from their banker.

Katie shrugged. "Well, we knew that taking over the firm would be a big risk. When do you think you'll start making a profit?"

"Our revenue should improve over the summer as clients pay for our tax services. Still, without more year-around clients . . ." Dave trailed off.

"Hasn't Jeremy done well?" Katie prompted to change the mood.

"I think our son inherited the best from each of us," Dave responded with a father's pride.

"You didn't think so when he removed all of the labels from our canned goods as a Halloween prank during elementary school."

"You're the one who made him eat whatever the opened cans revealed," Dave returned.

"Except for the dog food." Katie laughed before adding, "Jeremy isn't a kid anymore."

"No, he's not. Every time I think of him as a husband and father, I wonder where the time went."

Katie paused, enjoying the memory. Then she added her own concern. "Have you noticed that Denyse has become a bit short with Jeremy since we first met her in Australia?"

"No, I hadn't noticed."

"Well, I see them when they come home tired from work. She can be a bit harsh then."

━━◆━━

Dave had not forgotten his promise to Katie. Not one

to indefinitely postpone a difficult task, he spent hours pondering her questions about suffering. She had kept her word to not allow the situation to affect her enjoyment of Christmas or pestered him for answers through the winter or spring. But no answers had come to him. *Right now, I've got to generate more year-around business for the firm*, he thought. *I'll find the answers to Katie's questions later.*

—◆—

"You've all improved remarkably this year. Every one of you has passed basic maths. I'm proud of each of you," Denyse told her final class of the school year in late May. Applause and a few hoots acknowledged her praise. "I've enjoyed being your teacher. Thank you for your hard work."

The ringing bell interrupted Denyse's goodbye. Her students remained seated, waiting for their favorite teacher to finish. "Have a great summer. Any of you can advance to algebra or geometry next year. I hope you will." Denyse opened the classroom door. Anthony and her other students stood and filed out, each nodding or speaking to her for what everybody expected to be their last time. A couple of the girls wiped away a tear and stopped to hug Denyse as they departed for summer vacation.

Left alone in the classroom, Denyse started to gather her things to go home. *That was my last class at Central High. Too bad I don't have teaching certification in Alabama. Maybe I can substitute again next year.*

Denyse turned to find Caleb Fogle had entered after the students had left. "Thank you, Denyse. You did a remarkable job with these kids. You believed in them and made them believe in themselves."

Hardly trusting herself to speak, Denyse nodded. "Thanks." She managed, "I loved teaching them. Many of them are in difficult situations like I had growing up. Please call me whenever you need a maths substitute."

Caleb nodded himself. "What would you think about a full-time job this fall?"

Denyse shook her head. "I don't have the necessary Alabama teacher certification."

"I talked with the school board about you yesterday. They're willing to defer the requirement if you'll start taking part-time education classes leading to your certification."

Denyse stood still in surprise. "How many classes would I need to take?"

"You'd need to get an accredited school to review your transcript from Australia and lay out a curriculum leading to certification. The school board would expect you to take at least one class this summer. The University of South Alabama has an intense six-week course that yields five semester hours starting next week."

—◆—

"Okay, let's see how caught up we are," said Dave to his assembled staff on the last day of May. "Have all of the tax returns for which we had filed extensions been completed now, Jeremy?"

"Every last one. And I've started setting up a paperless filing option for next tax season. For clients expecting a refund, a local bank will allow us for a three-percent fee to offer an immediate payment. That will be an additional incentive to file through us next year."

Dave nodded approval of Jeremy's initiative. "Herschel, have all of our bookkeeping clients received a current balance sheet? And how about the audits we picked up after tax season?"

"Everybody's up-to-date. I've received the engagement letters from the new clients and requested their bank and credit card records for the audits. Once those are returned, we should be able to proceed."

"Have you completed all of the invoices for our services, Dorothy?"

"Nearly eighteen hundred of them. Payments are coming in mostly through the payment function Herschel installed on our new Parker and Company website."

"Anthony, have all the paper invoices been mailed out?"

"Yes, sir. I checked each of them three times before sealing the envelopes."

"Great! All of you have done a very professional job this tax season. Starting Saturday, I'm declaring a week of paid holiday for everyone. This is in addition to your personal discretionary vacations." A murmur of approval answered Dave's announcement. "And unlike our Christmas break, this time I'll set an example by actually taking off myself. For those who wish, I'll take you fishing in the Gulf on Tuesday."

"Not me," protested Dorothy. "I get sick just smelling fish in the market. Being on a rocking boat would send me over the edge. I'll promise to relax all week, though."

"Herschel? Candace can come along."

"Our boys are sick with colds. She won't leave them. But I've always wanted to try deep sea fishing."

"Alright, then. Anthony?"

"I'm invited too?" The young man looked surprised.

Dave nodded. "Of course."

"Sure, I'll go. Thanks."

Dave looked carefully at him. "Remind me how old you are, son."

"Almost seventeen."

"Okay. Jeremy, why don't you drive Anthony home and make sure he has permission to go with us from his mother."

"I'll be happy to. But you haven't asked if I would go," answered Jeremy.

"When have you ever turned down a fishing trip?"

"Try leaving me behind. I just didn't want you to take me for granted," Jeremy responded with a big grin.

"What about Denyse?"

"She may be starting a summer course next week. I'm pretty sure she'll want to spend the day with Katelyn. But I will bring someone."

—◆—

Katie approached Dave at his workbench in the garage. "Have you heard that Caleb offered Denyse a full-time job at Central High?"

Dave continued getting the tackle ready for the upcoming fishing expedition. "Yes, Jeremy told me."

Katie stared at her husband in exasperation. "Why didn't you tell me then?"

Dave put down the reel on which he had installed fresh line. He looked at Katie with apprehension. "I know you think a mother should stay home with her children. The job would also require some commitment to additional education by Denyse. If she doesn't accept, then upsetting you wouldn't be necessary."

Katie sat down in a folding lawn chair nearby. "Why doesn't Denyse want to stay home with Katelyn?"

"It's not that she doesn't want to be home with her daughter. Jeremy told me she just feels an obligation to help young people. I've seen pastors who didn't seem so dedicated. It isn't for money or a career. Denyse's motivation is genuinely altruistic. I have to respect that."

"Denyse *is* a wonderful mother when she's with Katelyn," Katie admitted. "She spends all of her time with her daughter other than her school hours. It's just that, even though I got plenty tired of Jeremy when we were together 24/7, I would give anything to have some of those moments back. I regret Denyse missing any part of that time with her daughter."

"Maybe Denyse looks at it as a worthwhile sacrifice. And she knows Katelyn isn't suffering any neglect when you're taking care of her," Dave added.

"You're right about Denyse being dedicated. It's like she feels a calling. And according to Caleb, she's making a big difference with at-risk kids. She identifies with them and makes a connection because of her own difficult start."

"Sweetheart, you're a part of that. God is using you to let Denyse serve others."

"That could be. But I still think Katelyn should be with her mother."

―◆―

At five a.m., Jeremy brought Herschel and Anthony along with Ripper to the marina where Dave kept his ocean-worthy boat. Dave emerged from the tiny cabin where he had been stowing tackle, lunch, and a cooler of soft drinks. "Can you swim, son?" he asked Anthony.

"Not very well."

"Well, I wouldn't want to get into trouble with your mother if you were to fall overboard. Put this on." Dave handed Anthony a life jacket. "Here's a pill to prevent seasickness. The water will be choppier once we leave the bay. And put on this sunscreen."

"Herschel?" Dave passed him the same pill and some sunscreen.

"I took lifesaving in PE at Auburn."

"Alright, I'll put life jackets for you, Jeremy, and myself under the steps to the bridge. I thought we'd try catching some deep reef fish today. We should be fishing in about an hour and a half. You two were both smart to bring hats and sunglasses. Sit down and enjoy the ride out." Dave waved toward the built-in seats.

A few minutes later, Dave backed the boat out of its slip, reversed the propeller, and headed into Mobile Bay. Jeremy busied himself with the bait and tackle. Ripper came to be petted by Herschel and Anthony.

"Nice dog," said Herschel.

"Yeah," Anthony answered nervously. After a few moments he added, "This is my first time fishing, except using a cane pole with my mother when I was little."

"Then this is a first for both of us," Herschel answered. "I was worried about getting seasick and being embarrassed. I'm glad Dave gave us those pills."

Herschel's response had surprised Anthony. "I thought people like you did stuff like this all the time."

"No, I'm just like you, Anthony. Grew up without much in Mobile. Went to Central High School. But I hope my two boys will get to do things like this as they're growing up."

Anthony stared at him. "Then how'd you get to be an important CPA?"

Herschel laughed. "Maybe I was lucky to be too small to play sports. I studied and tried to make good grades instead. I got an academic scholarship to Auburn. There I found that I could out-compete most of the ones who had received more advantages. Education and training your brain is a path that will work for those willing to work hard."

He talks just like Ms. Parker, thought Anthony.

Chapter Fifteen

———•◦•———

Katie picked up the ringing phone. "Hello."

"Hi, Katie. This is Denyse."

"Good morning, Denyse. Why didn't you take Katelyn fishing with Jeremy and Dave?"

"I wanted to spend the day with her. And Jeremy warned me that the water outside the bay would be rougher. We're going to the park to feed the ducks. Would you like to go along?"

"Thanks, but I'm catching up on some correspondence and checking on some of the marriage discussion groups I helped organize."

"Helping couples have good marriages *is* important. And it really affects their children as well."

"Thank you," Katie responded. "Your work educating young people is important too."

"That's the second reason I called. Principle Fogle offered

me a full-time job in the fall. I'd be teaching algebra. He also wants me to teach a class of calculus for the first time at Central High."

"Jordan told me that. Are you thinking of taking the job?"

"Truthfully, I'm torn," Denyse confided. "I know that I'll miss part of Katelyn's life that I won't ever be able to get back. But I know that I can make a big difference in these kids' futures."

"That's true," Katie conceded.

"And there's Jeremy. He's been great and has told me he'll support me either way. But I don't want to make life harder for him."

"I'm pretty sure Jeremy can handle it," Katie heard herself say.

"I've already decided that I won't put Katelyn into a childcare program."

That means I can control this situation, thought Katie. *If I refuse to take care of Katelyn, Denyse will stay home with her. But then I wouldn't get to take care of Katelyn. And Denyse sincerely feels a calling to help her students.*

Katie sighed. "You know that I think it's best for a child to be with her mother."

"Yes, I do. And I want to be home——"

"But this is your decision to make," Katie interrupted. "If you decide to take the job, I would love to care for Katelyn. I'll even feel a part of helping your students."

"Are you sure it's not too much to ask? I would split my salary with you."

Katie laughed. "Taking money for caring for my granddaughter would seem like stealing. You and Jeremy can add the money to your house fund."

"Thank you, Katie. I love you."

"I love you too, Denyse."

"If I do take the job, I'll need to take some classes to eventually get my teacher's certification. Jeremy can take care of Katelyn at night. But during summertime, day classes . . ." Denyse trailed off.

"I already know about that possibility. While you're in a class, Katelyn and I will be fine together."

Red Snapper

"If a fish pulls you into the water, let go of the rod," Jeremy teased Anthony once the boat had passed the old confederate citadel at Fort Morgan and entered the Gulf. More seriously he added, "Dad lost his father's best rod overboard when he was a kid. So hold on unless you find yourself in the water."

Dave piloted the boat from the bridge above the tiny cabin as Anthony sat like a statue gripping a stiff seven-foot rod. He cut the engine to allow the boat to drift over the artificial reef. Jeremy tied Ripper to the ladder to keep him from getting under the feet of those fishing.

"Relax, Anthony. The bait isn't in the water yet," Jeremy continued to tease.

The young man sat back in the deck chair looking embarrassed. "Why do you have those silvery metal things above the hooks?"

"Those are flashers to attract the fishes' attention. Then we put three baited hooks two yards apart to improve your chances." Jeremy pushed a walnut-sized hunk of cut bait onto each hook. Anthony saw an egg-sized lead sinker below the hooks.

Jeremy threw the assembly overboard. "Okay. Lower the bait down to about forty feet. The fish finder shows a school. They're probably snappers." To Anthony's puzzled look he added, "Back wind the reel about eighty times."

Jeremy threw in Herschel's bait next. Anthony watched Herschel release the line brake and start lowering the rig into the murky salt water. He lowered his own bait, surprised that the line angled behind the boat. "Why doesn't the line go straight down?"

"That's because the boat is drifting in the wind and current. We have to use the heavy sinker to get the bait deep."

Dave shouted from the elevated helm where he monitored the fish finder and GPS positioning unit, "We're almost directly over the reef."

Anthony felt a slight jerk and saw the rod tip quivering.

"Hold on just a few seconds," Jeremy instructed. Anthony could feel the rod vibrating as the fish below struggled. A much larger tug soon followed. Jerking replaced the vibration. "Now reel up." Anthony found cranking up the fish and heavy sinker difficult. His arm soon ached, but he didn't quit.

A reddish shape about a foot long appeared in the water. Strangely, the fish had stopped its struggle near the surface. A bulbous sack protruded from its mouth, like the fish was blowing bubble gum.

"That's the fish's air sack," Jeremy explained. "The air sack expands when the fish is brought out of deep water where the pressure is high. Keep reeling."

Jeremy peered over the side. For the first time, Anthony noticed Herschel next to him also reeling up a fish.

Jeremy said, "I thought maybe you could get a bigger one," as a second much larger reddish shape appeared connected to a lower hook. "Now that's a nice snapper," he added as he reached down with a gloved hand and pulled both fish onto the boat deck. Ripper cautiously sniffed at the fish. "Anthony got one about five pounds," Jeremy yelled to Dave.

"Way to go, Anthony," Dave called back. "After you get Herschel's in, I'll circle around for another drift pass over the reef."

Jeremy hoisted Herschel's fish aboard. "About three pounds," he announced. Ripper started barking at the new arrival.

As Anthony and Herschel watched, Jeremy unhooked the smaller fish Anthony had caught. "We'll need to throw this one back to grow up." To their surprise, he punctured the protruding air sack and gently pitched the small fish overboard. "With the air sack inflated the fish can't swim home," he explained. "Now these two are nice keepers." He held the other two fish up for everyone to admire and then put them into the cooler.

While Dave repositioned the boat, Jeremy rebated the hooks. "Let's try again. You know what to do."

"Wouldn't you like to fish yourself?" asked Herschel.

Jeremy shook his head. "Thanks, but I enjoy seeing you two catch fish more."

Fish came up sporadically until Anthony and Herschel had twenty-three between them. "I hope you both like cleaning fish," Jeremy resumed his teasing on their way back to the marina.

But at the marina Dave expertly filleted all the fish and split them between Anthony and Herschel.

"My mother won't believe this," said Anthony in amazement.

The next day, Dave puttered around the house catching up on chores and maintenance. "The phone is ringing," called Katie from where she defrosted the freezer. "Can you get it?"

"Hello."

"Dave, this is Buddy Oleson from Minnesota."

"Hi, Buddy. After your call last year, we went to Washita to see everyone like you had suggested. Thanks for telling us we could visit again."

"No problem. You and Katie made a big difference up there."

"We just fell into that situation. You and Richard are the real heroes. The Big River Mansion Museum is remarkable. And who could have expected Susie Holmquist to be the new mayor?"

"How about Billy at the university?" Buddy answered. "I remember when he and I both responded to the drive-by shooting. Oh, and remember when you and Katie rescued that young woman, Leslie, out at the Midnight Lounge? I wanted to slap you on the back. But being the chief then, I had to maintain an appearance of objectivity."

"I understand. Nothing ever looked better than seeing you arrive to take charge," answered Dave. "So, how is your retirement going? Have you gotten used to the warm, humid Florida weather yet?"

"Mary and I are happy in Florida. Our old cold bones have finally thawed out. And we're thinking about coming back through Mobile this summer. Katie had said something about fishing?"

"Sure, we'd love that. When could you come?"

"How about mid-July?"

"Perfect. The king mackerel should be hitting then."

—◆—

"You won't believe who called me this morning," began Katie while fixing dinner a week later.

"A Hollywood studio wants you to reprise your Down Under role as a gambler and sultry temptress for a blockbuster movie," guessed Dave.

Katie returned a wry smile at his subtle compliment. "Not hardly. But it does relate to Down Under."

"Trevor has run away again, and we're supposed to find him?"

"Closer. Beatrice and Dingo are coming to the United States. An American publisher has purchased the rights to distribute Dingo's book, *The Right Fight*, in America. They're bringing the Larkins over for a publicity tour."

"Will they have time to visit Mobile?"

"We're their first stop. They'll be in Mobile for a week starting the second week in July. Then they'll start the publicity tour."

"It's good that they're coming in July before Denyse starts her fall school term."

"That's true. Beatrice offered to stay at a hotel. But I told her they could stay at our house."

Dave winced a little at the thought of hosting Dingo. "I guess we owe it to them after we stayed at their house in Melbourne."

Katie shrugged in sympathy. "That's what I figured too."

Dave brightened. "The Olesons should be here then too. We can take all of them fishing."

And what will we do with them the rest of the time? Katie wondered.

Chapter Sixteen

———•—

The next day Herschel came into Jeremy's office. "Can I ask your opinion about something?"

"Sure thing, Herschel. Let me just make certain my work is saved." A few mouse clicks later, Jeremy looked away from his computer screen. "Whatta ya got?"

"One of my restaurant clients is showing large and unusual charges. See, he writes 'Security' on checks made out to cash and lists them as an expense. The restaurant already has a night watchman and insurance. Why would they have an extra expense for security? Although we don't like to pry, according to our Golden Rule policy, we have a responsibility to look out for our clients' best interests."

Jeremy looked at the printouts Herschel placed before him. "That does look extreme. Maybe someone is overcharging. Or maybe Mr. Jackson is adding bogus expenses to reduce his taxes."

"I know this man. He goes to my church and doesn't strike me as the type to cheat on his taxes."

What is the type to cheat on taxes? Jeremy thought, but said, "Something does look fishy. Let's ask my dad."

The pair found Dave on the phone with one of his former clients. They waited discreetly outside his open office door but could hear the conversation. "I'm glad your business is doing well, Bill. I just wanted to tell you that I'm back at the accounting firm now. We hope to offer the same high quality of service that you received from me for over two decades." Dave stopped talking, presumably to listen to Bill. "No, no. My former partners retired. I own the whole firm now. My son, Jeremy, is back from Australia and is with me. He adds to our services by understanding international transactions. And we have another razor-sharp young CPA from Auburn, Herschel Johnson."

Jeremy and Herschel heard another pause. Then Dave spoke again. "Thanks for your time, Bill. And let us know if we can ever serve you in any capacity."

Once they heard Dave hang up, Jeremy knocked on the corner of the door. "Can we ask you a question, Dad?"

Dave sat wiping his face with both hands in apparent disappointment. "Of course, come on in."

The two young men sat down on chairs facing Dave's desk. Jeremy looked at Herschel, who explained what he had found. "We guessed that the client is being grossly overcharged. Or he could be creating false expenses for tax purposes," Jeremy added.

"Something isn't right," Dave agreed. "And I've got a bad feeling about this. Why don't you two go see Mr. Jackson. And don't bill any hours for your visit. Watching out for our clients is part of our Golden Rule service."

⊸◈⊶

Anthony and three teenage companions had walked a couple of miles to a Cinema 10 movie theater to watch the latest blockbuster action movie. Ultimately, the bad guys met disastrous fates at the hands of the courageous male and female leads. The summer night outside felt hot and steamy compared to the air-conditioned comfort inside the theater. The boys hardly noticed the temperature while walking home along a busy road and arguing about the movie. Several inserted their own heroic fantasies into the story line. "They shoulda kept the money," one insisted. "They deserved it from savin' everybody."

"Ow!" shouted the boy who had wanted the movie heroes to keep the money. In wonder, he wiped raw egg off his shoulder. Something heavy and compact hit Anthony in the back. Anthony reached to check the stinging spot. His hand brought back raw egg.

A raucous laughter sounded behind them. The boys turned to see a pickup truck had pulled up forty feet behind them. Three white men older than themselves stood in the truck's bed and leaned on the top of the cab. One of them shouted a racial epithet as he hurled another egg. The boy who had been first hit leaned over to pick up a fist-sized rock. *Bang.* A bullet from a pistol passed over the boys' heads.

"African, you scratch my truck and there'll be real trouble." The truck's driver held a pistol in his hand and followed his threat with a racial slur. The trio in the back launched more

143

eggs. Anthony and his friends turned and ran, chased by more laughter and epithets.

⚊◆⚊

Jeremy and Herschel sat in the small office of the African American owner of a popular seafood restaurant along the causeway crossing the upper reaches of the bay. "We appreciate you taking time to meet with us, Mr. Jackson," started Jeremy.

"You're welcome. I've been very pleased with the work Herschel has done." Mr. Jackson smiled. "What can I do for you today?"

Jeremy and Herschel had agreed prior to the meeting for Herschel to explain. "Thank you, Mr. Jackson. Parker and Company hopes to give you more reason to be pleased with our service. The reason we're here is that we think you might be paying too much for security."

Mr. Jackson's eyes widened. He took a deep breath before asking, "What do you mean?"

Herschel showed him the entries and added, "We just wanted to make certain you weren't paying more than necessary and that the charges would be viewed by the IRS as legitimate."

Mr. Jackson sat still, breathing deeply. "I assure you that the expenses are real. I give you my word as a Christian."

"We couldn't find Cash listed as a business in Mobile. Do you have any bills or receipts the IRS would accept?" Herschel persisted.

"I'll just stop listing this as an expense then. I can pay them in cash."

"But undocumented cash payments or disbursements are problematic—"

"You're a smart young man, Herschel," Mr. Jackson interrupted. "I would sure hate to terminate your services."

Herschel froze, not knowing how to respond. Jeremy spoke up, "Thank you for your time, Mr. Jackson. Our job as your accountants is to give you our observations. How you run your restaurant is your business."

Jeremy rose to go. Herschel, somewhat flustered, followed him.

Outside the restaurant Herschel started, "Maybe you were right, Jeremy. He could be padding his expenses to lower his taxes."

Jeremy shook his head. "Could be. But I don't think that's likely anymore. Did you see the fear in his eyes? And did you see how sincerely he wanted you to believe he wasn't a tax cheater? But there's definitely something odd going on."

—◆—

All the Parkers waited for Dingo and Beatrice Larkin outside of baggage claim at the Mobile airport. Denyse waved and jumped as Dingo and Beatrice came out pushing a cart with two large pieces of luggage each.

Denyse rushed forward to hug her parents. "I'm so glad you're here," she gushed.

Beatrice immediately approached Katelyn, whom Jeremy held by the hand. "Do you remember me, luv? I'm your grandmum."

Katelyn hesitated for a moment before answering, "Yes."

Beatrice knelt before her. "You've grown so much that I hardly recognized you. Can you give me a hug?"

Katelyn stepped forward to wrap her arms around Beatrice's neck. Beatrice stood and picked up her granddaughter while still hugging her. Katie couldn't help but remember the trepid response she had received from Katelyn at the airport when her family arrived from Australia. Katie consoled herself, *But of course, Katelyn couldn't remember me. She was just a baby when we saw her in Australia.*

Dave noticed all the weight Beatrice had lost. With a free-flowing dress, professional hair styling, and makeup, she looked dramatically different from their hostess in Melbourne. Dingo, despite sharp clothes and an expensive leather outback hat, looked the same as always. "Welcome to Mobile," said Dave as the two men shook hands.

"Thank you, mate," responded Dingo.

Dingo then turned to Jeremy. "Denyse tells me you've taken right good care of her and my granddaughter." He reached out to hit his son-in-law in the shoulder, affectionately, but not gently. "I hear you're partners with your dad now and making a lot more money than you did in Oz."

Jeremy started to explain that technically he remained an employee, but Dave interrupted, "Our firm is called 'Parker and Company.'"

"First, you'll come to see our flat," Denyse proposed as Jeremy pushed the cart with the four pieces of luggage out of the airport terminal. Beatrice still carried Katelyn. "Dave and Katie will carry your luggage to their house in their ute. After supper, Jeremy will drive you to Dave and Katie's to get some sleep. I've made you an Aussie roast of beef and potatoes."

⊶⬦⊷

Katie rose early the next morning to prepare an American breakfast for her guests.

"Where's Dave?" asked Dingo when he emerged from the guest room.

"He's at the office already. Would you like breakfast now or wait for Beatrice?"

"I'm hungry. Let her sleep. She won't eat much anyway."

"Then sit down. Would you like coffee?"

Dingo sat at one of the two places Katie had set. "Don't I remember you two as tea drinkers?"

"Yes, but we make coffee for our guests. Want your coffee regular or strong?"

Dingo gestured strong with his arms bent at the elbow and hands raised to the sky, fists balled. He watched as Katie put two overflowing scoops of coffee into a French press, then poured in scalding hot water.

"Last night when I got up to use the loo, I saw photos of you and Dave with messed-up faces. That was Down Under, wasn't it? Dave got that bloody nose at the wedding. You must have been hurt when you crashed the rental car to save Lena."

Katie smiled while making a four-egg omelet. "That's right. Our guests have fun trying to figure those photos out."

"Yeeah. Beatrice still carries both of those videos on her cell phone. I'll need to razz Dave about punching the kidnapper in the face." Dingo turned serious. "We haven't had the chance to thank you in person since all of the drama in Oz. Thanks for all you did for our son. Good on ya, both."

Katie placed the omelet, a pile of pancakes, a platter of

147

sausages, a bowl of grits, and homemade biscuits on the table. "You're welcome," she responded while pouring Dingo's coffee. "You had some drama of your own in Melbourne, I remember. You saved Lena and your grandson. How is Vlady? Is he growing?"

"Yeeah. The little ankle biter is running around now. And talking. I bought him a rugby ball for his third birthday. I don't think Lena wants him in such a rough sport, though. I should have bought him an Aussie Rules football." Dingo laughed then and started taking most of everything Katie had set on the table. "Beatrice saved all of us in the end," Dingo said as if he were talking to himself. Then he noticed Katie listening and elaborated, "It changed something between us. She's like my wife and my mate now."

Katie sipped her tea while leaning against the kitchen counter. "That's really good."

"What's this?" Dingo asked before putting a spoonful of grits in his mouth.

"That's grits. It's made of ground hominy corn. We eat it at breakfast instead of baked beans. You might like it better with some butter and salt on it or syrup or . . ." Katie placed a jar of Vegemite before her guest.

Dingo grinned. "Now you're talkin'."

Chapter Seventeen

———•———

"I think I'll go for a walkabout," announced Dingo after eating. "See a bit of America up close."

"We have a trail that starts at the end of our street. It can take you up and down the eastern shore, and even into the town of Fairhope. You'll need to watch for snakes, though."

Dingo rolled his eyes. "Your poisonous snakes are like a mozzie bite compared to our snakes." To answer Katie's quizzical look, he added, "A mosquito bite."

Katie privately had to acknowledge the truth of that. "Should you wait for Beatrice?"

"Naw. She's not much for trekking. I'll be fine. Which way is the trail?"

Katie pointed the way to Dingo and watched him saunter away in shorts, khaki shirt, boots, and his outback hat. "The town is about four miles, I mean six kilometers," she called after him.

Dingo waved goodbye without looking back. Katie returned to the dining room to survey the breakfast she had prepared. Dingo had eaten nearly everything leaving little for Beatrice. Katie had started preparing an additional omelet when Beatrice struggled into the kitchen looking sleepy and disheveled.

"Just coffee for me, luv," said Beatrice. While Katie put new coffee grounds and hot water into the French press, Beatrice looked around Katie's house. "Isn't this lovely? I didn't notice much last night after the long trip and Denyse's dinner on top of it."

"Thank you. We downsized here right after Dave's early retirement about five years ago. A lot has happened since then."

Beatrice sat down at the table. "Where's Dingo?" She leaned over to pet Old Yeller, who had wandered into the kitchen. He started sniffing around Beatrice's feet. "I'll bet he smells my corgis."

"Dingo went on a hike." Katie poured the coffee. "Cream?"

"Yes, please. Likely Dingo will discover a bottle of beer somewhere. He's kept his word, though. Only two a day. I've seen him nurse one beer for three hours in a pub. I'll try one of those scones too, luv." Beatrice pointed at Katie's biscuits.

Katie placed butter and strawberry jam next to a plate with two biscuits. "How has traveling with Dingo been?"

"Oh, it's been wonderful," Beatrice spoke while

exhaling. "It's like Dingo has become my friend. We're having a lovely time traveling and meeting people together. He brags on me everywhere. How I saved him and all, though I don't remember myself. People listen to Dingo, especially the blokes. He just tells the same stories he did in pubs all his life. Only now, he adds a meaning to it. 'Take care of your family.' "

Katie laughed. "That's an important message."

Beatrice picked up one of the biscuits Katie had freshly baked. "You and Dave are our examples. And now you're making a good place for Denyse and Jeremy's family." She split the biscuit and spread half with a thick layer of jam. "I didn't know you Americans made scones."

"Well, we haven't really made a place for Denyse and Jeremy yet." Katie sat down and poured herself another cup of tea from a fine porcelain teapot Dave had given her for Christmas. "We hope to if—as you might say—we can make a go of it."

"What do you mean?"

"Dave and I spent most of our savings buying the firm back from Dave's former partners. Unfortunately, the firm wasn't in good financial shape when Dave took over. The previous owners had lost most of the clients Dave had served so well before his retirement. We had a good tax season. But not many of his old year-around clients have come back yet."

"Oh. That's too bad." Beatrice thought another minute before speaking again. "And you had a bout with cancer, I understand. You look good, though."

"Thanks. This was actually the second time I've had

cancer. This time wasn't as hard as the first time, since it wasn't invasive, and because Dave and I had learned how to better face a crisis together."

"Aren't you worried about a reoccurrence? Do you wonder why this has happened?" asked Beatrice.

"Sure, I worry occasionally. But Dave promised to find some answers about the why. Just knowing he'll find them relieves me from thinking very often about the cancer."

Katie finished her tea. "For today, when you feel like it, let me be the first one to take you shopping in America. We'll go to my favorite bakery. We have more guests coming. I think I'll get the whole hummingbird cake. It's to die for! Or at least worth every calorie."

⸺◆⸺

While she and Beatrice went shopping, Katie had left the front door unlocked in case Dingo returned first. Reaching home, the women found him asleep, catching up from the time change between the US and Australia. He emerged from the bedroom after a couple of hours. "What did you see on your walkabout?" prompted Beatrice.

"I found a croc floating in a canal by the trail."

"Actually, that was an alligator," suggested Katie.

"Oh yeeah. He was a little bugger, though. Only about three meters. A crocodile in North Australia can go six meters easy."

Beatrice looked at her husband. "Did you find any beer?"

Dingo grinned guiltily. "Only drank one bottle. I wouldn't want to walk back tipsy with crocs along the path.

Wasn't much company at the pub during the morning anyway. So I brought back a bottle. It's in the cooler."

"Tomorrow is Saturday. Dave and Jeremy are planning on taking you both fishing. There's an early season hurricane passing north of Venezuela," said Katie. "The forecasters expect it to go into Mexico. But the water might be a little choppy."

"Oh, no boats for me, especially in rough water. I get seasick in a bathtub," Beatrice insisted. "Let Dingo go for both of us."

"Okay. We have some other friends coming over from Florida. This fishing weekend has been planned for months. He was the police chief we met in Minnesota. His wife, Mary, doesn't fish either. We three women can go sightseeing and have lunch together. Denyse and Katelyn will come with us too."

Dingo grimaced. "I've never really gotten on with a copper."

"You'll like this one," promised Katie.

⊷⧫⊶

"Dingo, there's something you need to know," Beatrice whispered as she and Dingo got ready for bed that night.

"What's that?"

"Dave and Katie put nearly all of their money into buying Dave's old accounting firm. But his previous customers haven't come back." Beatrice added a few details to contribute urgency to her rumor. "Dave and Katie could lose everything if business doesn't improve. And her still recovering from cancer."

"Bugger."

"Don't let on to Dave you know about their financial or medical troubles, though."

—◆—

The next morning Buddy and Mary Oleson arrived at five a.m. from their condo in Florida's panhandle. Buddy appeared as they had known him in Minnesota—a gruff, bald man nearly seventy years old. Despite his years, the former chief carried the appearance of physical strength. Mary, a few years younger, gray-headed, and stocky, reminded Dave of a grandmother serving home-made cookies and milk. Mary immediately scooped up Old Yeller to hug him. "And this is the famous cat? I've heard stories about you, big boy."

Rrrow.

Jeremy pulled up shortly thereafter along with Denyse, a sleepy Katelyn, and always-raring-to-go Ripper. Katie had a big breakfast ready for everyone. Afterwards, Dave kissed Katie goodbye for the day and drove all the men and Ripper to the marina.

Dingo and Buddy eyed each other suspiciously. In Buddy, Dingo recognized an older no-nonsense policeman, the type he preferred to avoid. In Dingo, Buddy saw the type of miscreant he had spent a lifetime restraining. Both helped Dave and Jeremy load the boat rather than talk to each other.

By seven a.m., Dave had cranked up the engine and headed for the Gulf of Mexico. "I thought we'd try trolling for king mackerel today," he explained.

While Jeremy steered the boat toward the Gulf, Dave sat in the stern with the two mutually distrustful men. He started asking questions about Minnesota and Australia respectively. Soon the two traded stories like old friends. Dave served each of them hot coffee from a thermos and joined Jeremy at the controls.

"Yeah," said Dingo. "I worked hard and fought hard all of my life. Sometimes against your kind. Once I got a beer in my hand, blokes couldn't stop me from talkin'. Now that I'm some kind of celebrity, they pay me to keep talkin' without a beer in my hand. That was hard at first, but I got the hang of it."

Buddy rolled his eyes. "I know your type. I dreaded a call to break up bar fights as much as I did 'shots fired.' " Buddy opened his mouth to show a missing molar. "I lost that one when a drunk wearing a big ring cold-cocked me. Then they invented the Taser. After we had the Taser, we simply tased anyone who gave us an excuse. I didn't lose any more teeth."

After laughing in sympathy, Dingo asked, "How did you meet the Parkers, mate?"

"Nearly four years ago in Minnesota they became entangled with an extended family of professional criminals. Dave and Katie helped us to break up a network that had terrorized a town for over a century," answered Buddy.

Dingo leaned forward. "I heard a bit about that. Is that when Dave shot a man?"

"He certainly did and saved a policeman's life. Then he used an empty shotgun to bluff a second man who held a loaded automatic rifle."

"Fair dinkum, mate?"

"Yes, it's true," Buddy confirmed. "I heard that Dave and Katie had gotten mixed up with something pretty bad down your way too. How about that?"

"Yeeah. They located and saved my son, Trevor, from some thugs. When pimps tried to kidnap Trevor's wife, Katie crashed a car into their van. Then Dave punched out one of the kidnappers."

"Dave hit a suspect?"

"He did, mate, square in the nose. I've got the police video right here on my wife's phone." Dingo produced Beatrice's phone, tapped up the Auckland video, and held the screen so they both could see.

Buddy shook his head. "That's amazing."

"Yeeah, the New Zealand police arrested a lot of criminals and freed some girls from servitude." Dingo played the short video again for Buddy. "And if you liked that, look at this." Dingo found the wedding fight video. "Look, mate, see Dave take a sucker punch. My daughter, Denyse, is the one in the wedding gown. And there's Jeremy wrestling on the ground."

Buddy whistled aloud in amazement. "Where were you in all this?"

"There I am, mate." Dingo proudly pointed out himself exchanging punches with other men.

"Wow! Nearly fifty years ago I did some boxing myself."

"Were you any good, mate?"

Buddy mimicked Dingo, "Yeeah."

◄─◆─►

Both men stared at Dave when he came back to announce, "We're approaching the trolling ally between the reefs now. Usually we find fish at about twenty feet down." To himself, Dave wondered, *Why are they looking at me like that?* He proceeded to attach a tasseled pink lure above a two-inch steel hook to each of the stout fishing rods. He added a sixteen-ounce lead sinker a few feet higher to hold the bait at twenty feet below the surface. On each hook he secured a ten-inch mullet from the live well.

"What's that pink thing?" asked Dingo.

"We call that a duster. It helps attract the fish's attention."

From the elevated helm, Jeremy used the GPS to guide the boat alongside and between the reefs at slow walking speed. Dave threw the bait and downrigger overboard and let out about forty yards of line. He fitted the two rods into sockets on each corner of the boat's stern. Buddy and Dingo resumed swapping tales. Dave waited patiently while looking at the boundless ocean. *I love being out here*, he thought. *This is like being in heaven.*

Chapter Eighteen

———•———

Jeremy continued guiding the boat to skirt the reefs.

Dave realized that someone had spoken to him. "Excuse me?"

"I asked, 'How do you know where to steer the boat, mate?' " Dingo repeated while looking at the featureless ocean.

"The state of Alabama has built some artificial reefs to create a fish habitat a few miles south of the coast. We troll slowly near the reefs using GPS and the depth finder," Dave explained. "The reefs provide food and cover for little fish; bigger fish eat the little fish, and we hope to find the biggest fish looking for the others. The water color helps us too. We look for what they call 'king green'—not too brown or too clear."

"How did they build the reefs?" Buddy asked, looking over the side of the boat into the greenish water.

"They sunk all sorts of stuff: old cars, a hundred obsolete army tanks, culverts, old boats and ships, derelict machinery, construction rubble, oyster shells, a lot of crushed limestone, and even outdated voting machines. The rumor is that the voting machines were sunk before they could be counted in a local election. The reefs made fishing here productive for the fishermen as well as the local businesses."

"You know these waters well, don't you, mate?" Dingo responded.

"I think so. I've been fishing here all my life. And my family passed down a lot of lore from generations of Parkers fishing in this area. See Dauphin Island over there?" Dave pointed to a thin line on the northern horizon. "To the right of the island is where they fought the Battle of Mobile Bay."

"That's when the Union admiral, Farragut, said, 'Damn the torpedoes,' isn't it?" commented Buddy.

Dave smiled. "That's right! After the Union fleet ran through the minefield with the loss of one ship, the Confederate ironclad Tennessee along with three little gunboats came out to fight seventeen Union warships. My great-something grandfather Ezekiel Parker had been a fisherman on Mobile Bay. He was a rebel on the un-armored side-wheeler, Gaines, with six small guns. A Union cannonball holed them almost immediately. Before they could sink, the men beached the Gaines and ran away to avoid capture. Ezekiel had been wounded by a wood splinter thrown by a cannonball. He made his way inland to his parents' cabin. Our family hid him in the swamps until the festering wound healed. By then the war had ended. After that, he returned to fishing and collecting oysters."

—◆—

Buddy looked out on the endless water and took a deep breath of the salty air as Jeremy continued guiding the boat to skirt the reefs. Suddenly the rod in front of him bent nearly double. The reel screeched as a fish took out line.

"Stop, Jeremy!" Dave shouted. Buddy reached for his rod. "Reel in, Dingo, so your line won't snarl Buddy," instructed Dave. To Buddy he said, "Put the rod butt in your stomach and hang on until the drag stops the fish. You've got 250 yards of line to work with."

Buddy could feel the fish running and taking out line in surges. Gradually it tired and angled perpendicular to the line rather than directly away from the boat. Dave moved closer to Buddy and spoke calmly. "Now lift the rod tip. Don't exert too much pressure and break the line. As you lower the rod tip try to reel in a little." Slowly Buddy managed to pump the fish closer. His arms and stomach hurt.

I've almost got him, Buddy thought as he worked the fish nearly within sight of the boat.

Rrrrrr . . . sounded the reel as the fish renewed its efforts and took out fifty more yards of line.

Buddy simply held on. Once the fish stopped that run, he resumed pumping it back toward the boat; *raise rod tip, lower rod tip, reel in line.*

This time they saw the exhausted fish glide alongside the boat. Dave leaned over the side with a twelve-foot hooked pole to gaff the mackerel through the gills. He held the thrashing fish for a few seconds, and then with a smooth motion hoisted the fish onto the boat at Buddy's feet. "Watch its teeth," he warned. Buddy sat down feeling as exhausted as the fish.

Ripper barked with excitement, his eyes on the flopping fish.

"Good on ya, mate," said Dingo. Twenty-six minutes had elapsed fighting the fish.

"Loop back around, Jeremy," Dave called up to the helm. "We could find this one's brother for Dingo." To Buddy he said, "Maybe 45 pounds. What locals call a 'smoker.' Well done."

"How's that compared to catching a Minnesota Muskie?" Dave asked as Buddy recovered.

"I don't know. I've never caught a Muskie. Or a northern so big, for that matter."

Three more passes in the general area resulted in a fish nearly as large for Dingo. Buddy caught a mackerel about half as large as his first. Dingo hooked and lost one. Dave served each of the fishermen an ice-chilled beer after the fishing had slowed. Dingo and Buddy exchanged more stories that seemed to grow more outrageous as they sipped beer and got to know each other.

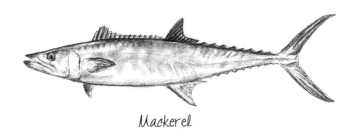

Mackerel

With their guests occupied, Jeremy told Dave about the encounter with Mr. Jackson earlier that week. "He seemed sincere to me, Dad. And he goes to the same church as Herschel. But I couldn't quite tell if he was afraid or ashamed, maybe both. What do you think?"

"That is unusual." Dave pondered Jeremy's description. "You say he's still our client?"

Jeremy nodded. "He might not remain so if we meddle. He pretty much said so to us. But he likes Herschel and wants to stay with him."

"Buddy is an expert in illegal activities. Let's ask him."

Together the Parkers approached the story-telling policeman. Dave started, "Buddy, Jeremy has a situation that doesn't make sense to me."

"I've heard a few stories from this Australian that don't make sense either," Buddy ribbed Dingo, who grinned.

"Would you tell us what you think?" Dave asked. "You too, Dingo."

Jeremy repeated his and Herschel's experience. Buddy without hesitation replied, "I can't be certain, but that sounds like a protection racket."

"How does a protection racket work?" Jeremy asked.

"Some thugs offer 'protection' to a businessman while dropping hints that they are the ones he needs protection from. Usually they threaten his business, but sometimes include his family. Their words are vague, nothing that even if recorded could convict them in a court. But the meaning is clear. Then the thugs collect money regularly for doing nothing. Restaurant owners are particularly vulnerable because there are so many ways a restaurant can be sabotaged like fire or food poisoning. Your client could have just been naive enough to think that he could write off extortion as a business expense."

"That's serious stuff," said Jeremy. "Should we call the police?"

"When I was a chief, I'd be obligated to tell you to contact the local authorities. But as a private citizen, I can tell you that there's not much the police can do. And if the police handle the situation clumsily, they could bring the wrath of the criminals down on your client. You don't want that."

❦

Returning to the marina with a cooler of fish in the late afternoon, the men discovered frenzied activity. "Hurricane Broderick has shifted course to head north. It's expected to make landfall somewhere along the Gulf coast in just over twenty-four hours," a harried worker explained. "Let's get your boat out of the water, Mr. Parker. We'll store it in a safe place with the other boats."

"I've got to get back to Santa Rosa Beach," said Buddy.

"Our house is on high ground. Why don't you stay here with us or evacuate inland before the rush?" asked Dave.

Buddy shook his head. "Mary's cats are still in our condo. She won't leave them with a hurricane approaching. She'll want to make sure her babies are safe."

Dave handed the car keys to Jeremy. "Would you drive Buddy and Dingo back to the house? You can send your mom to pick me up and then go home yourself with Denyse and Katelyn. I'll stay here, help with the boat, and clean the fish. Buddy, I'll freeze your fish for you to pick up next time you come."

"I'll stay and help you, mate," said Dingo. To Buddy Dingo said, "I'm calling Beatrice. She'll give you a present from me, mate."

"Thanks . . . mate," answered Buddy. The two men shook hands warmly. Buddy and Jeremy hurried away.

Forty-five minutes later, Beatrice came with Katie to pick up their husbands. Dave had filleted and sliced the fish while Dingo washed and bagged the portion-sized pieces. The ever-present brown pelicans, sensing the approaching storm, acted apprehensive. They still squabbled over the fish scraps, though.

"Buddy jolly liked the autographed book you gave him," Beatrice said to her husband. "The Olesons are a really fine couple."

"They aren't Aussies. But they're straight-up."

Back at the house, Dave retrieved his portable generator from their storeroom. It started easily when he pulled the cord. He found his chainsaw also in good shape. "Okay.

Now we'll need to go out and buy gas for the generator and top off both vehicles." To Dingo's puzzled expression he added, "Petrol. After that, we can have a fish fry. In tomorrow's light, we'll board up the windows and get ready."

"Will the storm be that bad?" asked Beatrice.

"A hurricane is the same as a typhoon," Katie, the former science teacher, explained. "Except that the winds rotate counterclockwise in the northern hemisphere. Along the coast, winds can push a flood onto shore. The pounding waves can destroy nearly anything."

"Why do the winds rotate at all?"

"The rotation of the earth swirls the air rushing into an area of low pressure. Just like the water running down a drain spins."

—◆—

The sound of hammering woke Dingo the following morning. He looked out the window to see Dave's neighborhood alive with activity. Most homes had people nailing pieces of plywood over the largest windows. Many applied strips of duct tape to smaller windows. He found Dave hauling out plywood from the crawl space under his house.

"Let me help you, mate," Dingo offered.

"Thanks. How are you on a stepladder?"

"No worries."

"Then you nail while I hold." Together Dave and Dingo started securing the window covers.

"Where's Katie?" asked Dingo.

"She's gone to pick up some supplies for us to stay here."

"Why would you stay?"

"You don't know when the authorities or the condition of the roads will let you return. The governor has only made evacuation mandatory along the coastline and in low-lying areas. Unless the hurricane reaches category four, we'll probably be okay here."

"Can I help, luv?" a female voice asked.

Dave turned to see Beatrice dressed in his slippers and bathrobe. Katie must have loaned them to her or she had helped herself. Either way, she looked funny. "Sure. Could you make us breakfast?"

"Glad to." Beatrice disappeared into the house.

As Dingo nailed the last piece into place, Dave noticed Jordan Fogle struggling to hold a sheet of plywood while Caleb nailed it. "Come on, Dingo," said Dave.

Together the men crossed the street. "Let me hold that," Dave told Jordan. She released her hold and stepped back.

"What can I do, mate?" Dingo asked Caleb.

"Thanks! You could bring the rest of the plywood from my garage," Caleb told him.

"What about me?" questioned Jordan.

"Do you need some supplies? Batteries and such?" asked Dave.

"I could use a few things."

"Call Katie on her cell phone. She's already at the superstore. She can pick up anything you need."

"What then?"

"You could help Beatrice fix breakfast for all of us. Everybody will be hungry before we're done."

Jordan talked to Katie on her phone as she crossed the street. In Katie's kitchen, she introduced herself to Beatrice and started cooking.

After securing all of Caleb's windows, the three men moved to Dave's kitchen where Beatrice and Jordan had prepared a breakfast mixing British and deep South cuisine. Katie pulled into the driveway. "Sorry for taking so long. The stores are jammed, and the traffic is murder. All of the tourists and other folks from Gulf Shores and along the coast are evacuating in a hurry."

Chapter Nineteen

―――•―•――

"Where will the people go?" asked Beatrice.

"They're safe from the storm surge a few miles from the water. Wind damage can be severe up to forty or fifty miles inland. Torrential rain could cause flooding in low-lying areas all the way to Kentucky. Schools and churches open their doors for refugees." Katie turned to her neighbor. "I got all the things you wanted, Jordan. Between us we got the last of the fresh bread. I also brought a bag of flour for each of us."

"I'll just bake up enough biscuits in advance of the storm for Caleb and me. Thanks, honey," Jordan answered.

After breakfast, the three men worked in the neighborhood helping those who hadn't finished preparing for the storm. The women filled every available receptacle with fresh water. Then they taped the remaining windows and picked up anything unsecured the winds could turn into a projectile.

In the early afternoon, Katie's cell phone rang. She heard Jeremy's voice. "Mom, our apartment complex is wood framed and has multiple floors. The police stopped to say that it probably isn't safe. Denyse told them she didn't want to leave. Then a deputy asked her to use a magic marker to write her name on her forearm, so her body could be identified. That really scared her. Can we come to your house?"

"Of course. Load up with everything you think might be useful and come right over. Put all your important documents and your valuables into your trunk. Don't take too long. Bring milk for Katelyn."

⬤

Two hours later, Jeremy and Denyse arrived with Katelyn and their fully loaded car. Of course, they brought Ripper too. The young dog had grown to about fifty pounds—about three-quarters full size for a male Labrador—but remained a puppy at heart. He felt excitement in the air and frisked from person to person for attention. Although Katie loved dogs, particularly Labradors, she remembered how troublesome large adolescent dogs could be inside a house. She looked at Ripper with misgiving.

"Pull your new car into the garage alongside mine, Son," Dave instructed him.

"But where will your truck go?"

"It'll have to take its chances outside," Dave responded.

"The weatherman is reporting that the storm has veered a bit east toward Pensacola. We'll be on the west side," Jeremy added.

The science teacher in Katie came out again. "That's good for us. The counterclockwise rotation won't create such a bad storm surge in Mobile Bay. Not so good for Pensacola."

"Santa Rosa Beach is east of Pensacola. I hope Buddy and Mary got through," said Dave.

"Oh, Mary called while you were out helping the neighbors. They passed Pensacola before the heaviest evacuation started and missed the worst of that traffic. They've retrieved her cats. But the Mid-Bay Bridge from Destin north is jammed. They've headed east on backroads toward Panama City."

"The highway patrol has closed I-10 from here toward Pensacola. They're using all four lanes for westbound traffic," reported Jeremy.

"Good thing the Olesons are past Pensacola. The storm will most likely come ashore between us."

⸺◆⸺

As the sky darkened and the wind started to rise from the east, the first splatters of rain smashed onto the windows. Katie took charge of the household. "Dingo and Beatrice, you already have a bedroom. Jeremy, you, Denyse, and Katelyn can have the bedroom your dad uses as an office. Just put all the file folders he keeps on the bed into a cardboard box from the garage. Please put Ripper in the laundry room."

"What about Old Yeller?" asked Beatrice as Jeremy led Ripper to the laundry room.

"He's a cat. He'll take care of himself." Old Yeller heard his name mentioned but didn't give up his safe spot under the coffee table.

All found seats in the living room while Katie served coffee and tea in the semi-darkness of the storm-shrouded early evening. She brought out the hummingbird cake on a pedestal. Once Ripper had been removed, Old Yeller left the security of the coffee table to brush against people's legs. He allowed Katelyn to pull his ears. "Old Yeller may have saved our lives in Minnesota, you know," Katie said as she served large slices of cake. She looked purposefully at Dave.

"That's right," he agreed. "Old Yeller woke us up just in time. He led us to the secret room in the Big River mansion too."

After serving the cake, Katie settled into her favorite rocking chair. "He turned out to be a more-than-ordinary cat alright." Prompted by a nudge from her mother, Katelyn tottered over to climb into Katie's lap. His favorite spot taken, Old Yeller returned to the coffee table and curled up underneath.

A nearby lightning strike made everyone jump. The Australians looked at the windows with apprehension. Wind howled around the house, which seemed to vibrate. The TV weatherman reported that the storm had strengthened to category 3 with sustained winds of 122 mph.

"Why don't you tell us the whole story of your adventure in Minnesota?" suggested Beatrice.

"You go ahead, sweetheart," Dave told Katie. "I'll help whenever you need me."

Katie started with a description of the old mansion and the charming town of Washita. Rain pounding on the roof and debris hitting boarded windows mingled into a menacing roar. The screaming wind added to the mysterious tone Katie used telling about the mansion.

Oool. Oool. Unhuman howling joined the wind. Katie's listeners looked at each other with alarm.

"That's Ripper singing with the wind," Jeremy told them. "He wants to join us. He's mostly house-broken." Jeremy looked hopefully at his mother.

Katie didn't appreciate the interruption of her tale. "Well, okay. But keep an eye on him."

Allowed into the living room, Ripper curled up near Jeremy and put his chin on his forepaws. Being alone in the laundry room had settled him down. His eyes remained alert glancing from human to human with occasionally a longer look of curiosity at Old Yeller. Everybody watched when the cat approached and rubbed against the young dog. For his friendly gesture, Old Yeller received a massive face lick from Ripper's pink tongue. The cat returned to lie under the coffee table.

Katie resumed her tale. Soon she had everyone alternating between suspense and laughter. Another bolt of lightning crashed, followed by a flash of blueish light and the bang of an explosion. Simultaneously the lights went out, leaving them in near-total darkness. A few startled exclamations involuntarily came from Katie's listeners. Old Yeller hissed. Katelyn cried briefly until comforted by Katie. Ripper jumped to his feet and barked until Jeremy shushed him. The dog settled back at Jeremy's feet.

"That must have been the transformer on our street," guessed Dave as he peeked through a crack at the edge of the plywood covering the window. "All of the houses are dark."

"Denyse, would you get some candles, please?" Katie asked without disturbing Katelyn. "We can't run the generator inside and risk carbon monoxide poisoning or put it out in the storm. The candles and matches are in a drawer beside the refrigerator."

"I'll help," offered Beatrice. Together the two women fumbled in the dark to find the drawer then placed and lit a half-dozen candles on saucers around the room. Yellow light soon illuminated the faces and cast dark shadows.

Katie continued her story, gradually building suspense up to the climactic confrontation. Then she ended with a humorous recounting of her and Dave's fear that they would be held financially accountable for the damage to the mansion.

"Blimey! That's quite a story," Dingo exclaimed after Katie had told about their early return to Mobile. "You should let Trevor make that into a book. Is that the way it happened, Dave?"

Dave looked bashful and nodded. "I guess that's the first time I've heard the story told all the way through myself. And that happened four years ago." The snapping of tree branches breaking in the hurricane drew everybody's attention. Something tossed by the wind crashed against the roof.

The Australians looked at the ceiling with alarm. "This house was built to local codes designed for an occasional hurricane. We'll be okay riding this out," Dave reassured them.

"My, that was a good story," began Beatrice. "I feel like I've been to a cinema, or something."

Murmured agreement praised Katie's storytelling ability. "Who else has a story?" Jeremy asked the group.

When nobody volunteered, Denyse spoke up. "How about yourself? Jeremy, tell about the first time you met Dad."

He feigned apprehension looking from Denyse to Dingo and back again to Denyse. "Do you think that's safe?"

Everyone laughed, Dingo the hardest. "Well," Jeremy began, "Denyse had warned me that her father was a bloke's bloke. When we didn't find Dingo at home, Denyse sent me to McGinty's pub to meet him. The barkeep pointed to an empty stool. 'That's Dingo's seat,' he said. I took the stool next to Dingo's place and waited. After a few minutes, the toughest, meanest, beer-guzzling, croc-wrestling bushman I could have ever imagined sat down beside me. He drained a tankard of beer without taking a breath. Then he took out a nail to chew on like a toothpick. I spoke to him, 'I'm Jeremy, Denyse's friend. Do you mind if I call you Dingo?'

"The rough man looked at me and asked, 'Is this Dingo's seat?'

" 'Sure is, mate,' the barkeep answered.

" 'Pardon me then, I've got to move before Dingo finds me sitting on his stool.' "

Everybody roared. Dingo himself doubled over laughing before adding, "I remember meeting Jeremy the first time. He looked scared to death. The lad proved out alright, though." After that Jeremy told more factual details about meeting Denyse and her parents. He poked fun at each of them in a lighthearted way—a sign of true Aussie friendship.

"Who's next?" Denyse asked when her husband had finished.

Katie spoke up, "What exactly happened when Dingo and Beatrice saved Lena in Melbourne?"

"I still don't remember much about what happened," Beatrice answered. "Dingo can tell you."

Her husband showed himself an adept storyteller as well. In the end, he praised Beatrice for sticking by him in a crisis. "I never heard the whole story of Dave and Katie finding Trevor," Dingo reminded everyone, passing the storytelling on to the others.

Dave orchestrated the story by calling on each one to fill in the details of their participation. During the telling, the wind and lightning ceased. "Is the storm over?" asked Beatrice.

"No, we must be in the eye," Dave explained. An eerie stillness seemed to engulf the house like the vibration had earlier. Even Old Yeller and Ripper seemed unsettled by the quiet.

"Can we go outside?" asked Dingo.

Katie answered, "Just for a minute. The storm will start again without warning and from the opposite direction as before."

The group couldn't see much in the darkness from the front door step. Dave's big flashlight revealed broken tree limbs and storm debris littering the yard. Piles of leaves and Spanish moss covered the ground. A light breeze blew from the south in damp air.

They saw another flashlight across the street. "You and Jordan okay, Caleb?" Dave shouted.

"We're alright. Y'all?" Caleb returned before both families went back inside.

True to Katie's prediction, the wind came back with a blast a few minutes later and from the west. "The second half could be worse since the wind will come toward us over Mobile Bay," she predicted. A tree crashing to the ground made everybody jump. After all had finished retelling their roles in Trevor's rescue, Beatrice prompted Dingo into telling some of his pub tales.

About one a.m. the winds and lightning lessened a little, indicating that the worst had passed. "Maybe we should try to get some sleep," suggested Dave. "Tomorrow will be a busy day for everyone."

—•—

"The Parkers are nice people, huh, Dingo?" Beatrice whispered as she and her husband listened to the wind and still-pounding rain while trying to fall asleep.

"Yeeah, Denyse did well to recognize that in Jeremy."

"I sure hope that Dave and Katie don't lose everything they own. They need more business at their accounting firm to survive."

"Oh. I'd forgotten about that."

Fallen Tree

Chapter Twenty

Dingo heard a two-cycle engine revving near dawn. The previous night's strong winds had diminished to a gusty breeze. Rather than a continuous downpour, occasional showers provided sporadic precipitation.

Careful to not waken Beatrice, Dingo slipped out of bed and headed toward the kitchen. He could hear Dave's generator humming to power the refrigerator, freezer, microwave, and a few lamps through extension cords. Katie had used a propane camping stove to heat water in a teakettle for hot tea or coffee.

She smiled at her guest. "Coffee? Strong, right?" She poured water from the kettle into her French press. "I can cook you some breakfast on this stove."

"Where's Dave?" Dingo asked.

Katie poured Dingo's coffee. "He's out back getting the chainsaw ready. A downed tree is blocking access to our street."

Jeremy passed by, taking Ripper outside for a morning toilet walk. "G'day," he greeted.

Dingo carried his coffee cup and followed the sound of Dave's chainsaw. The flashlight peek during the previous night's storm lull had not prepared Dingo for what he saw in the daylight. Storm debris covered the ground. Two beautiful live oaks had been toppled in the neighborhood. Fortunately, most houses only showed moderate damage: missing shingles, broken windows, awnings wrenched loose. A standalone utility building behind one home had been demolished. Finally, Dingo saw where a falling tree limb had smashed the hood of Dave's old pickup truck. "Sorry about your ute, mate."

"It'll still run. That ding just gives it more character," Dave said as he looked at a medium-sized oak blocking the entrance to the Parkers' cul-de-sac.

Dingo put down his coffee cup. "Need some help, mate?"

"Thanks, Dingo. There's plenty to do for days. Our first priority will be to get the roads clear. Let's eat something first, though."

Inside, Katie had abandoned the thought of a cooked breakfast and made sandwiches with luncheon meat warmed up in the microwave. She poured more coffee for Dingo and Jeremy, hot tea for Dave. The strong smell of coffee brought Denyse and Beatrice to the kitchen.

Twenty minutes later the trio of men started cutting up and removing the oak tree. "Let's stack the logs by the garage for firewood later," Dave told them.

Dingo proved to be a prodigious worker, as strong and energetic as Dave and Jeremy put together. Within an hour, the cul-de-sac had been opened. But no traffic passed on the main road.

"Mind if I check down the motorway, mate? I'll carry our cell phone in case you need me."

"No problem. Take the chainsaw and my truck. Don't forget to drive on the right-hand side. Jeremy and I will need to check on some of our neighbors."

━◆━

"What's holding us up, Bennie?" Charlie, a young reporter from KPIZ TV in Mobile, asked. "Can we get through to Fairhope?"

"Fallen trees must be blocking the road," his cameraman answered. "I see some locals trying to clear them."

"Pull over, then. Let's take a look. This might be just what we need for our human-interest story. Viewers love to see spots about everybody pulling together for the benefit of all."

To their surprise, Charlie and Bennie found a stocky Australian using a chainsaw and leading local volunteers clearing the road.

More interesting than I realized, thought Charlie. "Sir, could we have a word from you for our viewers?" Charlie asked Dingo.

"Sure, mate."

"Roll it, Bennie," Charlie instructed and held the microphone before Dingo. "You've come a long way to help in a cleanup."

181

"Oh, I'm not here in the States for this. I'm supposed to appear on some telly talk shows next week in New York and Los Angeles. I just happened to be here to catch the storm."

What have I lucked into? Charlie wondered. "Then why did you come to the east side of Mobile Bay?"

"I'm here visiting my daughter and her in-laws. The Parkers are straight-up folks. You wouldn't think they could be so tough, being they're accountants."

"You mean here in Mobile?"

"Parker and Company is their accounting firm. Dave Parker's son married my daughter in Melbourne."

"What did you mean about them being tough?" Charlie persisted.

"Here, look at this." Dingo pulled out his cell phone. "See, there's my daughter in her wedding dress. She teaches at Central High School. That fellow fighting on the ground is her husband, Jeremy. The bloke who gets sucker punched and then tackled by my daughter is Dave Parker."

"I've seen this on YouTube. It went viral when it was first posted. Are you telling me the older man who was punched is from Mobile?"

"Fair dinkum, mate."

"But how does getting punched make Mr. Parker tough?"

"Look at this one." On his cell phone, Dingo found the Auckland police video of Dave smashing one of Lena's would-be kidnappers in the face. "That's Dave Parker."

The reporter stood transfixed staring into the tiny screen. To himself he said, *This is a great story for after the storm story runs its course.* To Dingo he said, "That's great . . . mate. Could you forward these clips to me?"

"No worries. The Parkers' accounting firm needs some new customers. I'll bet the videos will attract attention."

"I'm sure they will attract attention," the reporter agreed. "Get some shots of the other volunteers working for tomorrow's news," he said to Bennie.

A day of hard work by Dingo and others had cleared the roads allowing power company crews to enter the area. Everybody cheered when the electricity came back on late that night. The next morning's early news showed a clip of Dingo using Dave's chainsaw to clear the main road.

In the afternoon, Jeremy and Denyse returned to their apartment with Katelyn. Katie felt sad to see them go, even Ripper.

Two hot and humid days of hard work made Dave and Katie's neighborhood somewhat resemble its previous appearance. Everybody agreed that Dingo had been tireless in his efforts to assist anyone who needed help. Beatrice, along with Katie, had provided sustenance to the neighborhood's workers.

Although the eastern shore of Mobile Bay had sustained wind damage from Hurricane Broderick, Pensacola to the east had taken the wind plus maximum storm surge from the ocean. National TV coverage showed devastated buildings and people begging for help. "Governor Cleveland of Florida is calling out their national guard. President Huffington has declared the western panhandle of Florida as a federal disaster area," reported the national network anchor. "FEMA is rushing relief supplies into the area. But many roads are impassable with storm debris. Some roads and bridges have been washed out by floodwaters due to thirty-four inches of rain."

"We barely missed the worst," said Dave. "That could have been us."

━•◆•━

Red alert. All available patriots to provide security in Pensacola. Bring field supplies and maximum armament, Jeremiah Wallace tweeted to his followers.

━•◆•━

"Come back when you can," Katie invited the Larkins at the airport. "We'll be watching you on the TV talk shows."

"Can you promise us better weather if we come back?" bantered Dingo. Beatrice started to cry.

"I'm so proud of you," Denyse told her parents as she hugged them before they went through airport security. Katelyn also hugged her Down Under grandparents. Beatrice cried harder.

Once through security, Dingo tried to comfort his wife. "You'll be happy to hear this. I've helped the Parkers and their financial problem."

Beatrice dabbed at her eyes with a tissue. "What do you mean?"

"Just wait and see."

━•◆•━

The following day Dave and Katie watched continuing national news coverage of the hurricane disaster in Pensacola. Reporters showed pictures of people struggling to clean out flooded houses and find fresh drinking water. Because of the difficulty FEMA had helping everyone immediately, some victims of the hurricane had resorted to ransacking retail

184

establishments. The network anchor announced, "Heavily armed men from all over the southeast are reported to be converging on Pensacola. Their spokesman, Jeremiah Wallace, has been linked to various white supremacist groups."

A tape showed Jeremiah speaking to a crowd, "If the government can't maintain order, then it's up to American patriots who won't back down."

The news anchor continued, "Sporadic gunfire between Wallace's supporters and local residents of Pensacola has been reported."

Katie stared at the struggling people with empathy. "That could have been Mobile," she said. "Jeremy and his family could need help. Or Herschel and his family. A lot of those being arrested for looting are young and vulnerable just like Anthony. Most of them are just desperate." Katie talked to herself, but out loud, "The destruction. The desperate people. The children without food or water. The violence. Why does God allow such suffering?"

Suddenly, Dave remembered his promise from before Christmas. "I'm sorry, sweetheart. I had promised to answer that question for you."

"I remembered. But you've been busy. What about now, though? Maybe we could talk about it or ask someone."

Typical of a woman, thought Dave. *Talk or ask someone. She was right about that in Minnesota, though.* "Who would I ask?" he asked.

Katie shrugged. "Maybe our pastor."

"I've heard his answer before. 'Don't worry. God is in control. Everything will work out.' But I'd like something a bit more substantive." Dave thought another minute. *Whom would I really trust?* "I've got an idea," he said to Katie.

"You always come up with an idea."

"Not always. But maybe yes, this time. Let's call Pastor Foster."

Katie stared at her husband. "You mean John? In Washita?"

"Why not? He certainly is a good man. Would you like to listen on the extension?"

"Sure. I'll let you do most of the talking, though."

A quick search on the Internet gave them the phone number of the Lutheran parsonage in Washita. After dialing, Dave listened to the ringtone. To himself he counted *one, two, three.*

A woman answered. "Hello."

Despite her promise to let Dave do the talking, Katie spoke first. "Ellie, this is Dave and Katie Parker in Alabama."

"Katie! So happy to hear from you. Did you have much damage from Hurricane Broderick? We prayed for you."

Katie and Ellie chatted for a few minutes before Katie got to the real reason for the call. "Let's catch up later, Ellie. Right now, Dave wants to talk to John about a spiritual issue, if he's available."

"Alright." The Parkers heard Ellie shout, "John, Dave and Katie Parker are on the phone."

A minute late the Parkers heard, "Hello, Dave and Katie. We loved seeing you last summer."

"Thanks, John," responded Dave. "Could we ask you a theological question?"

"Of course."

First Dave described the reoccurrence of Katie's cancer.

He shared the anxiety they both still felt over the firm and their finances. Then he referred to the situation in Pensacola. He concluded with, "We've been wondering, why does God allow such suffering?"

John whistled aloud. There was a slight pause before he spoke. "You want me to answer a question that theologians have been debating for thousands of years?"

Chapter Twenty-One

"I'll bet you know a lot more than we do," said Dave.

"Maybe. Actually the Bible gives a lot of clear reasons why God allows suffering. Sometimes God uses temporary suffering to help people in unexpected ways. Other times our suffering can help someone else. People like Ezekiel, Joseph, Esther, and especially Jesus suffered for the benefit of others. Maybe someone will be positively influenced by Katie's faith dealing with her cancer."

"She has certainly impressed me," returned Dave. "But what about the people in Pensacola?"

"I can't say for certain. Because, although the Bible does give reasons for suffering, nowhere does God promise to reveal the specific reason in a given situation. But God does allow suffering to give us the opportunity to demonstrate

His love by providing help and comfort. That could be one reason for the difficulties being experienced in Pensacola."

Katie broke in, "But what about the suffering of uncertainty Dave and I feel about our situation?" She described her anxiety over cancer and told a little about the challenge of rejuvenating the accounting firm.

"Those could be a test of faith. God allowed Satan to afflict Job to demonstrate the faith of his servant."

Dave resumed the query, "Why won't God reveal the specific reason for a particular suffering?"

"I don't know for certain. But maybe because for people in the midst of suffering, the reason wouldn't seem good enough. Try going to Pensacola and telling them that they are suffering so that others could have the opportunity to help them. That wouldn't make them happy."

Dave laughed. "You're right about that. Thanks, John. You've given us a lot to think about."

"Let me send you an email with other scriptures and divine purposes to read. Although we might not know the specific reason, the Bible gives many on-point scriptures and examples, so we can be confident that God does have a reason."

"Your family is always welcome to vacation with us in Mobile, John," Katie added. "If you men are finished, I'd like to talk to Ellie some more."

—◆—

Caleb and Jordan saw a bulletin flash onto the TV screen displacing the normal telecast. The camera view switched to the anchor desk where a hastily prepared reporter announced, "We interrupt our regularly scheduled program with breaking news from the hurricane-damaged areas in Florida. Gun battles have broken out in Pensacola. National Guard troops, unsure of what is happening, have drawn back into secure positions. Governor Cleveland of Florida had to be evacuated when bullets from unknown assailants forced him and his staff to take cover. The president has withdrawn FEMA until their safety can be guaranteed. Hospitals are receiving injured people. The governor of Florida is calling up more national guard troops. Once reinforced, the guard units will deploy in force."

The Fogles watched the report in horror. "That's just over in Pensacola, only forty miles away. I hope it doesn't spread here," said Jordan.

"It started here, remember?"

—◆—

Lighted outdoor basketball courts allowed for nighttime games at a local park on warm summer nights. Idle players waited their chance to play three-on-three in a you-make-it-you-take-it style. The winners of each game to fifteen baskets stayed on the court to take on the challengers in a king-of-the-hill fashion. Anthony noticed a group of those waiting had gathered around several somewhat older African American males. Curiosity made him join them. He recognized the most vocal of the men as Tyrone, whom he had seen fist fighting at the riot.

"You got anything to fight with, bro?" Tyrone asked him in front of the others.

"What do you mean?"

191

"Some firepower." The large man revealed a 9mm semi-automatic pistol. Several others also showed weapons.

"Why do I need firepower?"

"Haven't you been watching the news? The KKK is invading neighborhoods in Pensacola. We need to be ready to defend our people." To this Anthony made no reply.

"You got any money?" Tyrone asked.

"Yeah. A hundred dollars I made working after school and on Saturdays."

"I heard about that. You're a number-crunching accountant now." All the men laughed. "Show me your hundred," Tyrone demanded.

He took the hundred dollars Anthony produced, counted it, and pressed an older 38 revolver into Anthony's hands. "That will get you this." Tyrone added a handful of bullets.

"I don't want to get into any trouble," Anthony insisted as he looked at the gun.

"You think the people in Pensacola wanted trouble? Ready to fight makes for no trouble. And you got just as much legal right as any white man to bear arms."

Anthony felt something tightening inside. "That's all true."

⟶◆⟵

Parker and Company reopened for business a week after the hurricane. "Call for you on line two, Dave," announced Dorothy.

Dave stared into the computer monitor trying to re-engage himself after the delays of the guests and hurricane. "Who is it?" he asked Dorothy.

"Somebody claiming to be from KPIZ news."

What could they want from us? Dave wondered as he picked up the phone. "Hello, Dave Parker here."

"Mr. Parker, thank you for taking my call. This is Charlie Collins of KPIZ."

"You're welcome. What can I do for you, Mr. Collins?"

"I have a couple of videos showing you involved in physical altercations. That's unusual for a respected accountant. Would you care to comment before we air the piece tonight?"

"What videos?"

"One shows you in an altercation being tackled by a bride—Denyse Parker is your daughter-in-law, I believe—who teaches at Central High School. The same video shows your son, Jeremy Parker—your associate at Parker and Company—fighting on the ground."

Dave could not make himself speak.

The reporter continued, "The second video shows a car accident, after which you assaulted an occupant of the other vehicle."

"Where did you get those?"

The reporter spoke with equanimity, "I'm not at liberty to disclose my source."

"Then no comment." Dave hung up.

Dave sat at his desk utterly flabbergasted. *We're trying to reestablish a respectable accounting firm, and these videos show up.* He heard the phone ring again. "Dave, it's the same reporter asking for Jeremy," called Dorothy.

"Tell him Jeremy isn't available." To himself Dave said, *What I wouldn't give to know God's purpose for allowing this fiasco.*

"Welcome to the Morning Show," KPIZ's perky hostess greeted Jeremiah Wallace. "I believe you have an important announcement for us."

"I feel led to run to become Alabama's First District Representative to the US Congress. My campaign theme will be about law and order. The violence before Christmas in our own city of Mobile, now continuing in Pensacola, cannot be tolerated."

"What would you do to curb violence, Mr. Wallace?"

"It's time we started protecting our police from unwarranted persecution despite the dangers they face daily on our behalf. When I'm elected as your representative, I'll introduce federal legislation to protect police officers from vindictive prosecution whenever they're required to use any force during the performance of their duties."

The Morning Show hostess asked, "Are you referring to Mobile's district attorney's recent indictment of a white police officer for shooting an unarmed African American?"

Jeremiah's voice took on a patronizing tone. "Certainly, I'm speaking of protections for all police officers unjustly accused. But the case to which you are referring is an example of overzealous prosecution by those who haven't experienced the hazards our officers face."

"Then you approve of the dismissal of charges against the African American patrolman who shot and killed a white assailant."

Jeremiah shook his head. "I would approve if that murder had not occurred only a couple of months after the first shooting and before the white officer could be exonerated. The DA's office should be investigating the possibility of a payback."

—◄◆►—

Everyone from Parker and Company tuned in to KPIZ Action News at six p.m. The new anchor baited her viewers, "Tonight, we lead off with an exclusive report. KPIZ has uncovered a story revealing prominent citizens and business owners of Mobile involved in a public brawl. What do you have for us, Charlie?"

Charlie appeared on camera. "The following videos reveal accountants living a double life." He went on to describe the cursory details he knew. "We contacted Parker and Company for an interview. They only responded, 'No comment.' I guess that you can't count on a CPA to be forthcoming."

The reporter talked over the videos as they aired. After a few more comments by Charlie extolling public decorum, he ended the segment with, "The activities we discovered just don't add up."

The picture returned to the KPIZ anchor desk where the announcer tried her own quip. "Keep auditing the situation, Charlie."

—◄◆►—

"Aren't these the people you been workin' for?" asked Anthony's mother.

Anthony paused in front of the TV. He saw a picture of Mr. Parker and his wife, Katie. He caught the words, "These videos will be posted on KPIZ TV's website."

"Yeah, that's the place. What did the TV say about them?"

"They been fightin'."

"That isn't true," he insisted.

"Says you. You check it out yourself, baby. And you went out fishin' with them?"

In his bedroom, Anthony brought up the KPIZ website where he saw a replay of Jeremy Parker fighting on the ground and then a second clip of Dave Parker hitting a man in the face.

His mother came in to look over his shoulder. "Isn't that the math teacher you're sweet on in the wedding dress?"

"I'm not sweet on Ms. Parker."

"Well, you better not be. 'Cause looks like she's a tough cookie."

Chapter Twenty-Two

Dave sat down on the couch and put his face in his hands. "How are we going to get new clients with that circulating? Accountants are supposed to be responsible, dependable, dull."

Katie sat down beside him and rubbed him lightly on the back of his neck. "You're all of those things, Dave."

He looked up. "Dull? Thanks a lot!"

"Except for that of course." She paused. "Well, maybe sometimes."

Despite his dismay, Dave had to smile. "Thanks again."

"Where do you think they got the videos?" Katie wondered.

"I don't know. Maybe . . ." The phone ringing interrupted him.

"Hi, Dad. Did you see the news?" asked Jeremy.

"Yes, we saw. Have you thought of any way KPIZ could have gotten those videos?"

"Like I said at the office, I didn't give those to anybody. I couldn't think of anyone who would have done so either. But Denyse had a guess."

"What's that?"

"She remembered that KPIZ showed a segment of Dingo clearing the road after the hurricane. He had the videos on Beatrice's cell phone. Denyse suggested that Dingo gave Charlie Collins the videos. She isn't happy with her dad either. Denyse knows her students will see the videos too."

Dave spoke in exasperation. "Why would he share those videos?"

"You saw how hard Dingo worked after the hurricane. He wants to help everyone. And he looks on fighting as manly. I'll bet he thought that the videos would help us get new accounting business."

Dave remained quiet for a few moments before speaking in resignation, "You're probably right, Son. You're a good man. Better than me in some ways. You always see the best in people."

After goodbyes, Dave hung up. "Denyse and Jeremy think Dingo gave the videos to KPIZ. Jeremy suggests Dingo was just trying to help us get clients. Denyse says he should have known better."

"I did mention to Beatrice that the firm needed new clients," Katie admitted.

Dave sat back on the couch in despair. Katie sat beside him again. "I've been thinking a lot about what John Foster said about suffering. And I read all the Bible verses he sent to us.

The Bible does give a lot of possible reasons. Maybe God can use this for some good."

"I don't see how. But I do hope I can handle my suffering now as well as you handled your cancer."

"I think thanking God could be a demonstration of some faith."

Dave looked at Katie. "You mean thank God for this fiasco?"

"Yes, I do." Katie took her husband's hand.

"Well, why not?"

As Dave and Katie finished praying, the phone rang again. "Now I know what those black-eye pictures on your wall are all about," said Caleb.

"You've figured us out," Dave tried to kid along.

"Actually, we had picked up enough bits and pieces of your adventure Down Under to know a hatchet job on KPIZ when we hear one," Caleb continued. "They try to come up with something sensational every day to attract viewers."

"But what can we do?" Dave lamented.

"Something, I think," Caleb insisted. "Listen. I know the editor of the newspaper pretty well. That is, if you'd be willing to set the record straight."

⏤◆⏤

A week later Dave arrived late to the office after going with Katie for her follow-up doctor appointment. *Today I'll resume phoning the tax-return clients we served last spring. Maybe some of them need year-around accounting services,* he thought. The prospect of making such likely fruitless calls did not cheer him. *There's nothing I hate more than soliciting.*

He walked by Candace talking on the phone where Dorothy normally sat at the front desk. *Candace?* he wondered.

Dave turned around. He saw Candace's two young sons quietly building a Lego castle in the corner. "Candace, why are you here?"

"Dorothy called me in to help answer calls. The phone is ringing constantly."

"What's going on?"

"Haven't you seen the morning newspaper? Look on the conference table."

In the conference room, Dave found the local paper laid out. The front-page headline proclaimed, *Local Accountants Heroes Down Under.* A picture apparently lifted from Parker and Company's website showed Dave and Katie smiling. The article, continued inside, told the story of Dave and Katie's experiences in Australia and New Zealand.

"That newspaper reporter did a thorough job, huh?" Jeremy said from behind Dave. Dave turned to see his son standing with a big grin. "After he talked with you and Mom, he called Denyse. He called the police in New Zealand too. He even managed to get a phone interview with Dingo and Beatrice."

"Jeremy, we need you on the phones," Dorothy, unaware that Dave had come in, shouted from somewhere within the offices. "Candace and I are screening out the curious. We're just taking name, number, and promising a quick call back from a CPA to the others. Herschel needs help calling back the prospective clients and explaining the process of signing engagement letters. You should handle all the additional media inquiries too. Every other news outlet in the area wants an interview, even KPIZ."

Jeremy explained while returning to his office, "Other news outlets are wanting to carry the story. But most of the calls are about accrual-basis bookkeeping or audits. Some even quip, 'I want someone who will fight for me.' Businesses need the financial statement from an audit to apply for insurance claims and loans after the hurricane. A few potential clients have inquired about help with international financial reporting. I'm eager to take on those accounts myself."

"I'll help Herschel," Dave shouted in Dorothy's direction.

—◆—

Anthony's mother yelled to him, "Baby! You better come see this. Here's another report about your boss on the TV. They say he's a hero or somethin' down in Australia and New Zealand. And they got a picture of that math teacher again. Says she's a hero too."

Anthony came running into the living room and stared at KPIZ on the TV screen. He saw that the station had changed their approach from skepticism to praise. He heard the words, "Tonight at six we'll run an expanded report on the story first broken on this station about our local accountants in heroic action. The Parker family broke up a human trafficking operation and rescued two victims. David Parker is a lifetime resident of the Mobile area and the owner of Parker and Company Certified Public Accountants. His wife, Katie, is well known in the city for supporting local schools. Their daughter-in-law, Denyse Parker, teaches mathematics at Central High School. Tune in at six."

"Did you know any of this?" his mother asked. Anthony shook his head in response. "These folks are maybe somethin' special," she added. "And they sent you home with all of those fish too."

Anthony nodded while staring at the images of the Parkers on the screen.

—◦—

The following week, Denyse stood in front of her first class of the fall term. "A car drives for a hundred miles at sixty miles an hour. How long does the trip take? That's arithmetic. Two cars start a hundred miles apart and drive toward each other at forty and seventy miles per hour. How long until they meet? That's algebra. Two cars start a hundred miles apart at forty and seventy, but one is accelerating, the other decelerating. That's calculus. Welcome to Central High's first calculus class." Only twenty-three students sat in the seats before her, none of them from the basic math classes she had taught the previous term. Caleb Fogle had gathered Central High School's best students from the previous year's algebra and geometry classes.

In the rear of the classroom, Caleb Fogle rocked on his heels watching. Denyse called on him, "Principal Fogle, do you have an announcement to make?"

Caleb cleared his throat. "Those of you who pass an achievement test at the end of the year will receive six semester hours of credit at the University of South Alabama. We hope you'll be the first of many Central High students to take college-credit classes."

"Thank you for arranging this, Mr. Fogle," responded Denyse as the students turned their faces back to her. She then spoke firmly to them while looking them in the eyes. "Let me assure you that every one of you will pass that exam and get the uni credit."

All her new calculus students waited with quiet trepidation. They had heard about Ms. Parker's passion for mathematics and expectations of her students. They listened to her continue, "Those of you who aspire to be engineers, chemists, physicists, or mathematics majors will need calculus." The students glanced at each other. None had previously aspired to those professions.

She raised the screen that had blocked their view of a blackboard. The students saw where she had drawn a grid with 81 squares, some of which had numbers in them. "This is called a sudoku puzzle. The object is to fill in the blank squares with the numbers, one through nine, so that no row, column, or box has the same number twice." She pointed at the blackboard. "Let's fill in this one together."

Caleb continued watching. To his surprise, in a few minutes Denyse had the twenty-three students participating and teasing each other over mistakes. Most had voluntarily left their seats to cluster around Denyse at the blackboard. Once the example had been completed, she shooed her pupils back to their seats and passed out a unique sudoku puzzle to each student. "Now fill this out. And this isn't a test. Helping each other is permitted." Soon the classroom buzzed as the kids worked on the puzzles and helped each other.

Caleb sidled over to where Denyse watched her pupils. "This is an unusual start to a calculus class."

"Most of them learned algebra and geometry by rote and formula. This will start them thinking on their own. Plus, we want maths to be fun, like solving a puzzle. And solving the sudokus will give them confidence."

"That was quite a promise you made that all of them would pass South Alabama's exam."

Denyse showed a little uncertainty by biting her lower lip. "I know. But when they do pass and get the uni credit, then every kid at Central High will be encouraged to take their maths seriously."

—•◦•—

"Massive deployment of the national guard by Florida's Governor Cleveland has stabilized Pensacola," the national news anchor reported.

A clip showed the governor saying, "I want two armed men with loaded weapons on every street corner. Curfew from dark to dawn will be enforced. Guardsmen are authorized to defend themselves if fired on."

"This follows the last three days of gunfire between local African Americans and members of white supremacist groups," the network anchor reported. "Police had been forced to withdraw due to sniper fire from both sides. Three policemen struck by bullets are in stable condition at local hospitals." The screen showed faces of three young men, two white and one black.

The TV screen switched to a clip of Jeremiah Wallace standing outside White America's headquarters. "If the governments of the United States and Florida had taken responsibility to maintain order sooner, patriotic citizens would not have had to act," he claimed. "When I'm elected to the US Congress, I'll enact legislation that equates any illegal acts by a distinct minority group to an act of terrorism."

An African American pastor in Pensacola appeared on the screen next. "Most of the provocateurs aren't even from Florida. If they had stayed away, our local police could have arrested any looters taking personal advantage of the difficult situation. No gun battles would have started."

"Twenty-three people have been hospitalized by the skirmishes," the network anchor concluded. "Four others have been pronounced dead on arrival at local hospitals. Both sides are invoking Florida's stand-your-ground law, which allows citizens to react with deadly force when they feel threatened. In other news, the US Congress is at an impasse over raising the national debt limit."

Dave clicked off the TV. "What else is new?"

"Well, gun battles in Pensacola are a recent development," Katie answered.

"I meant the Congress. But the gunfire is frightening. I just hope it doesn't spread to Mobile."

Chapter Twenty-Three

What are they looking at? thought Denyse. All her third period algebra students had gathered around something in the back of the classroom. Nearly all had been part of her basic math classes the previous year. They certainly knew to take their seats when the bell rang.

Rather than alert them, Denyse quietly joined the group from behind. One student held a newspaper and read aloud to the others. ". . . currently employed as a mathematics teacher at Central High School." Denyse also noticed several of them using cell phones to show the videos from Down Under.

"What is this?" Denyse interrupted the reader and phone viewers. The students startled at the closeness of her demanding voice. Then every face turned her way.

Anthony spoke for all of them, "Is this you, Ms. Parker?" He pointed to the picture printed in a newspaper showing the fracas in Melbourne. "We saw a video of this too."

"Yes, that's me in my wedding dress," admitted Denyse. "I told you all that I came from a rough background. Maths gave me a chance to make something of myself."

All the students took their seats without being told. A girl raised hand her. "What is it, Sherri?" Denyse called on her.

"Could I say something, please, Ms. Parker?"

"Go ahead."

"You bad, girl," Sherri responded in an exaggerated accent.

All the students laughed. Denyse had to laugh with them as she recognized a culturally delivered compliment.

"You'll know just how bad I am if you don't reach college entry level on your achievement tests next spring. Please solve the following sheet of single-variable equations for X. Remember that you perform exactly the same operation on each side of the equation until the X is left alone."

Anthony raised his hand. "Ms. Parker, why don't we get to do puzzles like your calculus class?"

"You want sudokus?"

"Yeah," several students answered.

"Alright, I'll made a deal with you. If every one of you gets 100% on this exercise, I'll bring in some puzzles tomorrow. But if anyone misses a single problem, you all start over."

The class murmured agreement. "Can we help each other?"

"Sure, but not just with the answers. I get to call four of you to the board to work one problem on the sheet. If any of the four can't solve the problem, then you all . . ."

"We know. Start all over."

"Right."

"Look at this!" Dave held up a check for Katie to see on the last day of August. "This is our first pay from Parker and Company. We only needed nine months to get to above breaking even."

Katie took the check from Dave's hands. "Congratulations! Your first paycheck." She looked more closely at it. "But isn't $350 a little light? Your forensic accounts alone brought in a lot more than that."

Dave reached to take the check back. "You're missing the point, sweetheart. This is the first month we haven't had to write a check to keep the firm in business."

Katie nodded appreciation. "That is a milestone. How much have we had to subsidize since you took over last year?"

"Only $178,000. Less than I had expected. Of course, you and I haven't had any outside income for nine months. That drew our savings down a lot too. But we wouldn't be where we are without Jeremy's marketing instincts."

"And Dingo's intervention didn't hurt," Katie added.

Dave grinned in agreement and reluctantly acknowledged, "And Dingo."

Katie hugged her husband. "What's your next move?"

"We've got more clients now than Jeremy, Herschel, and I can handle. Jeremy is looking for new associates to hire."

"CPAs?"

"Yes, and bookkeepers. We'll have the CPAs check and sign off on the bookkeepers' work."

⬦

The next day, Katie waited with Katelyn for Denyse and

Jeremy to return home from work. Ripper relaxed in the corner on a pallet Jeremy had arranged for him. A hunk of knotted rope lay between his paws. The young dog, then teething, had spent much of the day chewing on the rope. Katelyn toddled toward him reaching for the rope. She picked it up to put in her own mouth. "No, no, Katelyn," Katie shouted. The little girl turned to look at Katie and quickly dropped the rope back at Ripper's feet.

I had better remove the temptation, Katie thought and reached for the rope herself. Ripper surprised her by jumping to his feet with the rope in his mouth. Once Katie had her hand on the rope, Ripper started to shake his head violently. He jerked backwards until Katie had to release her hold. She left Ripper with the rope and returned to the couch with Katelyn. The dog followed her, rope in mouth, and held the rope within easy reach. When Katie grabbed the rope, Ripper pulled it out of her hand. Immediately the dog resumed his position, hoping for another tug-of-war. Katie watched as Katelyn reached for the rope. Ripper released it to her without a contest. Katelyn dropped the rope and threw her arms around Ripper's neck. He stood still allowing her to squeeze him tight. *He knows she's a child*, Katie realized. *He's a good dog, just young and boisterous.*

Katie heard the garage door opening. Ripper started jumping around in anticipation. "Hey, boy," Jeremy spoke to him as he entered with Denyse. Ripper jumped against his master and licked his hands.

"Take that dog outside," Denyse ordered. "He'll be knocking Katelyn over."

Jeremy engaged in a pulling contest with Ripper and the rope. "Getting knocked over wouldn't kill her."

"If you were more responsible, you wouldn't have gotten such a big dog."

Katie saw Jeremy bite back a retort. "Come on, boy. Let's go for a walk."

"Aren't you going to spend some time with your daughter?" Denyse demanded as Jeremy closed the door after himself.

<hr/>

"And what is this I found?" Anthony's mother gestured toward the kitchen table.

There Anthony saw the 38 revolver he had been coerced by Tyrone into buying. "I'm just keeping that for a friend," he lied.

"Mm-hmm. Then why do you need to keep it hidden in a drawer under your clean clothes?"

Anthony tried to go on the offensive. "Why are you going through my stuff?"

" 'Cause this proves that I need to." Anthony's mother stood glaring at her only remaining son. "Baby, I've had such high hopes for you. Your grades are gettin' better. You've got a job workin' for good people. You got a real chance to make somethin' of yourself. Now I see a hardness growin' in you. I saw the same thing in your older brother. Now he's dead. Don't you spoil your chance by hanging out with people who carry guns. You'll find yourself dead too."

Anthony reached for the revolver. He felt a sharp pain on his wrist. "Ow." His mother had hit him with the flyswatter.

"No, you don't." She stood defiantly facing him. "You think I like workin' graveyard shift to put food on the table for you to eat and paying the rent to give you a place to sleep?

You think I'm going to do all that just so you can get yourself killed?"

Anthony knew he was beaten. He looked away. He knew his mother hated her job at the all-night discount store. "I'll get rid of it," he promised.

"You better. 'Cause if I find it around here again, your 'friend' will have lost it forever."

━•◆•━

"Ms. Parker, you stay away from our neighborhoods. Go straight home when trouble starts."

Denyse took a long look at the teenage girl who had approached her in between classes. "What is it, Sherri? Is another demonstration coming?"

Sherri looked right and left in concern someone might hear her. "Maybe."

"Do you expect problems?"

"Some men, some women too, are getting ready."

"What are they getting ready for?"

"Big trouble." Sherri hurried away.

━•◆•━

"So what price range are we looking at?" the perky real estate agent asked. "Most people multiply their combined yearly income by three to decide how much loan to take."

"That would put us at about $320 to $340 thousand dollars," answered Jeremy.

"Good. A lot of new houses are on the market in that range."

"We don't need a house that big, though. And newer isn't a requirement for us," Denyse insisted.

212

"This house is an investment, Denyse," Jeremy explained.

"That's just so much money. A waste of money."

"A waste . . ." Jeremy's voice rose.

Denyse interrupted him, "We don't need a huge house. You know that."

The real estate agent sat quietly as the argument played out. She had seen this argument many times before.

—◆—

"Dad, can I use the Audit on Saturday?" Jeremy stood in the doorway to Dave's office.

"Sure, Son. Are you taking Denyse and Katelyn out?" Dave kept his eyes on the computer screen.

"No, just me and Ripper."

Jeremy's unexpected response made Dave turn around. "You and Ripper on the boat alone? No house hunting for you this weekend?"

"I've been house hunting enough lately. I'd rather enjoy this Saturday."

"You're welcome to the boat. The marina has spare keys."

"Thanks, Dad." Jeremy paused as if he was going to keep speaking but instead returned to his office.

House hunting should be a lot of fun for a young couple, thought Dave.

—◆—

"Jeremy, I've been looking at the new bookkeeping accounts." Herschel came into Jeremy's office with some printouts in his hands.

"You'll get a thumb-up or thumb-down decision on any bookkeepers before I hire them to work under your direction,"

Jeremy promised and waved a stack of job applications he had been reviewing.

"Thanks. But that's not why I came in. I've found some more security charges to several of our new clients that appear to be bogus. Remember Mr. Jackson?"

Jeremy blew out his cheeks. "He pretty much told us to back off."

Herschel nodded. "You're right about that. But I know some of these men. All the ones I know are African Americans. And the addresses would indicate that at least some of the others are too."

"Herschel, with the hurricane and all the new clients, there's something I forgot to tell you," Jeremy confessed. He explained to Herschel about Buddy's diagnosis of a possible protection racket. "Sorry, with all that's happened, I haven't even thought about Mr. Jackson since that day we took Buddy and Dingo fishing."

"That's okay. But do you think somebody is running a protection racket on African Americans?"

Jeremy laid the job applications aside. "It sure looks that way."

Herschel sat down. "What are we going to do?"

"Let's talk to my dad."

Restaurant

Chapter Twenty-Four

Two days later, Dave pulled into the crushed-oyster-shell parking lot of a popular seafood restaurant on the causeway east of the city linking the two sides of Mobile Bay. Seabirds wheeled in the air and periodically dived for fish. A few sat on posts of abandoned piers protruding from the water. The ramshackle establishment had been built on telephone-pole-sized posts to lift it above possible flood tides. Stepping inside he smelled the distinct odor of frying fish and hush puppies. He wished he and Katie had come there to have lunch. He politely asked the girl welcoming diners if he could speak to the owner. After being ushered into the owner's small office, he saw a wiry African American man about his own age wearing a look of trepidation.

215

"Mr. Jackson, I appreciate you seeing me without an appointment. I was afraid you wouldn't meet with me otherwise. I'm Dave Parker with Parker and Company CPAs. I'm not here to talk about your account."

Mr. Jackson sat back in his chair and gestured for Dave to take a seat. Curiosity overcame his concern. "Then why are you here, Mr. Parker?"

Dave sat down. "Please call me Dave. May I call you by your first name, Timothy?"

"Yes, certainly. I've read about you in the papers. You solved a missing person case in . . . where was it? The South Pacific somewhere . . . New Zealand? And everybody in the church knows about how you've been good to Herschel and that high school kid, Anthony. Caleb Fogle is my friend. He also speaks well of you."

"Thank you, Timothy." Dave looked him in the eyes. "Herschel is the reason I'm here. He's discovered a pattern of unusual security charges among some of our *other* clients."

Dave's statement seemed to surprise Timothy. But the restaurant owner remained silent.

Dave went on, "I think that you and the others might be victimized by some sort of protection racket. I'd rather risk losing your business than not inquire."

Timothy sat without speaking for a long minute. Dave watched him glancing around his office at various mementos and especially the photos of his family. "There are others?" he asked without looking directly at Dave.

Dave nodded. "Yes, there are."

Timothy leaned forward. "How many?"

"We don't know for sure. At least seven or eight. All appear to be African Americans."

Then Timothy looked directly at Dave. "Who knows about this? Am I the first one you've told?"

"Yes. Only myself, my son Jeremy whom you met, Herschel, and Buddy Oleson, a retired police chief from Minnesota, know about this. In case this is some sort of extortion racket, we all know to keep our mouths shut to avoid any type of retaliation against our clients."

"Mr. Parker, Dave, I . . . I . . . I . . ." Timothy's words trailed off.

"You don't have to say anything, Timothy. I just wanted to tell you that we're concerned and that maybe we could help."

"Are you like one of those TV mystery solvers?" Timothy attempted to lighten the mood.

Dave laughed. "Not hardly. But Katie and I have worked with the authorities in a couple of dangerous situations." Dave stood to go. "I've taken enough of your time."

"I appreciate your concern. We should be alright. Just don't divulge any of your suspicions to the local police or tell any others right now, please."

"Yes, sir," Dave indicated compliance before adding, "Your restaurant is one of my wife's favorite places to eat."

"Thank you." Timothy stood up. "Can I get you something from the kitchen to take home to her?"

"That's more than generous. But we'll come again soon for dinner. Katie loves to look out at the birds and the marsh as she enjoys your always-fresh seafood."

"Let me walk you to your car," Timothy offered.

In the parking lot, Dave and Timothy lingered chatting about fishing, the recent hurricane damage to the bay area, and the current college football season. Once in his car, Dave said to himself, *Without saying anything, Mr. Jackson told me a lot.*

◄─◆─►

A week later Katie answered the Parkers' home phone to hear an unfamiliar voice. "Could I speak to Dave Parker, please?"

"Sure." Katie held her hand over the phone to yell, "Dave, phone for you!"

Coming from the kitchen where he had been making what he called his 'world-famous seafood gumbo,' Dave asked, "Who is it?"

Katie only shrugged.

"Would you stir my roux for me?"

She whispered, "Are you sure you want me to touch your precious gumbo?" and took the wooden spoon.

"Hello," Dave spoke into the receiver.

"Dave, this is Timothy Jackson. I appreciate the concerns you expressed last week. The situation has gotten worse since then. Could we talk again?"

"Of course, Timothy. When would you like?"

"Why don't you come to the restaurant Wednesday night as my guest. That will be inconspicuous. After dinner stop by my office."

"Okay. Can I bring my wife, Katie? She's been my partner dealing with other difficult matters."

"I meant both of you. The same newspaper article I read about you included your wife's participation. She crashed your car into the kidnappers' van to rescue that Ukrainian girl, I believe. She'll make you even less conspicuous."

⸺◈⸺

Katie, normally a seafood lover, could not enjoy her dinner at Timothy's restaurant overlooking Mobile Bay. Dave had filled her in on Herschel's discoveries and his previous meeting with the restaurant owner. She hurried through her entree and skipped dessert.

Once in Timothy's office she waited while Dave chatted with Timothy a few minutes. Then she heard her husband ask, "So you say the situation we discussed before is worse? Can you tell us about it?"

Timothy took a deep breath before beginning. "It's like you suspected. A couple of years ago a man came offering extra security. I told him we didn't need any. Then he told me that some restaurants had gone out of business because of accidents or poisoning by contaminated food. The man suggested that he could provide undercover surveillance to prevent anything from happening. He charged $5,000 a month. The man hinted to me that if I tried to go to the police, he would know it. How could that be?"

"They could have a collaborator within the police department," answered Dave. "How do you pay them?"

"Men come around the first of each month. They usually meet me in the parking lot after the restaurant closes. I first gave them checks made out to 'cash.' But I put 'security' on the check's purpose line, so it would at least be tax deductible. After Herschel and your son talked to me, I started collecting the cash some of our customers used to pay their bills to pay the men."

"Timothy, do you know the IRS would interpret what you're doing with the cash as concealing revenue? You could go to jail for failure to report revenue."

"I could go to jail?" Timothy exclaimed.

"Yes. If you must continue paying these men, give yourself a bonus. Then use that personal money to give them. You'll have to pay income taxes on the money, but your payments wouldn't technically be illegal."

"I could go to jail?" Timothy repeated in disbelief.

"On the phone you said that the situation had gotten worse," Dave prompted.

"Yes, the man who came three nights ago said that the fee would double starting next month. I just can't afford that much, especially after the repairs I had to make from the hurricane. I told the man that could put us out of business. He didn't seem to care and offered me a ridiculously low price to buy the restaurant."

"Do you know the man's name?"

"No, different men come each month. I don't know any of their names. They're all white men, though."

Dave could sense Katie's outrage growing. He looked at her pointedly. She spoke for the first time. "Do you have surveillance cameras, Timothy?"

"I could have the tapes available tomorrow."

—◆—

The next evening the Parkers and Timothy met to review the surveillance tapes at a camera shop that rented video editing equipment for an hourly rate. Katie sat at the controls with Dave and Timothy looking over her shoulders. "Even lightened by the computer, that picture isn't very bright," she commented with regret. The trio watched again the video showing a blurry image of a large man. "And you say that this is the man who first approached you? And the same man who recently doubled your payment?"

"Yes. I'm sorry I didn't stand closer to the floodlight," answered Timothy.

Dave punched a key to freeze the picture on the monitor. "His face is recognizable, though. Maybe some of the others will know who he is." He gave Katie a USB drive to save the image.

"You mean the other men Herschel identified as victims?" Timothy asked.

"Yes. They probably all think they're the only one being extorted. And if we found a handful of victims just among our clients, there could be many more."

—◆—

Jeremy and Herschel wondered why Dave had invited them out to a late breakfast at a fast food restaurant. The three men sat in a booth in the nearly empty establishment.

"I didn't want Dorothy listening in on this one," Dave explained. Then he told them about the meetings with Timothy. He showed a still picture they had captured from the surveillance video. Neither young man recognized the man in the photo. "Herschel, I need the names, phone numbers, and addresses of the others you suspect to be victims."

"What can I do?" Jeremy asked.

"This is going to take up a lot of my time. You can run Parker and Company in my absence."

"Dad, I can do more than that!" Jeremy persisted.

"Yes, you can, Son. And we'll call on you when you're needed like we did in New Zealand." Dave paused before speaking to Jeremy and Herschel together. "But I want both of you young fathers to stay out of this right now. Let Katie and me figure out what's going on first. And besides that, I need a paycheck from Parker and Company. If we all get involved in this situation, none of us will get paychecks."

To that Jeremy and Herschel had to agree.

—◆—

Dave read a list of nine names to Timothy over the phone. "Here are the names Herschel suspects could be victims."

"Four of these men go to my church, Calvary Baptist."

"Herschel also said that."

"Then what should we do?" asked Timothy.

"Probably each of them thinks they alone are being forced to pay. Let's get them together. There's courage in numbers. Somebody might even identify the face on your surveillance video."

"Do you want me to call them, Dave?"

"Would you, Timothy? But don't tell them why we want to meet."

"Why not?"

"Remember how you first reacted to Herschel and Jeremy?"

"Yeah. I'm embarrassed by that. Those young men were just trying to help."

"Don't worry about that now. Where would we meet?"

"Why not at the church? Nobody watching our places of business would notice that."

Brown
Pelican

Chapter Twenty-Five

Seven African American men sat with Dave and Katie at a folding table in a small upstairs Sunday school classroom at Calvary Baptist Church.

"Since we're in a church I feel like we should start with a prayer," Timothy suggested. After none of the others objected, he prayed, "Lord, give us wisdom, and give us courage. Help us to lean on each other. Amen." A chorus of "amens" followed his conclusion. Timothy gestured toward Dave to begin.

Dave alternated looking at each man as he spoke. "You're all clients of Parker and Company. I'm Dave Parker. But we're not here to talk about tax law. We suspect that some or all of you may be victims of a crime." Several of the men started shifting nervously in their chairs. "Timothy, would you tell your story, please?"

As Timothy told everybody about the veiled threats and payoffs, Katie saw varying reactions of outrage and fear among the men. The group sat quietly when Timothy had finished.

"Anybody else experiencing something like this?" Dave prompted.

The group remained motionless and silent. None of them looked at the others. Each one seemed to have isolated himself into a world of his own. Finally, one man spoke as if he were sitting by himself thinking aloud rather than in the presence of others. "Yeah, something like that happened to me. But what can I do about it? They got the police on their payroll. I report this to the cops and my business gets burned down."

Katie, encouraged by the few words shared, spoke up for the first time. "What makes you think they have the police on their payroll?"

"The White America agitators were waiting for us when we staged that march last December. We had told the police in advance. Somebody on the police force must have told the racists where and when they could confront us."

Another man added, "The thug who collects the security money from me said that he would know if I called the police. I didn't know others had also been threatened."

Once the silence had been broken, all those attending except the oldest man bitterly revealed the circumstances of their victimization. One man complained, "When I tried to refuse, they returned with pictures of my kids."

The release of pent-up anger and despair spilled out of the men, filling the room. Finally, their emotions expressed, the men turned their eyes to Dave. The first who had spoken then repeated his question. "But what can we do about it?" Katie noticed that he had changed his question from "I" to "we."

Dave shook his head. "I'm not sure what exactly to do. But I know that most men and women in law enforcement are honest. We just need to find the right ones. Maybe even the FBI."

"The FBI?" Timothy wondered out loud.

"Yes, they have jurisdiction over racketeering as part of the federal RICO Act. They can even intervene in local criminal activity if there's clear evidence of organized crime."

"What should we do?" the man persisted and indicated himself and the other men seated.

Katie spoke up again. "First, do any of you recognize the man in this picture?" As she passed around the picture taken from Timothy's surveillance video, each of the men indicated he did, but no one knew his name.

"There are a couple of others who sometimes come to pick up the money. But this man is their boss," one man suggested. Several others nodded. "How did you get this picture?" he asked.

Katie collected the photo and held it for all to see again. "We took this from a surveillance tape taken in Timothy's parking lot. Would each of you please review any surveillance tapes you might have that could show this man or his subordinates? Don't do anything with the tapes. Just send them to us."

The men started glancing at each other. Understanding and a solemn bond passed between them. Timothy spoke for all, "They'll do it."

Dave looked around the table. The men could discern respect in his eyes. "Now I'm going to ask you to do something harder. I'd like to record each of you telling your story. Don't say your name. I give you my word to *not* reveal your identity." Katie brought out a recorder from her purse and laid it on the table.

The men recoiled as if the recorder were a venomous snake. "Why do you need our stories?" one demanded.

"Your stories could be probable cause to allow the federal authorities to get court approval for a more thorough investigation."

The men started shifting in their seats again. "You mean like wire taps."

"Maybe. Or searches."

"But what if the judge is crooked or someone hears the recording who recognizes our voices?"

"I'll take the precautions to get a clean judge," Dave promised without any clear idea of how to do so. "And I'll avoid the local authorities."

One of the quieter men spoke up, "I appreciate your concern, Mr. Parker. But you have nothing to lose in this. My business, and more importantly my family, are at risk. I don't think that's a risk I'm willing to take."

The men looked at each other. Timothy spoke slowly, choosing each word carefully, "You're right. The risk is major; our livelihoods, our families. But what else can we do? The criminals will keep demanding more. Should we keep paying until we have no livelihoods left? Keep paying until we can't provide for our families anymore? We have no control that way. At least we might have some control over our futures if we try to end this. And we'll be making a stand against wrong." Timothy looked around the table. "Are we going to lean on each other, brothers? All together?"

Dave thought that he could hear his own heart beat in the silence that followed. Each man had to decide the right course of action for himself and his family. Very slowly, one by one, the men nodded allegiance to a chance at a new future.

"Okay, we're all together in this. Each man has made his choice," said Dave. "Everybody should keep paying the demands for now. Don't let the criminals suspect anything has changed. And don't tell anyone!"

A chorus of heartfelt amens confirmed their individual commitment to them all.

"Before we record our stories, I got one thing to say," said the oldest man who had yet to speak. Everyone looked his way and waited. "I don't know the man's name in that picture." He tapped the photo Katie had shown with one finger. "But I know where to find him. I saw him on TV. He was standing behind that Jeremiah Wallace during a press conference."

—◆—

"Yeah, we survived the hurricane," Buddy said in response to Dave's question over the phone. "After we evacuated east with Mary's cats, I think we got the last hotel room available in Tallahassee. Our condo had only a little damage. But

Mary had to throw out all the food that had spoiled in the refrigerator and freezer because of the power outage."

"Your mackerel fillets are safe here. I used our generator to keep our freezer going until our electricity returned."

"I loved that day out fishing with you and Dingo. But I've been curious. What, if anything, have you done about that possible protection racket?"

"Actually, I called for your advice about that." Dave told Buddy about the discovery of other victims, the meeting, and the reaction of the businessmen. He explained their fears of police and potential judicial corruption. He revealed the possible link to white supremacists.

"That could be," Buddy agreed. "White supremacists frequently become police officers. Nearly all cops are on the up-and-up. But like every profession, a few bad apples get in. There could easily be a sympathizer or even a deliberate plant within the local police. You'd better be careful. This time you could put a lot of innocent people at risk, not just yourselves."

"Then what should we do?" Dave asked.

"You say one of the victims identified the photo of the extortionist as a man who attended a White America meeting? Maybe even one of the close associates of Jeremiah Wallace? I've got an idea. I could come over there, attend a few meetings, pose as a sympathizer, find some names. I'm too old to be suspected of being an undercover officer."

"What about your retirement?"

"I've been getting bored. How many times a day can you walk on the beach or go play mini-golf?"

Dave laughed. "I know the feeling. Before my forced retirement I had thought I'd never get tired of fishing. The primary reason we went to Minnesota was to find a new life."

"Bet you didn't think your new life would include criminals," Buddy kidded.

"That's for sure. How does Mary feel about your retirement?"

"Mary is tired of me moping about. She's been urging me to find something to do with myself. Mary married a cop. She's used to some tension. And my wife has a spunky streak herself. I think she'll want to go to the meetings with me. She'll add to my cover."

—◆—

A mob of reporters congregated in front of the courthouse in Mobile. A makeshift news conference started with handheld microphones in front of the district attorney. "I'm disappointed that we had a hung jury," he stated. "Apparently two of the jurors were not convinced beyond a reasonable doubt."

"Where is the police officer who had been accused of shooting an unarmed black suspect?" a reporter asked.

"He was released on his own recognizance. His attorneys slipped him out of the courthouse through a side entrance."

"Will you retry the case?"

The DA glanced at the mayor, who stood nearby. "We haven't decided yet."

Mayor Hunt stepped forward and spoke into the microphones, "I think the community would be best served if this matter were to be put behind us. Your government tried the case before a jury and couldn't get a conviction. Let's let it go at that."

"Chief Floyd!" one reporter shouted to the uniformed police chief standing with the other city officials. "Do you have a comment?"

The chief appeared reluctant to approach the microphones. "No, I don't."

"Are you going to reinstate the police officer in question to Mobile's force?"

The chief hesitated and glanced at the mayor himself. "Failure to secure a city-provided body camera is a violation of procedure. This officer somehow misplaced his body camera after the incident. For this reason, he will not be reinstated to Mobile's police department."

—◆—

"I'm happy that the citizens of Mobile saw through the witch hunt that constituted the prosecution of a public servant performing his duties to protect law-abiding citizens," announced Jeremiah Wallace in front of a TV camera.

"Interviews of several who served on the jury indicate that ten out of the twelve voted for a conviction. What does that say to you?" the reporter asked.

Jeremiah gave her a condescending look. "That tells me that patriots are frequently in the minority and have to take a stand. I'm ahead in most polls leading up to the election. That proves that the citizens of Mobile feel the same way as I do."

After broadcasting the sound bite by Jeremiah Wallace,

the TV station showed the reporter standing alone. "The latest polls in the race for the US Congress do show candidate Wallace with a one-percent lead over his incumbent opponent, who is recuperating from open-heart surgery. Forty-two percent of probable voters remain undecided."

—◆—

Walking home from school, Anthony saw a group of young men and a few girls standing around Tyrone in a convenience store parking lot. Joining them at the back of the group Anthony heard, "They're letting that murderer go. He shot one of our brothers in the back. That tells all of the racists that they can kill us without fear. We got to stick up for each other. Nobody else will."

Anthony could sense outrage growing among those listening. He could feel it in himself.

"Did you see the other news?" Tyrone went on. "That bigot Jeremiah Wallace is winning the election to be our congressman. We got nobody to depend on but ourselves. Some of us will be meeting in the park tonight to get ready. Come and join us."

Chapter Twenty-Six

On Saturday night two weeks later, Buddy and Mary parked in front of Dave and Katie's home shortly after 2:00 a.m. Immediately the front door opened. The Parkers came to the car to greet their guests. Dave and Katie shook both their hands. "Please come on in," Dave encouraged. "Let me carry your bags."

"You must be exhausted from the drive and a long evening at the meeting," Katie added. "Your room is ready. You can go right to bed if you like."

"Thanks. But I'm not tired. If you can stay up awhile yourselves, I'd like to debrief," answered Buddy. "You know, while the impressions are most fresh."

"Of course. We're dying to hear what happened." Dave directed the older couple toward the front door after taking their bags from the car trunk.

"I can make coffee if you'd like some," Katie offered.

"I could use some," Buddy admitted. "I drank so much beer at the rally that Mary had to drive us here."

Dave showed Buddy and Mary their bedroom while Katie made them coffee. She then made tea for herself and Dave. In a few minutes, the two couples sat down in the Parkers' living room.

"We showed up early at the White America rally," Buddy began. "In the parking lot, I saw license tags from all over the southeast. A lot of people had been tailgating like before a football game. A few had even erected canopies. The first thing you notice is the smell of grills cooking burgers and brats. Loudspeakers from the venue played patriotic music outside.

"At a long registration table, Mary and I signed up for membership, paid $100 dues each, and went inside. The old discount store White America had purchased gives them a lot of floor space. Inside, some booths had been set up to sell weapons of all types, survival supplies, and racist literature. Even with all the space, most of the seats—maybe a thousand—filled up fast. Some people stood or sat on the floor. Nearly everybody attending carried some sort of firearm," Buddy explained.

"The program started with a color guard presenting the American flag alongside the rebel flag while a live band played 'America the Beautiful.' No one seemed to notice the contradiction in the flags. Then the drummers started a long cadence rising in tempo. I could tell something was coming. When the drums paused, the crowd yelled 'charge.' The band broke into a rousing rendition of 'Dixie.' Rebel yells nearly drowned them out.

"The first speaker talked about the decline of civilization due to the mixture of races. A couple of other speakers talked about guns and survival skills in a dystopian society. A lot of the same stuff you see on their racist website. Between speakers the band played and the crowd chanted slogans. Then Jeremiah Wallace stood up as the featured speaker. He warned the group about the imminent doom of America, played on their fears of losing their livelihoods, extolled the founding fathers and Confederate heroes, and quoted Old Testament scriptures about the pagans living among the children of Israel. He finished by urging locals to vote for him and leading the crowd in a pledge of allegiance to the white race. The finale was the drum cadence followed by 'charge' and 'Dixie' again. The organizers knew how to create excitement among their followers.

"After the cheering tailed off," Buddy continued, "Wallace announced free beer and ribs for all members. They must have had a hundred kegs of beer ready and thousands of pounds of catered ribs.

"The crowd broke into smaller groups drinking beer and eating ribs, while the band played the kind of music you might hear in a country honky-tonk nightclub. Mary and I circulated, listening to the conversations. Whenever we overheard something interesting, we stopped to jaw a little."

Mary broke in, "I felt scared. But Buddy was wonderful. I guess from all those years he spent on the force. Whenever someone asked his opinion, he just growled, 'We all know why we're here.' " Mary mimicked Buddy's gruff voice so well that the Parkers had to smile. Mary glanced at her husband. "Buddy talked a lot about guns with them too."

Buddy looked fondly back at her. "Maybe a quarter of the crowd were women. Mary being there really made me seem less suspicious to the other attendees."

"Must be my honest face," Mary offered as Buddy sipped his coffee. "Being undercover was exciting, though."

Buddy put down his cup. "I overheard a group talking about the confrontation in Mobile. They complained that more of the patriots—as they called themselves—would have shown up if they had gotten the warning earlier in advance. That adds to our suspicions that someone in the police is tipping them off.

"Next we mingled with a group talking about converting semi-automatic rifles to full automatic. I explained that using full automatic cuts down on accuracy and wastes ammo. One man said, 'With the right ordnance you don't need much accuracy.' "

"What does that mean?" Katie asked.

"That means they could have military weapons, perhaps explosives of some sort."

"Oh."

"Mary and I just kept mingling and listening. A lot of the men started to get a bit loose after drinking beer like water. That's when I heard one bragging that the 'Africans' had paid for the beer and ribs."

"That could be a reference to the extortion racket," Dave suggested.

Buddy nodded. "My hearing and repeating that wouldn't help a prosecutor to get a conviction in a court. That would be considered hearsay. But it is an indication to us that we're on the right track."

"What about the man caught on Mr. Jackson's surveillance video?" Katie wanted to know.

"I'm pretty sure he was one of the early speakers. Again, that wouldn't help much in a trial. Since nobody attending wore name tags, I didn't get his real name. But everyone referred to him as 'Lightning.' All the ones wearing colored arm bands were surrounded by people after the rally. I got close and shook his hand but didn't get a chance to talk to him."

"What did the arm bands signify?" Dave asked this time.

"They're probably a rank within a militia. An officer or unit leader. Most militia groups are organized on a quasi-military basis."

"See anybody else prominent?"

"I saw the policeman who had been put on trial for killing the unarmed black kid. His pictures were all over TV after the trial resulted in a hung jury. The crowd at the rally treated him like a hero. The organizers had even set up a spot for people to have a picture made with him."

"For twenty dollars a snap," Mary added.

"That line was a mile long."

⊷◆⊶

The next morning Mary entered Katie's kitchen after sleeping in from the late night. She found Katie waiting. "Good morning."

"Good morning to you," Katie greeted warmly. "What would you like for breakfast?"

"Just coffee for me, please." Mary thought for another

minute. "On the other hand, I could use a couple of scrambled eggs if that wouldn't be too much trouble."

"No trouble at all." Katie flipped the switch on the kettle to make hot water for coffee and took three eggs out of the refrigerator.

Mary leaned over to pet Old Yeller, who had heard voices and come to join them. "Have you done anything else heroic lately?" She picked him up for a hearty hug.

Rrrow, responded Old Yeller.

Mary took a stool at Katie's breakfast counter. "Dave was really nice to take Buddy fishing this morning. I just don't understand why they had to leave so early after talking so late."

"Men and fish. The early morning departure is part of the ritual. It's not to understand, only to accept."

Mary laughed. "That's for sure."

Katie broke the eggs into a bowl. "It would be easy enough for me to add some cheese and ham to make a simple omelet." To this Mary consented. Katie beat the ingredients all together and poured the bowl contents into a hot skillet. When the kettle clicked off, Katie poured hot water into her coffee press.

Mary watched as Katie poured her a scalding cup of the freshest possible cup of coffee. "Working with Dave on this is good for Buddy. He enjoyed leisurely walking on the beach and sightseeing for a year after we retired. Then he started getting bored. He missed the opportunity to feel like he was making a difference with his life."

Katie flipped the omelet to the other side for a minute and then slid it onto Mary's plate. "Dave was the same way when his partners forced him into early retirement. That's why we went to Minnesota."

"I'm sorry I didn't meet you then, and Old Yeller. Buddy used to come home talking about a crazy cat." She gestured toward Old Yeller, who, having been ignored for a couple of minutes, had lain down in his warm box. "Buddy never wanted to be or liked being the police chief. He only accepted the position when Richard Christensen called because he knew a change was needed for Washita. Buddy always preferred field work. It's wonderful to see him acting like a young detective again."

"Don't you worry about him?" Katie poured herself a cup of tea.

"Of course. I used to worry all the time. Whenever I couldn't reach him by phone, my mind would start to think up all sorts of bad situations. But a cop's wife can't continue like that. She has to learn to put her fears into a compartment and live on. This takes effort, but most wives manage it. Or they aren't married to a cop for very long. But last night was different. While I could see Buddy unharmed, I didn't need to worry. And my being available to drive allowed him to drink beer as part of his cover. I can't believe that I actually helped in an investigation."

"We really appreciate you helping us, both of you. Without you, Dave and I wouldn't have had any idea what to do."

"That's not what I hear about you." Mary tasted her omelet. "This is wonderful."

Katie smiled. "I'm glad you like it. Did you shop at Hansen's bakery in Washita?"

"Oh, I loved Hansen's. I haven't found any place in Florida like it."

"You'll like where I take you today."

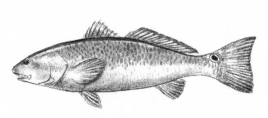

Redfish

Dave guided the boat to a river mouth that emptied into Mobile Bay. "I thought casting lures today would help keep us awake. You might want some of this." Dave handed Buddy a can of insect spray containing DEET.

"Mosquitos?" asked Buddy while spraying his arms and legs.

"Hordes of gnats coming out of the salt grass. Locals call them 'no-see-ems.' They're small enough to pass through a screen. But their bite stings as much as a mosquito."

Buddy gestured toward the water. "And these are redfish, you say?"

"Yeah, great fighters, and they're delicious. Maybe we'll catch a snook too. They both live in the brackish water of an estuary. We'll cast for them a lot like you cast for northerns in Minnesota." Dave passed Buddy a heavy-duty open-faced spinning rod. On the line he had tied a shallow diving plug with a silver spinner.

Buddy proved himself no slouch with a fishing rod. He laid out a sixty-foot cast alongside some rushes lining the bank and started a slow jerking retrieve. "So then what's our next step in the investigation?"

Dave privately rejoiced in Buddy's use of the word *our*. "I'm just an accountant. You're the expert in law enforcement. What do you think we should do?"

The two men stood on opposite ends of the boat working the water in a systematic arc around them. Dave let Buddy think.

After nearly five minutes, Buddy cleared his throat to speak. "I'd like to go to the feds and ask them to invoke the RICO Act. That was passed by the US Congress in 1970 to combat racketeering. But with only what we suspect, they might feel obligated to immediately involve the local authorities. If what we think about an informant is true, the feds going to the locals could bring retribution onto your clients. Even the local office of the FBI could be compromised. We need some evidence that White America has a man inside the Mobile police to convince our feds to act unilaterally."

Dave jerked back his rod as a snook attacked his lure. Three minutes later Buddy netted a seven pounder. "Nice fish," he told Dave.

"Lots of bigger ones are around here," Dave promised. He removed the snook from the hook and dropped it into the cooler. "So how would we get evidence of an informant?"

Buddy started outlining his plan. Dave only interrupted him to point out a V ripple indicating a passing redfish. "Cast right in front of where it's going."

Buddy did so and caught a five-pound redfish. "They're especially good eating," Dave reminded him.

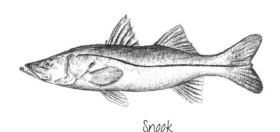

Snook

Chapter Twenty-Seven

---◦---

"You want me to lie to the police?" Herschel sat stunned at the request.

"Think of this as planting a rumor. It's not like you'd be giving false information to a question," Dave tried to ease Herschel's concern.

"Still sounds like lying to me."

Dave made a hands upward gesture of concession. "Okay then. It is lying. Will you do it? You know that we're trying to help Timothy Jackson and the others you identified. They're convinced that White America has an informant inside the police department. We need proof to take to the federal authorities."

"Why me?" Herschel persisted.

"We think your voice might be most convincing."

"Because I'm an African American?"

Once again Dave's gesture indicated concession.

Another voice came before Herschel could respond. "I'll do it," volunteered Jeremy. "Offisa, they's gonna be a demonstration tonight of our foke in de white neighborhoods. I jest don't want no trouble."

Despite himself, Herschel had to smile at his friend's clumsy effort. "You do know we don't talk like that, right? Except in 1930s movies. Nobody would believe you." He turned to Dave. "Okay, I'll do it. What do you want me to say?"

"Pretty much what Jeremy said, only in a convincing way."

While Dave recorded him, Herschel called 911 on the disposable cell phone Dave had purchased from a kiosk. The call lasted less than fifteen seconds. Herschel looked shaken afterwards. "I've never done anything like that before."

Jeremy spoke in sympathy. "Bad circumstances sometimes require doing things we wouldn't ordinarily do." He told Herschel about watching his mother play a temptress in New Zealand.

"You mean, your mother? Katie Parker?"

"Yeah, my demure wife." Dave supported Jeremy's story. "Jeremy did some playacting himself in that situation."

"Tell me about it, Jeremy."

━━◆━━

Forty-five minutes later Buddy received a text message from White America. *Red alert. White neighborhoods to be invaded in Mobile. Full turnout tonight. Assemble at the headquarters. Come fully armed.*

As the sun set, Buddy mingled with hundreds of men in the parking lot at the White America headquarters. The outdoor loudspeakers instructed the men, "Remain near your vehicles. We'll convoy to the affected areas as soon as our scouts identify the Africans' direction of advance." Buddy saw many men sipping from bottles and passing them around.

A recorder in Buddy's pocket captured angry words from the men assembling. "The Africans are going to invade white neighborhoods. This is our chance to teach them a lesson." Other voices coached novice militiamen, "Remember to aim carefully. Remain undercover until your unit leader gives the order to advance. Be careful to not expend your ammo in the first few minutes." The outdoor loudspeakers played martial music.

The assembled men waited until after midnight for the call that never came. Buddy recorded voices of disappointment. Finally, the loudspeakers announced, "The Africans learned that we had mobilized. You saved Mobile tonight." The crowd cheered and dispersed.

—◆—

"Will we need an attorney to approach the FBI?" Dave asked Buddy later that night.

"I don't think that will be necessary. They're protective of informants. I'll use my former police credentials and connections to get a meaningful appointment. Otherwise we'll only get to talk to the greenest recruit delegated to the crackpot detail."

"Okay, when do we go to Montgomery?"

"As soon as I can get us an appointment."

"Can Katie come?"

"Certainly. I'll bring Mary too. If we go in two cars, Mary and I can go back to Santa Rosa Beach after we put the feds onto the scent. She's getting anxious about her cats."

◄╍●╍►

FBI Senior Agent Mark Whitten met the Parkers and Olesons in the reception area of the FBI's Montgomery office.

He shook hands first with Buddy. "Chief Oleson, our Minneapolis office spoke well of you. I understand you have something concerning the White America militia. We've been monitoring them. Their website looks pretty reactionary."

"This is my wife, Mary," Buddy introduced. Agent Whitten nodded respectfully to her and lightly shook her hand.

Agent Whitten turned to the Parkers. "And these are the informants you promised?"

"We're Dave and Katie Parker," said Dave as they each shook hands with the FBI agent.

Agent Whitten looked carefully at Dave and Katie. "The Minneapolis office? Chief Oleson?" he murmured to himself. "Isn't there a story about an older civilian couple in Washita? That's where you were police chief, right? The civilian couple helped to break a big case. That wouldn't be you two, would it?"

Chief Oleson spoke for them. "Yes, the Parkers were the ones who provided the key clues that led to the arrest and conviction of dozens of criminals. And maybe you saw the news reports from Mobile about a missing person rescued in New Zealand. Dave and Katie are the same civilian couple."

"I had never put those two stories together." Agent Whitten spoke thoughtfully, "You two seem to get around. Around trouble, that is. And you're an accountant. Isn't that right? Now you've uncovered something else?"

Dave maintained a professional posture. "Maybe we have. Unfortunately, closer to home this time. We appreciate you hearing us out."

"Let's go to the conference room to see what you think you've uncovered." Agent Whitten signed them in to the FBI's offices and led the way to a luxurious conference room in the back corner of the building.

"Would you like coffee, a soft drink?" All declined. "Okay then, who starts?" asked Agent Whitten.

"Are you recording this?" asked Buddy.

Agent Whitten shook his head. "Technically we have the legal right to because this is our facility, you've come to us voluntarily, and you haven't been accused of any crime. But, no, we aren't recording. Let's just make this a discussion for now."

"Go ahead, Dave," said Buddy.

"Alright, as you surmised, I'm a CPA. I have a firm, Parker and Company, down in Mobile. One of my associates identified several of our clients who had questionable and excessive security charges. At first, we suspected some sort of tax evasion. But our friend in law enforcement, Chief Oleson, theorized some sort of protection racket might be the cause. One of these clients admitted that he was being extorted and asked for our help. Katie, would you bring up the records?" While Katie booted up her laptop, Dave continued. "The first client contacted the other clients whom our records indicated could also be victims."

"Ready," Katie reported and moved to sit where Agent Whitten could see the screen without any glare.

"These are excerpts from the records showing the possible extortion payoffs. The questionable entries are highlighted in red."

Agent Whitten pointed as he commented, "I notice that you've obscured anything that would disclose the identity of your clients."

"That's because we need to protect them in case the extortionists were to seek retribution. And we didn't know, still don't know, how you might react."

Agent Whitten nodded acceptance. "Fair enough. Please continue."

Katie then explained, "When we met with the probable victims, we asked permission to record their stories. These are recordings of them speaking. The entire tape will take about twenty minutes." She looked questioningly at Agent Whitten who nodded in response. Katie hit the play icon.

Fear and anger infused the words from those Katie had recorded. A few questions from her helped the speakers be clear and thorough. Katie saw Agent Whitten's jaw tightening. Although Dave had listened to the compilation before, the injustice of the situation still unnerved and angered him. When the recording finished, all in the FBI's conference room sat in silence.

Agent Whitten was the first to speak. "Those all sound like African American voices." Katie nodded agreement.

Whitten continued, "Did they give any indication of who the extortionists might be?"

"By careful screening of surveillance videos at their various businesses, we came up with several photos of suspects," Dave answered.

Katie clicked through four photos of men who could be recognized. "This last one appears to be the primary one who approached the victims." She hit the play icon on her computer again. The words of an elderly man reported having seen the man on his TV at a White America gathering.

Agent Whitten whistled. "So we have African Americans claiming to be forced into giving protection money to a white supremacist group?"

"That's what we suspect," Dave answered. "And the victims are all scared to death."

"I attended a White America rally with Mary." Buddy pointed at the screen where Katie had left the photo of the last man up. "I identified that man at the rally. They call him 'Lightning.' He's apparently one of the leaders of an associated militia." Mary nodded to support her husband.

"I don't blame the victims for being afraid," Agent Whitten agreed. "But why didn't they go to the Mobile police? They have a first-class department down there. I know the chief of police, Harmon Floyd. And he's an African American himself. We even have an FBI office in Mobile."

Dave shook his head. "The victims are all convinced that White America has a sympathizer within the police who is reporting to the supremacists. Several of the victims had been told by the extortionists that going to the police would be quickly discovered and dealt with. The victims are even afraid of the local FBI."

Agent Whitten shook his own head. "Do you have any evidence of that informer within the police?"

"Well, white agitators knew beforehand when a march was planned in Mobile and had assembled along the route. That's when the riot took place before last Christmas. The organizers had kept the march secret from the community until the last minute except for notifying the police."

Agent Whitten rubbed his face with his hands. "The FBI's relationship with local law enforcement agencies is always strained. Unfortunately, Alabama doesn't have a RICO statute of their own. We'll need more to go on than the rumor of a police informer before we act unilaterally. Otherwise we can't invoke the RICO Act without including the locally responsible authorities in a joint investigation."

Chapter Twenty-Eight

——•◦•——

Dave and Buddy looked at each other. Buddy's head nodded an almost indiscernible amount. Dave glanced at Katie, who hit play again. Herschel's words to the 911 center came from the speaker.

"Forty-five minutes later I got this text message from White America." Buddy held up his cell phone. "Then, when I reported to the assembly point, I recorded these words." Katie played the words he had taped using a pocket recorder at the assembly.

Once again, silence filled the conference room. The Parkers and Olesons waited for Agent Whitten to draw his own conclusion.

"The 911 call was a fake, right? Then a summons to White America's militia members arrived just forty-five minutes

251

later? Finally, those summoned knew the contents of the 911 call, which was fake. Have I understood that correctly?"

After both Dave and Buddy agreed, Agent Whitten concluded, "Someone in the police department must have tipped them off." He continued talking to himself without seeming to realize the others were listening. "That would explain why our efforts to infiltrate . . ." He broke off after remembering the others could hear him.

Agent Whitten turned to Dave. "Who is that making the bogus 911 call?"

"Do you need to know?" Dave asked respectfully.

Buddy broke in, "I'll take full responsibility for the fake 911 call, Agent Whitten. I'm the one who knows the seriousness of abuse of the 911 line."

"No, never mind. The 911 records can confirm the call, if needed. Are the victims willing to testify?"

"Not without some sort of protection," Dave answered. "They're all scared for their families and businesses."

"We can't promise them all witness protection based on just this. And they wouldn't be eager to leave their homes and communities either." Agent Whitten looked at the Parkers and Olesons. "Would you be willing to testify, if needed, at least before a judge or grand jury to establish probable cause?"

"I have 35 years of experience as a policeman," Buddy answered. "I've testified hundreds of times."

"I'm certified as a forensic accountant," Dave said for himself.

Agent Whitten laughed out loud. "You both should be credible. And you ladies," he said to Katie and Mary, "would be very believable if called to testify."

Mary surprised everybody by speaking up. "Buddy, you forgot to tell Agent Whitten about the weapons. I heard them talk about weapons too."

"I did forget, Mary. Agent Whitten, while I drank beer with some of the White America members, some of them alluded to fully automatic weapons and even ordnance."

Agent Whitten's face reacted in surprise and concern. "That's very good to know. Over 70% of domestic terror acts are done by white groups. This threat could add to the urgency of our investigation. Ms. Parker, would you mind if I had copies of the files and recordings you've used, please? With these, your in-person testimonies might not even be necessary at this point."

Katie handed him a pre-prepared USB flash drive. "Yes, of course."

The federal agent paused. "Is that everything you have?"

"Yes, sir," responded Buddy for all.

"Then I want to thank you for your work and for coming in. Let me emphasize that you shouldn't publicize what you've found for the safety of your informants and for the security of our investigation. Just step away from this for now. The FBI will carefully consider what you've discovered."

—◦•◦—

After saying goodbye to Buddy and Mary, Dave and Katie drove down I-65 toward Mobile. "Well, it's in the hands of the FBI," Dave temporized. "We're out of it now. I just pray that they'll handle things carefully without jeopardizing Timothy and the others."

Katie scooted over to sit close to her husband. "You didn't

reveal the names of the victims. How could the criminals find out who accused them?"

Dave grimaced. "Criminals have a way of finding things out."

Katie remembered some of their previous experiences and agreed. "You're right about that. I'm glad this worked out without all of the drama we had in Minnesota and Down Under."

Dave reached out and squeezed her hand. "So am I."

"Tomorrow I'll be back to taking care of Katelyn like nothing happened." Then Katie changed the subject. "I'm worried about Jeremy and Denyse, though. Denyse has started treating Jeremy like she learned to deal with Dingo. She handles unruly male students the same way. But Jeremy isn't like them."

Dave nodded slowly as if thinking. "I'm certain that Denyse genuinely loves Jeremy. But that's the communication pattern she developed at a young age to deal with difficult males. Old habit patterns are hard to break."

"And new ones are even harder to begin. That's especially true when you're juggling a lot of balls like Denyse is."

—◆—

"And that's what we told the FBI," Dave concluded his update to Jeremy and Herschel. "They don't know who made that bogus 911 call. And they don't really care."

Herschel relaxed at Dave's report about the 911 call. "And you didn't reveal any of our clients' names?" he clarified.

"No, we didn't. And Agent Whitten understood our desire to protect them. Now we just wait to see what the FBI does, if anything."

"Dad, you should call Mr. Jackson and tell him the status," suggested Jeremy. "Let him tell the others."

"That's a good idea, Jeremy. After that I'll need to get back to work. I appreciate the two of you running the firm while I've been preoccupied."

"No problem," said Herschel.

Jeremy had picked up some Aussie lingo from Denyse. "No worries, Dad."

—◆—

A local TV news anchor reported, "In political news, polling results show Jeremiah Wallace's lead increasing three percentage points among probable voters with only a month until the election. Apparently, his stand on law and order is drawing support from a lot of South Alabamians. His opponent is still affected by recent surgery and only able to attend a limited number of meetings. Mr. Wallace is spending three times more money than his opponent."

A commercial break immediately followed with a campaign ad showing Jeremiah being congratulated by a group of handsome actors dressed as policemen and soldiers. Patriotic music played over local icons of patriotism: the battleship Alabama, fishing boats going out in early morning, families walking up the steps to a church with white columns.

—◆—

A large crowd of teen to middle-aged African American males gathered in James Seals Park. *There must be two hundred here*, thought Anthony.

"We got to be ready," Tyrone shouted for all to hear. "We'll have the advantage because we know our neighborhoods. If they come at night, we'll hide undercover in dark corners and wait for them. Once you fire, you fall back, take cover, and wait for them again."

"Wait for who?" someone shouted.

"Where you been?" Tyrone responded derisively. "The White America goons will invade our neighborhoods like they did in Pensacola. Some police may try to support them."

"Don't trust anyone white," another voice shouted.

Anthony felt the revolver under his hooded sweatshirt. Competing emotions confused him. *Protecting my people is my duty*, he thought. Then he remembered Denyse's commitment to her students. He remembered Jeremy helping him to correct the foul-up with the envelopes and taking him fishing. *All white people aren't bad*.

"And arm up!" Tyrone demanded. He brandished an AR-15 automatic rifle over his head for all to see. "White America is buying weapons. You got just as much legal right as them to bear arms."

—◦—

Katie looked up as the garage opener signaled Denyse and Jeremy's return. Katie nudged Katelyn to greet her parents as they came through the door. The little girl needed no urging. Katelyn ran to Jeremy, who picked her up.

"Hello, sweetheart," Jeremy spoke to his daughter. "What did you do today?"

Katelyn extended a little hand toward the kitchen. "We made cookies."

Indeed, the smell of sugar cookies permeated the apartment.

"Cookies? Oh, that's what smells sooooo good. Could I have one?"

"Yes."

Denyse looked pointedly at Jeremy and instructed, "You shouldn't set a bad example for her by eating cookies before dinner." She came over to take Katelyn from his arms. Denyse hugged Katelyn tightly. "You helped Grandkate make cookies? We'll eat some later."

Katie saw Jeremy squeeze his lips together to prevent responding to Denyse. She watched him curtly turn around and lean over to pet Ripper. The dog wagged in delight with his whole body.

"Hey, boy. You ready for a walk?"

"I made a lasagna for your supper," Katie volunteered.

"You and Katelyn go ahead with supper," Jeremy told Denyse. "I'll take Ripper to the park. Then we'll go look at pickup trucks."

"You don't need a pickup truck," Denyse responded. "And you should be here with your daughter for supper anyway."

Jeremy jingled the car keys to excite Ripper and opened the door for them without speaking. Katie heard his and Ripper's footsteps going down the stairs to the garage. The garage door opening indicated their departure.

Denyse sat down on the couch with Katelyn. Katie heard her sigh. "Do you mind if I have supper with you and Katelyn?" Katie asked. "Dave is meeting with one of his forensic clients in Atlanta."

"You're welcome, of course." Denyse tried to smile.

Denyse continued to talk with and amuse Katelyn as Katie set three places at the table and served the lasagna with a green salad.

"I'm afraid I let her eat too many cookies," Katie confessed as Katelyn played with her food.

Denyse helped her daughter down from her high chair to return to the children's TV program. "Katelyn won't need this high chair much longer," she said with obvious sadness. She tried to smile at Katie. "Don't worry about the cookies. I just wish Jeremy was here with us."

"I couldn't help noticing that things are a bit . . . strained between you and Jeremy."

"Yes," Denyse admitted. "We both come home tired from work. And we've had major disagreements looking at houses. Jeremy wanted to buy a bigger house than I thought we needed. He said something about it being an investment. But I'm not comfortable with taking on so much debt. Now Jeremy is thinking about buying a pickup truck. I know two vehicles would make things easier for us. But they might allow us to be apart all the time, rather than just most of the time."

"Maybe there's something else going on too," Katie suggested.

Denyse put down her fork without having eaten anything and asked, "What could that be?"

Katie took a deep breath. "Well, when you were growing up, Dingo could be difficult."

"What's that got to do with Jeremy?"

"You had to . . ." Katie hesitated, ". . . develop a straightforward manner of communicating with your father. We've seen how effective it is with Dingo. The same method works well with your sometimes-unruly male students too."

"Men need us to be direct," Denyse insisted.

"Sometimes, yes," Katie agreed. "For example, if you have something specific in mind you want for your birthday, you need to tell your husband directly. He likely won't guess what you want. But regarding everyday activities, women need to be more discrete. Dave and I talked rather directly with Jeremy occasionally when he was a teenager. But we were his parents, not his wife."

Denyse sat still after crossing her arms across her chest. "But—"

Katie interrupted to complete her point. "Jeremy usually went away to sulk after we had rebuked him." She pointed at the door where Jeremy had left with Ripper.

"Why would he sulk at what I said?" asked Denyse in a defensive tone.

Katie took another deep breath and forced herself to speak. "Jeremy is non-confrontational like his father. His response to conflict is to withdraw. And Denyse, your tone, appropriate with Dingo, would sound reproachful to Jeremy."

"Reproachful? What makes something sound reproachful?"

Then Katie smiled. "Almost any time we women use the word 'you' followed by describing a behavior change, men hear that as reproachful. Men like Dingo respond. Men like Jeremy, or Dave, withdraw to sulk." Katie pointed at the door again before adding, "You didn't talk to Jeremy like that when we first met you."

Denyse stared at the ceiling for a moment before speaking. "Things are different now. We have Katelyn to consider. We're both so busy."

"Yes, things are different now. But you still need to be

careful how you speak to Jeremy. Men need to be respected by their wives. Most of our respect or lack of respect comes through in the way we communicate. And Jeremy needs to realize that in hectic circumstances, words can feel reproachful when the words are just meant to be efficient. He also needs to understand that his withdrawing from potential conflict doesn't show you respect either."

Denyse uncrossed her arms and reached toward Katie's hand. "Would you tell him that?"

"I'll have Dave tell him if we need to. But I think it would be best if you and Jeremy worked this out without our interference." Katie pointed at Katelyn. "And as you said, there are other ears in your home now. The best gift you can give your daughter is a mom and dad who really love each other and treat each other with respect."

Denyse hung her head. "This is hard. I probably do have some bad habits that need to be changed."

"Yes, a great marriage is hard. But you're a good woman, Denyse. Jeremy is lucky to have you for his wife. And you're as smart as anyone I know. This isn't a major problem. I'm sure you and Jeremy can fix it before it becomes major."

Denyse looked at the door. "Can you watch Katelyn awhile longer? And can I use your car? Jeremy took ours."

"Of course." Guessing Denyse's intentions, Katie added, "Don't tell Jeremy you and I talked."

"Why not?"

"The stinker would be embarrassed that his mother intervened. But he'll love you more for rescuing him from himself. Dave did."

"You had to rescue Dave?"

"Do you remember me telling you how he had become obsessed with work? He greatly appreciated my encouragement to set some limits and actual goals for having fun together as a family. Men like Dave and Jeremy love goals."

"Oh, I remember now. Maybe you could tell me more about that another time, Mum."

Katie smiled at Denyse's calling her 'Mum.' "I'd be happy to, honey."

"I need to go now."

"Good on ya."

Chapter Twenty-Nine

Jeremy stood on the banks of Mobile Bay at a park he frequented. Ripper dropped the tennis ball at his feet and looked at him expectantly. Jeremy picked up the dog-drool-soaked ball and threw it as far as he could into the water. Ripper whirled and plunged into the water as if retrieving that ball was the most important activity in the universe.

I should be home with Katelyn and Denyse, Jeremy thought. *But I just need a calm place to unwind a bit from work.* Still he felt guilty.

"Mind if I throw it this time?"

The words startled Jeremy. He turned to see Denyse standing beside him. Inwardly he cringed and thought, *She found me. She's probably here to berate me for not staying home.* He gestured *go ahead* with a throwing motion.

Ripper came dripping out of the water and without even shaking, dropped the ball and stood ready for another throw. Denyse picked the ball up and heaved it as far as she could.

Ripper dashed into the water as if the ball would drown without his intervention.

The couple stood silently until Jeremy spoke. "Where's Katelyn?"

"Your mother is taking care of her."

Jeremy winced. "Sorry I disappeared. I know you don't get to spend as much time with Katelyn as you would like."

"We're both pretty busy. And I haven't made things any easier by being crabby lately."

Jeremy didn't deny her admission. "I've been a bit touchy myself."

"I thought I'd go with you to look at the utes."

"I don't need to buy a pickup."

"But we are going to need another vehicle. Why not a truck?" Denyse picked up the ball Ripper had returned and held it as the dog stood ready. She pointed to the dog. "Otherwise we'll always be hauling a wet animal in our car." She smiled at Jeremy.

Jeremy laughed. "Dogs do love trucks." He paused. "Maybe we could buy an inexpensive truck."

"Spending money is hard for me," Denyse confided. "We never had any growing up. Then I scrimped to get through uni. Next you and I paid off debts plus saved for the baby. Afterwards we saved for a house. At first, we didn't know if the firm and your job would survive. Changing old habits is difficult. But I know you're very good with money and will help us make the best long-range decisions."

"What would *you* like to buy, Denyse?" Jeremy took the ball from her and threw it for Ripper.

"I'd like to start looking at houses again. And we should pick one big enough for Katelyn's little brother to have his own room."

Jeremy jerked his head around. "You mean you're . . ."

"No, no. I didn't mean that I'm pregnant. But hopefully someday soon . . ."

—◄•►—

Katie heard the garage door open followed by the sounds of Jeremy and Denyse coming up the stairs. They hardly noticed her as they amicably bantered about pickup trucks and houses. Ripper, tired from having rescued every tennis ball thrown, went to his bed.

"Your mother made a wonderful lasagna. Would you like some?" Denyse asked.

"I'm starved. I'd love some. Where's Katelyn?" Jeremy looked around.

His face showed disappointment when Katie answered, "She fell asleep on the couch. I put her to bed."

"We can spend all day tomorrow together," Denyse promised. "Let's you and I have a late supper now. Maybe we could set some goals for purchases and having fun as a family."

"I'd like that. Let me set the table for you and me." Jeremy went to get the plates. "Do you really think we need four-wheel drive?" he called from the kitchen.

"I'd rather have it and not need it, than need it and not have it," Denyse called back as she winked at Katie and returned her car keys.

"We have more than enough saved for a house down payment. We can save money in the long term by paying cash for the truck," Jeremy continued as Denyse dished out the lasagna.

Katie quietly let herself out.

———◆———

A week later, Dave caught up on some reading at home with a college football game playing on TV in the background. Katie sat nearby connecting with friends using her laptop. The ringing phone interrupted their peace. "Hello," answered Dave.

"Have you seen the news?" a gruff voice asked.

"No, Buddy. What's happening?" Dave motioned to Katie to listen in.

"The feds are acting on the information we gave them."

Katie rushed to change the channel on the TV. A twenty-four-hour news channel showed pictures of blocked-off entrances to the White America headquarters. Men and women wearing jackets boldly proclaiming *FBI* and *ATF* manned the barricades.

"Buddy, can you give me any insight into what's going on?"

"They've probably gotten search warrants for everything associated with White America and locked down the entire complex. They're likely also executing freeze orders to banks on all of the organization's assets."

"Why would they freeze assets?" Dave wanted to know.

"That's done to prevent the leaders from absconding with or hiding the money. If the search warrant reveals criminal activity, they'll use the rules of civil forfeiture to claim all the assets. They'll want it all protected in that eventuality. And they certainly don't want the suspects using the money to hire fancy-pants defense lawyers, either." Buddy chuckled at the last portion of his answer.

"Civil forfeiture would allow them to take all of White America's assets?"

"You betcha. If the feds had waited until a meeting was underway, they could have confiscated the vehicles of everybody attending. Civil forfeiture is a wonderful tool for law enforcement."

Dave whistled. "Or more likely they would have incited a gun battle. Generally, the white supremacists think of the federal government as their enemy."

"I'm sure Agent Whitten thought of that. There could be trouble anyway. I'm going to come over to Mobile. I'll sniff around and find out how the militia's rank and file are reacting. Can I drop Mary at your house?"

"Sure. You be careful, Buddy."

Chapter Thirty

After Buddy hung up, Dave and Katie continued to watch the TV.

The picture showed a clip of a furious Jeremiah Wallace standing in front of several microphones. "This is an outrage! A clear violation of our constitutional rights by the anti-white forces controlling our federal government," he shouted. "All God-fearing Americans should realize that this is the time to stand up for liberty. When I'm elected I'll introduce an investigation to bring the criminals responsible for this attack on law-abiding citizens to justice."

The TV anchor then transitioned, "Our reporter is currently at Mobile's city hall. Mayor Dan Hunt of Mobile is addressing the public's concerns."

Flanked by the police chief and city's DA, Mobile's mayor stood at the top of the steps in front of city hall. "We did not have any warning of this raid. I'm very troubled that federal agents failed to notify local authorities. They have no legal right to be in Mobile. I've called the governor and asked him to intervene with the president to order the overreaching federal agents to withdraw."

"Doesn't a warrant by a federal judge make their actions legal and give them the right?" a reporter asked.

"When did trampling on the rights of the law-abiding citizens of Mobile become a right?" the mayor retorted.

A reporter from the back shouted out, "Do you know what they're looking for, Mayor Hunt?"

The mayor looked disgusted. "No, and we resent the fact that federal agents did not consult with the duly elected officials in this community."

The TV picture quickly changed to show Agent Whitten standing in front of microphones at the headquarters of White America as agents behind him scurried to remove boxes of confiscated materials and computers. A reporter asked, "Can you tell us what you are searching for?"

"Not at this time. All I can say is that our warrants have been authorized by federal courts."

"Why didn't you involve local authorities?" another reporter demanded.

"No comment at this time."

"Have you found what you are looking for?"

"No comment at this time."

"Are you going to arrest the leader, Jeremiah Wallace?"

"We are searching for Mr. Wallace as a person of interest."

—◆—

After dropping Mary at Dave and Katie's house, Buddy drove to a nightclub he had heard frequently mentioned by members of White America. Inside, he ordered a beer and waited at the bar.

He didn't sit alone for long. A man sat down beside him and said, "Didn't I see you at the White America rally? Later you responded when we assembled to repel the African invasion of white neighborhoods."

Buddy turned his head to see the man called Lightning. "Maybe," he growled and took a swallow of his beer.

Lightning leaned toward Buddy and spoke with breath reeking of tobacco and alcohol. "Have you seen the news about the feds trying to shut us down?"

"Why do you think I'm sitting at this bar? But what can I do? No orders have come from Wallace."

"I haven't gotten any either. But it don't mean we can't do somethin' ourselves."

Buddy turned to look at the man sitting beside him. "What do you have in mind?"

The man leaned closer. "We need to maintain our action-ready organization. The stinking feds must have got Colonel Wallace's cell phone. Our roster of members and their contact information is on the computer they took. That's why our communications have been limited. We're trying to get as many phone numbers and addresses as we can since we can't put out a call on Colonel Wallace's phone."

Buddy wrote his cell number on a napkin and handed it to the man. "What's your name?"

"Just call me Captain Lightning. And stay vigilant." The man slapped Buddy lightly on the shoulder and moved away.

"Dave, an Agent Mark Whitten of the FBI is here to see you," Dorothy notified Dave over the intercom. "I have him waiting at the front. He says you know him."

Dave left his office and went to the reception area. Dorothy met his eyes and arched her eyebrows in a silent question. Dave ignored her and found Agent Whitten leafing through an old Sports Illustrated magazine. "Mr. Parker, could I have a few minutes of your time?" asked the FBI agent as he tossed the magazine onto the table.

"Of course. Let's go to my office. Would you like anything to drink? Coffee? Soft drink?"

"I already asked him," Dorothy volunteered from behind her desk. "He declined."

"Right this way then." Dave nodded to Dorothy and indicated the hallway which led to his office. Inside the office he uncharacteristically closed the door behind Agent Whitten.

The FBI agent began before they could sit down. "Mr. Parker, I presume you've seen the news reports."

"Yes, I have." Dave waved the agent toward a chair and took the seat behind his desk. "Were you able to take advantage of the materials Chief Oleson and I provided?"

"Yes, they were the primary basis for the federal warrants."

"Have the warrants been fruitful?"

"Yes, we've also gotten an arrest warrant for Jeremiah Wallace and some of his closest associates based on unlawful weapons discovered at the headquarters. But we think the most significant evidence will be found in the financial records. You have a good reputation within law enforcement circles. I've come today to contract your professional services."

—◄●►—

Buddy's cell phone rang. "Who is it?" he growled.

"This is Lightning. You know the feds have tried to decapitate us by taking out Colonel Wallace. Those of us officers remaining are reorganizing the militia. You got military experience, right?"

"Vietnam, Marines, '69 and '72."

"What rank?"

"Master Sergeant."

"We need you to step up and help us put back together our units with new leaders until we get Colonel Wallace and the others back. Some of the boys are pretty green."

"Alright. When do I meet them?"

"Tomorrow is Saturday. Most of the key ones I've managed to contact can come."

"Is there a safe place we can meet?"

"There's a farm. Highway 87 off of I-10. The exit is not far from the Florida state line. Go north about five miles. Then take 112 east. Look for the confederate flag. I live there protecting the cache."

"The cache?"

"That's the materials we've collected. We want you to train some of our boys how to fight."

"I can do that."

"You'll need a code name."

"Call me Thunder."

"Lightning and Thunder. I like that. You'll be my top sergeant."

━◦◉◦━

After Agent Whitten left Parker and Company's offices, Dave summoned Jeremy and Herschel to his office. He again closed the door behind him. "I've got a new client," he began. "I'll need the two of you to run the firm without me for a couple of months. You're both junior partners as of now. That means the firm's owner, me, gets two shares, the senior partner, me, gets two shares, and each of you get one share. One share is a sixth of all profits after the firm's other expenses are paid but in addition to your guaranteed salaries. The new clients and associates should make us rather profitable."

Jeremy and Herschel looked at each other in surprise. Dave didn't give them any time to celebrate. "Just don't forget that the quality of our work is the key to long-term success. How are the new associates working out, Jeremy?"

"Fine so far. Herschel is checking their work. No error gets by him."

Dave looked at Herschel. "What do you think of the associates' abilities?"

"A couple of them are more experienced than me about various aspects of auditing. Jeremy made great choices of who to hire. And he's good about getting everybody to pool their knowledge. All of us are learning from each other."

"Fine. You make sure their work is perfect, Herschel. Anything else?" asked Dave.

274

Jeremy spoke, "I'm starting to network a little in the community. Some of our new clients are inviting me to various social activities. Mostly I think they just want to meet Denyse. Those videos made her a bit of a celebrity."

Dave smiled. "I was never any good at networking. Tom and Randy did that for us at Bayside Accounting. But I know networking is important for our long-term success. Go for it as much as you're willing. Better you than me."

At that, Jeremy had to smile. "Who's the new client, Dad?" he asked.

"Some law enforcement agencies."

Jeremy leaned forward and spoke softly even though they talked in a closed office. "You're mixed up in this FBI investigation of White America, aren't you?"

When Dave appeared reluctant to answer Jeremy's question, Herschel spoke for him. "Yes, he is."

"How would you know?" Dave asked Herschel.

"The man I saw waiting in the reception area is the same one who represented the FBI on TV during the raid at White America's headquarters."

Jeremy's mouth gaped open. "Just when were you going to tell us, Dad?"

"You knew about the evidence we had provided to the FBI. Also remember that 911 call Herschel faked for us," Dave spoke before Herschel could.

"Well, listen then," said Jeremy. "The White America outfit isn't the only threat. Denyse told me that something is brewing in the African American community too."

"I'll try to ask a few questions and find out what," volunteered Herschel.

"Stop it, you two," demanded Dave. "I need you to stay out of this mess and run Parker and Company."

"Okay, Dad. Calm down. We'll let you do the sleuthing while we conduct the bookkeeping and the audits."

"Sure, Dave. We wouldn't think about butting our heads into something that's none of our business," Herschel added.

Dave knew a fib from his son when he heard it. Herschel wasn't any better at fibbing than Jeremy.

AR-15

Chapter Thirty-One

Finding the farm on Highway 112 wasn't difficult for Buddy. An eight-foot stake dangled a rebel flag by an open gate. He followed a long driveway past palmetto plants and longleaf pine trees. Pickup trucks had been parked haphazardly near a mobile home mounted on cinder blocks. A padlocked steel shipping container rested nearby. A few large dogs of various mixed breeds lay watching or walking around the premises. He saw about twenty young men drinking beer under a shade tree. Several of them smoked or chewed tobacco.

The man Buddy knew as Lightning left a group of them and approached his car. "Have any trouble finding us?" Lightning asked.

"No problem at all," growled Buddy. "Where are the others?"

"We can't contact all of the members yet. These are to be the leaders in our reorganized battalion. Since we've suffered some casualties, a lot of them are new to leadership."

"Casualties?"

"Arrested or in hiding," Lightning explained. He led Buddy to the group, then spoke to all, "I'm Captain Stewart. Codename Lightning. Thunder here will be my top sergeant and second in command during your training. He fought in Vietnam as a marine. The rest of you have been selected as unit leaders under my command."

Buddy looked at the young faces. None of them appeared to be older than thirty. They seemed eager. "Permission to speak to the men, Captain?"

"Yes, Master Sergeant."

"Any of you have military experience?" When none of them responded, he continued, "Any ROTC?" Two of the younger men raised their hands. "How about police experience?"

One stepped forward. "Me. Four years as patrolman in the Mobile police department."

Buddy stared at him. "And your name is?"

"Johnny Simpson."

"Colonel Wallace called Simpson one of our best intelligence assets," Lightning told everyone. "We have him to thank for the warnings of African activity."

"You got anybody inside higher up?" Buddy asked.

"Maybe. Maybe at the highest level," Lightning bragged.

Buddy nodded gravely at Simpson. "Good work, soldier." He stared at the men a moment. He pointed at one who had raised his hand. "You, how many years ROTC?"

"Just one so far."

"Just one so far, Sergeant."

"Yes, sir."

"Just sergeant. Only say sir to the captain. Okay then, show these others how to stand at attention."

The ROTC cadet did so. "The rest of you, an officer is present. Attention!" Buddy demanded. He snapped to attention himself.

After the men had more or less stood erect, Buddy commanded, "At ease." The men mimicked the two ROTC cadets with their feet spread and hands behind their backs.

"Captain, with what weapons do you want me to train the men?"

Lightning, obviously delighted at the way Buddy had initiated discipline and respect for himself said, "I'm not supposed to show you this. But these are new circumstances. Wait just a minute." He ran for the mobile home.

A couple of minutes later he returned and approached the padlocked container. He unlocked and removed the padlock then pulled up the garage-like tracked door. Buddy had remained in the at-ease position. "Come over here," Lightning invited.

Buddy moved to the opening. The others broke rank and followed him. Lightning stood proudly and pointed inside. "Look at this."

Buddy stood at the entrance beside Lightning. The others crowded behind them. Inside they saw M-16s, cases of ammo, hand grenades, rocket-propelled grenades, several shoulder-fired missile launchers, night-vision goggles, a couple of machine guns, a stack of demolition charges, and other military gear. The container had been filled to the back.

"The Africans won't be able to stand up to us with this stuff," Lightning boasted.

"I should think not . . . Captain."

"And we're supplying likeminded groups all over the country."

Buddy answered slowly, "That's good to know . . . sir."

—◆—

"What have you found from the records?" Agent Whitten asked Dave over the phone.

"Well, I'll need several weeks to complete my review. But these records aren't hard to decipher. I'm finding well-documented revenue through 'security services,' likely a euphemism for protection rackets. The sources of payments correlate with some names of those we had recorded. There are also donations to a 501 tax-deductible organization, dues from members, and cash from unknown sources. I'm seeing regular business disbursements, and some lucrative salaries to Mr. Wallace and his inner circle. And maybe I've found something even more troubling."

"And what could be more troubling?"

"The records show purchases and sales of what they designate 'equipment.' If I didn't know better, I'd say the model numbers represent some pretty dangerous weapons."

"Weapons?" asked Agent Whitten. "We did find some AR-15 rifles converted to fully automatic during the raid."

"I'm no military man. But these could be more serious than that."

"Any reference to where the weapons physically are?"

"I haven't found any yet. But I did find what appears to be financial transfers to an offshore bank account in Colombia. I found the account number and a password. Because Colombia is a signatory of the UNCAC treaty, that money could be frozen and recovered."

Agent Whitten's voice revealed his anticipation. "How much money are we talking about?"

"About nine million dollars."

"Good work. That could help us get some local authorities on our side. What about the records of Jeremiah Wallace's political group?"

"I haven't gotten to them yet. I'm sure they're linked, though. We'll probably find illegal use of campaign contributions or failure to report them. Have you made many arrests yet?"

"We got the ones at the headquarters when we raided. Most of the other suspects are on the run."

"Too bad."

"We'll find them if we can get some local help. In the meantime, Mr. Parker, I need you to briefly summarize what you have regarding the assets of White America. Then I'd like to bring in some local officials to your offices after hours for a meeting. You'll tell them only what you've found in the seized records. Share nothing from what you revealed to me in Montgomery."

"Why my offices?"

"We don't want any scrutiny at this point. And Police Chief Oleson will attend, too."

"Have you heard any more from your students about something brewing?" Jeremy asked Denyse.

"Nothing specific. But they're scared of something." Denyse finished putting away the dishes Katie had washed before she left.

"What do you think is going to happen?"

"I don't know. Maybe we could ask Caleb if he knows anything."

❧

"Hi, Anthony," Herschel greeted the teenager after church. "When are you coming back to work at Parker and Company?"

Anthony broke into a big grin. "Ms. Parker says that I'll have a better chance of getting a university scholarship if I concentrate on my schoolwork right now."

"She's probably right. I noticed your name in the paper on the honor roll last week. I know your mother is proud of you. What do you want to study at the university?"

The teenager acted bashful at Herschel's praise. "I want to be an accountant, like you."

"You could make a good one. When you need someone to recommend you to the university or scholarships, you can use me." Herschel put his arm around Anthony's shoulders.

"Thanks, Herschel."

Then Herschel's voice took on a confidential tone. "Anthony, are you as concerned as I am about what's coming down?"

The boy looked uncertain. He wouldn't have expected an important man like Herschel to be involved in their clandestine preparations. "Yes, I'm pretty scared."

"What are you scared of, Anthony?"

"I'm not scared of dying, you know."

"Me either," Herschel confided.

"I'm more scared that I won't be brave. Or that I'll get shot in a place that cripples me. What would my mother do then?"

"Have you got a gun, Anthony?"

"Yes," the younger man admitted.

"Where did you get it?"

"One of the leaders made me buy it. It's only an old revolver. I haven't gotten an automatic rifle or pistol like most of the others."

Herschel continued his confidential tone, "My leaders have been a bit vague. What did your leaders tell you?"

"Just to be ready for when White America comes. Report to Central High when the word goes out."

"Anthony, will you call me at home when you hear about something starting?"

"If you want me to."

◄─◆─►

Jeremy met Denyse at Central High after her last class of the day. Together they found Principal Fogle encouraging the students in detention to act more responsibly. They waited outside the detention hall for him to finish. Surprise showed in Caleb's face when he found them in the hallway.

"Could we talk with you a minute, Caleb?" asked Jeremy.

He walked slowly down the hall. "Of course. What's on your mind?"

Jeremy motioned to Denyse, who spoke for both. "I've been hearing whispers among my students about something bad about to happen. Are you aware of this? Can you tell us anything?"

Principal Fogle stopped walking without a response. After a moment of contemplation, he said, "Let's step outside where we're unlikely to be heard."

He led the way to the school's courtyard. There he turned with his back to the building and faced Jeremy and Denyse.

"I'm afraid that in any community, black or white, there are some who look for trouble. We saw both sides in action during the riot last year. Right now, a few are reminding the African American community about the confrontation in Pensacola after the hurricane. Some of our local men have formed a sort of militia to get ready. And they've heavily armed themselves. As if those neighborhoods didn't already have enough guns," Caleb finished with some bitterness.

"What is the militia planning to do?" asked Jeremy.

"I'm not certain. But I think they're planning to resist any incursion of the white supremacists into what they consider their territory."

Denyse looked at her principal in amazement. "How do you know about this?"

"I think of every kid in my school like my own son or daughter. As the only father figure many of them have, I feel responsible to be aware of what's happening in the community. Wouldn't you try to find out about anything bad Katelyn might get involved in?"

Jeremy and Denyse looked at each other. Together they nodded to Caleb.

"Is there anything we can do?" asked Jeremy.

"Just let me know if you hear about anything starting. I'll protect as many Central High kids as I can."

"Should we alert the city authorities?" asked Denyse.

"I've already told the mayor and police chief."

Chapter Thirty-Two

Dave and Katie returned to Parker and Company's offices after all the others had left. Agent Whitten and an agent from the ATF agency arrived at sunset. Buddy came in just after them. Katie served coffee to the men while trying to calm her own nerves.

Three other cars individually brought Mobile's mayor, police chief, and the city's district attorney. Dave met them personally at the door and ushered each to the firm's conference room. The first to arrive waited in tense silence until the last had taken a seat. Agent Whitten and the ATF representative sat on one side of the long conference table, Mobile's officials on the other. The Parkers and Buddy sat at the table's opposite ends.

Agent Whitten started, "Gentlemen, I appreciate your response to this unusual invitation. As we speak, FBI and ATF agents are executing a federal court-approved search warrant at a location on Highway 112 in Baldwin County. We have reason to believe that we'll find military-grade weapons. We also have reason to believe that the police department has been compromised by a collaborator."

The trio of officials reacted with surprise. "A collaborator on my force! That's quite an accusation!" the police chief blurted out. "Who is this so-called collaborator?" he demanded.

By way of an answer, the federal agent continued, "I'd like to introduce you to former police chief Robert Oleson from Minnesota. Chief, please tell them what you've seen."

Buddy described his infiltration of White America and the weapons cache. He concluded with, "The police collaborator is Patrolman Johnny Simpson."

Agent Whitten added, "Patrolman Simpson has been arrested by federal agents and has already agreed to cooperate with the investigation in return for leniency. We plan to interrogate him at a secure location tomorrow."

"I can't believe it. I want to talk to my patrolman," the police chief demanded.

"Why are they here?" The DA pointed at Dave and Katie.

Agent Whitten explained, "Parker and Company has been retained by the FBI to examine the records seized in our raid last week on White America's headquarters complex. Mr. Parker, could you give us an initial summary of White America's business dealing and assets?"

Dave gave the briefest of summaries and ended with, "Plus

the physical assets, we've discovered about nine million dollars in an offshore account."

Katie noticed that both the police chief and DA brightened at that report. The mayor looked troubled.

"Thank you, Mr. Parker," said Agent Whitten. Then he spoke to the trio of public officials, "And so, by civil forfeiture, we'll have a nice pot to share with you. We'd now like to initiate cooperation between federal and local authorities. We need your help apprehending the fugitives. Here's a partial list of suspects we are seeking." The FBI agent handed a typewritten list of names to the police chief.

After some questions, which Agent Whitten answered politely yet vaguely, the three local authorities departed, leaving the federal agents with Buddy and the Parkers.

"Are you ready to leave, Chief Oleson?" Agent Whitten then asked.

"I'm ready."

"Your wife . . ." Agent Whitten looked at his notes, ". . . Mary, and two cats are being guarded at a hotel near the airport."

Katie burst in, "Where are you going, Buddy?"

Agent Whitten answered for Buddy, "He doesn't know himself right now. We're putting the Olesons into federal witness protection."

"Why do they need protection?"

"The Olesons infiltrated a criminal organization and are now betraying them. Their testimony will be part of any subsequent trials. We also suspect that one of the three men who just left is also a conspirator."

Dave and Katie looked at each other. "Then you let the criminal get away," Katie protested.

"No, we didn't. While we were meeting, federal agents placed court-approved listening devices and GPS trackers in their cars. If one of them bolts due to your disclosure, we'll know and arrest him."

Dave and Katie sat stunned. "You knew about this, Buddy?" Katie managed.

Buddy nodded. "Yes. This was the best way to expose the criminal. Not likely that it's the police chief considering that he's African American himself."

"But what about Simpson's testimony?" Katie persisted.

"We haven't even found Simpson yet, much less arrested him. We lied to smoke out the highest-level collaborator before we started cooperating with the honest locals. We need their help finding the suspects," Agent Whitten explained.

"The alleged conspirator, whoever he might be, saw us too," said Dave. "What about witness protection for Katie and me? Maybe some of the White America criminals will figure out that we were the ones who put you onto them."

"You can have witness protection, if you wish, Mr. Parker. But as far as White America knows, you're just the accountant we hired. Because our searches are uncovering plenty of evidence, we won't need the probable-cause evidence you had provided earlier for a trial. The FBI protects its informants. You're called 'un-named informant' in the records. Chief Oleson told us that you have a life and family here in Mobile and will probably want to stay. But we'll relocate and hide you too, if you want."

Dave and Katie looked at each other again. Katie saw Dave's shoulders slump. "We'll stay here," Katie answered for them.

Jeremiah Wallace had holed up, hiding at a riverside cabin north of Mobile. He had kept his personal phone idle to avoid disclosing his location while considering options and following events on TV. A burner phone purchased for emergencies buzzed with a message marked urgent. The message urged him to call Dan. He activated the cell phone he hadn't used since the FBI's raid and punched Dan's number. "What is it?"

"The feds are finding everything in the records. Simpson is giving us up as part of a plea bargain. The Africans are organizing to fight. Meet me at the rendezvous point. I'll take you south of the border along with me. We split the money sixty to you, forty to me like agreed?"

"Right. I'll be there in forty-five. Meanwhile I'll distract the police."

Mobile's mayor hung up without comment. Jeremiah thumbed into his phone, *All units. Full response. Africans mobilizing to attack. Assemble in James Seals Park on Texas Street just off of I-10 in downtown Mobile. Come fully armed with personal weapons and ammo. This is what we have been waiting for. Liberty forever.*

＝•◈•＝

"That was the mayor on the listening device we planted in his car," an FBI technician reported to his superiors.

"Voice recognition indicates the other end to be Jeremiah Wallace," another technician added.

"Too bad we don't know where the rendezvous point is," commented Agent Whitten.

"The GPS tracking device shows the mayor headed in

the direction of a private airport. Doesn't the mayor own an airplane?"

"Scramble the helicopter," ordered Whitten. "If necessary, shoot out the airplane's tires from the air."

"Wallace also said something about distracting the police. Tell our people to be on the alert. And where is Mobile's police chief?"

"The GPS tracker says Harmon Floyd is at police headquarters."

"Get him on the phone."

———◆———

The phone in Denyse and Jeremy's apartment rang. "Jeremy, I just got a call from Anthony." Urgency filled Herschel's voice. "He says that white supremacists are showing up heavily armed in James Seals Park. The police have disappeared. Runners and phone calls are calling on all able-bodied African American men to assemble with their weapons at Central High School."

The circumstances felt surreal to Jeremy. *Is this really happening?* He yelled to get Denyse's attention. Then he dialed Caleb's home number.

———◆———

Caleb hung up the phone after talking with Jeremy. "I've got to go downtown," he told Jordan. "I'll be back in a while."

"Is it another demonstration?"

"Maybe something worse."

"Then I'm going with you."

"Jordan, you can't—"

"Says you," she interrupted him. "I'll be in the car."

―•―

After Jeremy had talked to Caleb, Denyse took the phone to call her in-laws. "Katie, can you come take care of Katelyn, right now?"

"What's the emergency, Denyse?"

"There's a potential race war about to start in Mobile. I need to go talk to some of my students. Jeremy has our car keys in his clenched fist. He says he won't let me go alone."

Good for Jeremy, thought Katie. "Why do you need to go now?" she asked Denyse.

"Caleb is going to try to keep Central High students out of trouble. My kids will listen to me."

Katie put her hand over the phone and yelled, "Dave, get on the extension." She removed her hand and spoke into the phone again. "Settle down, Denyse. Caleb can handle this," she urged.

"I can help him. I'm losing time. Won't you come over?"

"Then why don't you take Katelyn downtown with you?"

Denyse's voice revealed shock. "That's too dangerous for a child."

"Then it's too dangerous for a child's mother." Katie gave Denyse several moments to consider that idea. "I respect your courage and commitment to your students, Denyse. But no, I won't enable you to put yourself at physical risk." Katie continued firmly, "Denyse, being a good mother means that you don't have that freedom. You'll need to decide what type of mother you are right now. Who is most important to you? Jeremy and Katelyn or your students? You can't have it both ways."

Chapter Thirty-Three

---•◦•---

Dave had picked up the bedroom phone. "Denyse, please put Jeremy on the phone." Katie's firm words had stunned Denyse so badly that she couldn't speak. Mutely she handed the phone to Jeremy.

She heard her husband say, "Hi, Dad," and then describe what Herschel and Caleb had told them. To herself Denyse thought, *I can get someone else to care for Katelyn. That couple who lives in the next building. They have a young son. I could call Dorothy or Candace.*

She sensed Jeremy speaking to her. "I'll go to Central High for you," he repeated.

Denyse stared blankly at her husband. Katie's words rang in her head. She walked across the room to pick up and hold

Katelyn. *Leaving Katelyn with a grandmother who loves her more than life while I teach is one thing. But do I have the right to risk depriving Katelyn of her mother? No, I don't,* she concluded.

Her eyes focused on Jeremy. "I'll go help Caleb," he offered again.

Still putting her thoughts together, Denyse thought out loud, "No, if Katelyn needs a mother, she needs a father too. We don't have the luxury of risking our daughter's parents."

"That sounds like something Dad would say," returned Jeremy.

"Sometimes making the safe choice is more difficult than being heroic."

—◦—

"I heard what you said to Denyse," Dave said to Katie.

Katie lifted her head from where it had drooped in despair. She turned her face to look directly at Dave. "I hope Denyse won't hate me. I've never spoken to her that way before. Never refused to care for Katelyn before."

"Doing the right thing is hard, isn't it? But you're correct. Neither Denyse nor Jeremy should get involved in this tonight," Dave consoled her.

Katie surprised Dave by saying, "We could go, though."

Dave looked at his wife in disbelief. "What? Us go?"

"Why not? I could die of cancer next year. And without me you'd be as good as dead." She smiled at him.

"You're right about me being no good without you." Dave smiled back and gave Katie a quick hug. "And we sort of started this mess anyway."

"Me and you together, dinosaur? More than ordinary again?"

"Yep. You and I together, more than ordinary again. That is, unless Old Yeller wants to join us."

"I seriously doubt he's interested." Old Yeller confirmed their suspicion by remaining asleep on the couch.

"But you know what, sweetheart? I'll bet you and I could be more effective at James Seals Park rather than Central High," Dave suggested.

"You're not going to try your dumb-guy routine again like you did in Minnesota, are you?"

"No. This time I really am dumb."

—◄◆►—

Dozens of heads turned to watch Caleb and Jordan drive up and park in front of Central High School. The Fogles saw perhaps a hundred and fifty mostly young men standing in groups around a few who spoke passionately. Every one of the men appeared to be carrying firearms including an alarming number of assault rifles.

"Principal Fogle?" one voice exclaimed. "I never expected to see you here." Several of the men clustered around the Fogles. "Are you with us, Mr. Fogle?"

"Yes, I am with you. But not in violence. This is my school. Most of you attended school here or still attend here. You're all my kids," Caleb shouted. Jordan stood next to him and held onto his arm.

Nearly all the men left their places and circled the Fogles then, standing a respectful few feet away. Tyrone, who had sold Anthony the pistol, shouted, "We got to fight for our people."

"Violence isn't the way to fight," Caleb shouted back for all to hear. "You can do better for our people by making something good of your lives."

"How we gonna do that?" Tyrone persisted. "Bein' the white man's donkey? Doin' the minimum wage jobs? Letting the racists intimidate us?"

One man pushed through the group to stand beside Caleb and Jordan. "I'm trying to fight by doing something good for my wife and kids," Herschel shouted.

"You're like a coconut. Brown on the outside and white on the inside," Tyrone sneered and brandished his AR-15 rifle. "The white racists are assembling at James Seals Park. The best defense is an offense. We can go get them before they attack our neighborhoods. Teach them a lesson that all racists will remember."

"What are you saying?" Herschel retorted. "That black men can't succeed in the business world? That being a thug is the answer? The racists win if they provoke us into a reaction."

Tyrone spoke with disgust, "You're the white man's donkey, then."

A teenager stepped from the listening crowd. Herschel realized it was Anthony, who then turned to face Tyrone. "No, he's not a donkey or a coconut. He's a good man. He's doing right for our people."

Another voice shouted, "Herschel thinks and acts like a white man."

Anthony shouted back, "All the whites aren't bad. Some of them are helping me to make something of myself. I'm not going to waste that opportunity." He then threw the pistol he had purchased at Tyrone's feet. "Let the police deal with the white racists."

Tyrone hadn't given up. "Where are the police who are supposed to protect us?"

"They're coming," Caleb promised. "And when they come,

every man with a gun will be a threat." He raised his voice so that all could hear. "I want each one of you to go home, lock your doors, turn out your lights, and stay put, even if the white racists start roaming your streets."

—◆—

Unlike Caleb and Jordan's arrival at Central High, Dave and Katie's entrance to James Seals Park drew no attention. Dave parked their car among dozens of cars, jeeps, and pickup trucks. He and Katie walked to where more than a hundred heavily armed white men gathered around an impassioned speaker. Most of the men wore some sort of camouflage clothes. A few had black grease paint under their eyes like football players.

"In Colonel Wallace's absence, I'm in charge," Lightning instructed. "We'll form up in our units and march through town to show the Africans our resolve. They won't dare try anything when they see we mean business. If they do attack us, we'll unleash hell and start the war right here."

"What the African Americans will see is an invading army," Dave shouted for all to hear. "What would you do if a group of armed men paraded through your neighborhood?"

"We've got to maintain law and order," Lightning yelled.

"You're about to provoke disorder. And a lot of you will die for no purpose," Katie answered.

"Listen to me!" shouted Dave as loud as he could. "My great-great-great-grandfather Ezekiel fought for the South in the battle of Mobile Bay." He pointed toward the bay. "My ancestors were dirt-poor fishermen. They never owned any slaves. But when Ezekiel saw armies invading his home, that made him fight."

299

A murmur of approval came from some of those gathered around him and Katie. "If you leave this park looking for an armed confrontation, you will be seen as the invading army, just like our forefathers saw the Yankees. They'll fight you by firing in ambush from cover. Many of you will be killed."

"But Colonel Wallace—"

"Where is he now? He's sent you to die while he gets away with millions of dollars embezzled from the White America organization. He's been manipulating you."

"Don't you disrespect Colonel Wallace!" Lightning bellowed. He pushed his way through the militiamen. "Colonel Wallace is a patriot, you African lover." Lightning stepped to within a few inches of Dave, an AR-15 held diagonally across his chest.

Dave did not flinch or retreat. He spoke directly to Lightning in a clear voice that all present could hear. "African Americans are US citizens, just like you and me." He changed his gaze to look into the eyes of the militiamen listening. "African Americans hope for the same things as you do: to have a good job, live in freedom without fear, and build a decent future for their children. The important things in life we all have in common."

"In common with you maybe. You're a traitor to your race," responded Lightning. He thrust the AR-15 suddenly forward, knocking Dave to the ground, and raised the rifle muzzle upward, preparing to smash Dave with the butt. He stopped when Katie stepped in front of him.

Lightning held back from striking and turned away from Katie. "Colonel Wallace left me in command! Form up in your units to march!" he shouted to the men. To Dave and Katie he

growled, "Interfere with us patriots and I'll shoot you myself."
All present saw Lightning click his rifle safety off.

━◆━

A Piper Cub taxied from one of the small airport's hangers.
"Please state your flight destination," the tower controller
requested.

"Uh, we're going to Albuquerque," the pilot responded.

The plane approached the runway facing into a moderate
breeze. A helicopter appeared out of the darkness. From it, a
spotlight illuminated the small plane. Above the chop of the
helicopter's blades, a thunderous loudspeaker announced,
"This is the FBI. Shut down your engine."

"Damn," said Mayor Hunt. "Maybe airborne we can
outrun them or lose them in a dark cloud." He revved the
single propeller in preparation for takeoff. The plane started
accelerating down the runway. Suddenly it veered to the left.

"What's the matter with you? Take off!" demanded
Jeremiah.

"We have a flat tire. They must have fired on us. We couldn't
hear the shot over the helicopter and our own prop. I won't be
able to hold our plane straight on the runway if we try to take
off."

"Shut down your engine," the loudspeaker ordered.
"Throw any weapons you have from the plane to the ground.
Then leave the plane and lie on the ground face down. Extend
your arms past your heads."

Through the plane's windshield Dan and Jeremiah saw
the helicopter land on the tarmac. Three figures carrying
automatic rifles jumped out and moved into the cover of
darkness in preparation to approach the airplane.

"You're under arrest. Don't make us open fire on you," the loudspeaker warned them. "Throw your weapons out and lie face down on the ground."

◄►

Caleb could sense uncertainty growing in some of the men facing them. Jordan surprised all by speaking up. "Each of you have mothers who love you. Some of you have wives, girlfriends, and children. Go home to them."

"Are we just supposed to sit like cowards in our homes while the racists parade through our neighborhoods?" Tyrone responded.

"You can sit and live or fight and die. Which do you think your mothers, wives, and children would choose for you?" Jordan answered back.

Caleb shouted, "Your dying might sound noble, but it won't help our cause of freedom and equality. A battle between whites and blacks here will cause people all over the country to choose sides. Many will choose the racists. Dr. King won the freedom we have by refusing to meet violence with violence. Many African Americans who used guns in Pensacola are crippled for life. Others have been arrested and face prison. How has that made anything better for our people?"

Jordan could feel the numbers facing them shrinking. Men slipped into darkness without speaking. Finally, only a handful remained.

"I know you want to do the right thing for our people," Caleb pleaded with them. "Avoiding violence takes more courage than resorting to it. Give the authorities a chance to stop a racial war in Mobile." More men followed the others into the darkness.

Finally, only one armed man remained opposing Caleb. The principal spoke personally to him, "I remember you, Tyrone. You scored a winning touchdown for us in the state playoffs. You were a great team captain. Make a good choice right now."

Tyrone tried to speak and couldn't. He disappeared into the darkness himself.

Herschel slumped in relief. He felt his thumping heart slowing to normal. "Thank God. We've avoided a gun battle."

"Maybe for now," Caleb answered. "They're listening to us by not attacking the white militia in James Seals Park. But if the racists enter their neighborhoods and taunt or provoke them, a few hotheads will use their guns. Once a battle starts, many others will come to the hotheads' aid. We won't have accomplished anything."

Chapter Thirty-Four

———•◦•———

As Dave scrambled to his feet, Katie pointed at Lightning and shouted, "Don't listen to this man. He'll get you killed or imprisoned. He's just a criminal henchman."

Lightning raised his right arm to strike Katie. Dave used the moment to reach out and snatch the AR-15 from Lightning's left hand. Lightning froze in surprise. Dave stepped back, removed the magazine from Lightning's gun, and threw it into the darkness, leaving the rifle unloaded. In a fury, Lightning reached for a gun held by one of the militiamen. That man stepped back, thereby depriving Lightning of a weapon to use on Dave and Katie. Lightning stood enraged.

"I know who you are," one man shouted at Dave. "You're that accountant. I saw you on TV punching a kidnapper to save a girl." Several other voices murmured recognition.

"Right now, I'm trying to save *your* lives. The lives of your children's fathers. Don't leave your kids fatherless." Dave let those words hang in the air. When he sensed their positive effect on most of the men facing him, he smiled disarmingly and added, "So please don't let this man have a gun to kill me." Dave indicated Lightning, who looked appealingly at the militiamen for a weapon. Despite the dire circumstances, a few of the watching men laughed at Dave's semi-mock appeal.

"The Africans want to take away our southern heritage," another man shouted.

Dave responded, "Debate them with an accurate understanding of history. And acknowledge that the slavery of Africans that enriched an elite class was wrong." Katie could sense the intensity of emotions easing among those she and Dave faced. Yet most could not concede without some argument.

Questions from the group of militiamen settled into irritated voices rather than angry shouts. Dave and Katie answered respectfully and truthfully. Dave shared details of what he had discovered in White America's financial records. The debate stretched into an hour, then longer. *At least we're stalling them*, Katie thought.

"Just give us a few days, please," Dave pleaded. "Evidence will prove that what we're telling you about the finances of White America is true. In the meantime, please go home to your families. Don't take a chance on a confrontation that will take a lot of your lives. Even the lives of those who survive would be changed forever. An armed fight will completely discredit you."

Anthony picked up the pistol he had thrown down. He handed it butt first to his principal. "Would you get rid of this for me, Mr. Fogle?"

"Sure, son. Good choice." Caleb took the weapon, unloaded it, and handed it to Jordan. "Honey, would you hold onto this until we can give it to the police?"

Herschel spoke to Anthony, "Walk with me to my house. Your mother is probably worried about you. We can phone to tell her you're okay. I'll bet you're also hungry. I'm sure my wife, Candace, will be happy to fix us both a late supper." Herschel turned his attention to the Fogles. "Caleb, how about you and Jordan coming too?"

"Thanks, but we'll stay here until the police arrive."

The White America militiamen started showing anxiety. Weapons previously held at ready sagged in their hands. Many glanced fearfully at the darkness surrounding them. A blue flashing light drew everyone's attention. A police squad car with a white flag extended from the driver's window drove slowly into the park. The car stopped by the edge of the crowd. The driver's side door cracked open. Two dark-skinned hands extended upwards raising the white cloth. Slowly, Mobile's police chief emerged waving the flag above his head. "I'm unarmed. I'm alone. I'm Mobile's police chief, Harmon Floyd," he shouted. "Many of you can remember me playing football at the University of Alabama." Then he said, "I'm reaching for the squad car microphone. I'll broadcast through the car's loudspeaker so that everyone can hear me."

Without any quick motions, the police chief raised the microphone. "Listen, men. I've held back our police officers to avoid sparking a gun battle. But the governor has called out the Alabama National Guard. He's declared a dusk-to-dawn curfew. The guard will start deploying in less than an hour to enforce the curfew. In case you don't know, the guard is based on Broad Street less than a half mile from here. Two hours from now this entire area will be swarming with soldiers and federal agents. Anybody carrying a firearm will be considered an imminent threat. The guardsmen will be scared after the Pensacola incidents and are likely to shoot to kill."

The police chief paused to let his first words sink in, then continued, "The federal government is indicting various leaders of the organization known as White America according to the US Congress' RICO Act against racketeering." A chorus of a few boos answered him.

"All the evidence will come out in court during fair trials. You can decide then for yourselves if those men are guilty or not. In the meantime, I need you to disperse and go home." Boos, fewer this time, expressed the group's displeasure.

"Now let me warn you about something else. When the national guard comes, they will cordon off downtown Mobile. Anybody found inside without lawful purpose will be subject to probable cause associated with the racketeering. Under the legal principles of civil forfeiture, the federal agents can and will confiscate everything you have with you except your clothes. If you want to save your guns and your vehicles, you need to leave right now."

Silence reigned after the chief's warning. "You're wasting time," he added.

Everybody heard a pickup truck starting. Heads turned to see it bounce over a curb and roar away. Two more trucks started. Suddenly everyone ran for their vehicles. Lightning reached out to grab his unloaded AR-15 from Dave then ran with the others.

"Come on, Katie." Dave pulled her arm in the direction of their car.

"Why should we run?" she asked. "We're here trying to defuse the situation."

"You want to try explaining that to national guardsmen and federal agents eager to take our car?"

Katie hurried after Dave as they joined the stampede. "I never expected this."

Dave laughed. "Me either. But compared to being beat up or shot, this feels great."

Katie felt the absurdity of the situation. Relief from the abrupt end of a dangerous confrontation overwhelmed her. She laughed hysterically as they ran for the truck. "I only wish Jeremy and Denyse could see us now."

In just eight minutes, the police chief stood alone in James Seals Park. He spoke over the police radio, "All units start moving in. Secure the area. Expect and assist the arrival of national guardsmen and federal agents. Announce a dusk-to-dawn curfew all over town using your car speakers."

As they made their escape, Dave and Katie saw dozens of lights-flashing patrol cars carefully entering downtown Mobile. "I wonder how the governor knew so quickly?" Katie choked out amidst their giddy laughter.

"I'll bet Old Yeller called him."

The ringing phone woke Dave and Katie early the next morning. Being Sunday, they had hoped to sleep in after the previous night's drama. "Are you watching the news?" Jeremy blurted.

Dave blinked away sleep. He and Katie hadn't gotten to bed until after four a.m. "No, what's going on?"

"There was nearly a racial war in downtown Mobile. The governor called out the national guard. They're on every street corner ensuring the peace. White America tried to create a confrontation. Dingo stopped it!"

"Dingo prevented a gun battle in downtown Mobile?" Dave repeated for Katie, who stood bleary eyed in her nightie. He saw her shrug and smile at him.

"Well, Dingo called the governor."

"How did Dingo know to call the governor?" Dave gestured for Katie to pick up the phone in the bedroom.

"Denyse tried to call the governor herself. The state's operators said he wasn't available. So she tried calling Dingo. Because the governor had read Dingo's book, he took Dingo's call." Jeremy's excitement could not be concealed.

"Did the news report any others who may have been involved?" asked Dave.

"Yeah. Mobile's police chief apparently went downtown alone and unarmed to face the White America militia. They dispersed when he told them the national guard would be arriving. The national news is calling Harmon Floyd a hero."

"Anybody else mentioned?"

"Local reporters say Caleb and Jordan Fogle reassured the African American community. They prevented a group of armed men from attacking the White America militia at James Seals Park."

Dave looked out the window to see three local news vans parked in front of the Fogles' house. Reporters and cameramen stood knocking on the front door.

"Then the news media isn't crediting Denyse and Dingo?" Disappointment sounded in Jeremy's voice. "No. The governor didn't mention them during the press conference."

"Well, politicians are like that," Dave consoled him. "But Denyse must feel good having played a role in diverting a possible tragedy for her students."

"She really does." Jeremy absorbed a little of the credit for himself. "And I feel good just for having brought her to Mobile. Denyse wants to speak to Mom now."

"Sure. Put Denyse on."

"Katie," Denyse began, "Are you and I alright? I was pretty upset when we talked last night. I'm not sure I spoke very reasonably."

"You just felt the urgency to do something, Denyse. I understand your commitment to your students. And it sounds like you were able to do the most important thing from home. God may have used you and Dingo to save a lot of lives."

"But Katie, what you said is right too. I have a responsibility to Katelyn and to Jeremy. They need to be my priority from now on."

"You're a good wife and mother, Denyse. You did well to think about what you were going to do before you did it. Emotions can lead us to do all sorts of things that bring harm to ourselves or those we love. Clear thinking, especially in a crisis, will always yield the best answer. You have my respect. Dave's too."

"Thanks, Katie. What did you and Dave do last night?"

"Oh . . . we went out and had some laughs together."

Denyse changed the subject. "The other thing I wanted to say is that Jeremy and I have found a beautiful house in a quiet, established neighborhood. We'd love to get your and Dave's opinion about it before we put down an offer. The house has a shady fenced-in backyard for Ripper, four bedrooms, live oak trees—one with a swing— and is walking distance from a park on the bay. It's on the eastern shore, only a few miles from you and Dave. I never in my life even hoped for such a nice place to live. And it doesn't cost the maximum we could borrow."

"We would love to look at it. How about late this afternoon?"

"That would be lovely."

"Back to bed?" Dave asked after Katie had said goodbye to Denyse.

"Absolutely."

—◦—

Before leaving to meet Denyse and Jeremy and tour their prospective home, Dave noticed Caleb outside his house. He drifted across the street. "Hey, I hear you're a hero."

Caleb rolled his eyes. "I just did what I always do, try to keep my kids out of trouble."

"They're lucky to have you as their principal and guide."

"Thanks. But I wasn't alone down there. Your associate, Herschel, showed up and stood right beside me. I told the news reporters that. And that boy, Anthony, spoke up too. I think Herschel is his role model."

"Anthony couldn't find a better one. And Herschel is a junior partner at Parker and Company now."

"That's great. I'd like to see Central High produce hundreds of Herschels."

Chapter Thirty-Five

---•---

Two months later, Dave sat at the computer in his office at Parker and Company. Out the window he could see city employees putting up public Christmas decorations. He finished the last entries on a report summarizing the findings he had made in the records taken from White America and Jeremiah Wallace's political group. After Dan Hunt's arrest, the FBI had subpoenaed the mayor's financial records as well. The records proved collusion between the two men to profit from a racial crisis of their own making. They had recruited thugs, like Lightning, to execute their schemes. The records had revealed payments for illegal military weapons to individuals who worked for arms companies. Payments received had proved White America's willingness to sell such weapons to anybody able to pay escalated prices.

"Dave, there's a call for you," Dorothy announced over the intercom. "He says he's Richard Christensen, the District Attorney for Minnesota."

"Put him through, please."

"Can't you and Katie stay out of trouble?" Richard chided Dave.

Dave laughed. "It would seem that we can't."

"Buddy and Mary told me quite a tale about racketeering, mob violence, weapons, and if that wasn't enough, a hurricane too."

"You talked to Buddy? I thought that he and Mary are in federal witness protection."

"They are. But being a state DA brings some privileges. FBI Agent Whitten let me talk to them on a secure line. Even so, I don't know where they are or what their new names are."

"So how are they doing?"

"Mary just said that they're somewhere warm. Her cats like the climate. Buddy is excited that the FBI offered him a consulting job. Apparently, he and Mary together can infiltrate where FBI agents have difficulty."

"Well, the Olesons broke quite a case here. The FBI has our former mayor and congressional candidate on RICO charges, plus a half-dozen henchmen who ran the extortion racket for them. They helped stop an illegal weapons operation too."

"I think you also had something to do with that."

"A lot of people played a role."

"I'm sure of that. But one thing hasn't come to light. According to Agent Whitten, FBI interviews have revealed that before the local police chief dispersed the militia of White America, an older white couple had already delayed and calmed the white supremacists down. The FBI is happy letting their Mobile police counterparts be the heroes. But would you perhaps know anything about that older couple? A tall, distinguished, gray-headed man with a petite and attractive wife about his age?"

Dave laughed. "Maybe."

"I thought so." Richard laughed himself. "Apparently even the white supremacists credit Mobile's police chief for saving their vehicles and firearms from civil forfeiture. His action made them more reasonable afterwards."

"Yeah, our African American police chief and the city's Caucasian DA are co-chairing a bi-monthly public forum on racial relations here in the Mobile area. The discussions can get a little heated, but understanding between the factions is growing."

"Progress is never easy," agreed Richard. "But Dave, this is actually an official call. I've uncovered a likely Ponzi scheme up here in Minnesota posing as an international real estate investment trust. Looks like maybe ninety million dollars have been filtered through numerous accounts. Dubious real estate transactions are recorded in Eastern Europe, especially Hungary. Could I hire your professional services? Working for the state government now, I can even afford to pay you."

"I'd be honored to work with you again, Richard."

"Can you come up next week to look at what we've subpoenaed?"

"Katie too?"

"Of course."

"We'll let you know when we expect to arrive."

"A state patrolman will pick you up at the airport. And

don't you forget that you've invited us to go fishing down your way. Buddy told me some great fishing stories."

"Anytime, Richard."

—◆—

Dave greeted Katie that night when she came home from caring for Katelyn. "Are you ready for another adventure?" He told her about Richard's phone call and offer. "Can you go with me to Minnesota next week?"

"I'd love to go to Minnesota next week. Does this also mean I'll be traveling to Budapest later?"

Dave grinned. "Could be. What about Katelyn?"

"I love my granddaughter to death. But I could use a break. We've had a pretty intense year."

Dave agreed, "We have suffered through a lot during the last twelve months. We've had a personal financial crisis when we had thought ourselves secure, your cancer, racial conflict, danger from criminals, even a hurricane, all while trying to resurrect the firm."

"A lot of good has come from our troubles though."

"Yes, it has. My learning to listen and both of us trusting God in difficult circumstances. But, like John said, maybe we'll never know all the reasons for what has happened. I'm just confident God has good reasons for everything."

Katie nodded. "Me too."

"When you're in Minnesota, what will Denyse do with Katelyn while she's teaching?"

Katie shrugged. "I don't know. Katelyn is her and Jeremy's responsibility. But Denyse has made friends with several mothers in the subdivision where they bought their house. They all help each other out."

316

"Then it's you and me, sweetheart."

Katie collected her suitcase and opened it on the bed. "All the way, dinosaur."

Authors' Note

All the characters in this novel are purely fictional and created in the imaginations of the authors. However, most of the locations and the descriptions of south Alabama are as detailed and accurate as space and our readers' attention would allow. Central High School is a composite of several high schools imagined to be within hiking distance of James M. Seals Jr. Park and Community Center. James Seals was a jazz musician and community leader in Mobile.

Drew grew up along the Florida Gulf Coast and in Alabama. His memories have been incorporated into this story. Since our first *Challenge Series* novel took place near Kit's home in Minnesota, both of our childhoods have found purpose in our writings.

Although somewhat knowledgeable about the Gulf Coast and Alabama, we had never heard the remarkable story of Mobile's Can't-Get-Away Club until our research uncovered it. That history seems a bit obscure even in local knowledge. The excerpt from the last letter of John Wesley Starr is real. It brings tears to our eyes and challenges us to greater dedication to Christ and our fellow man.

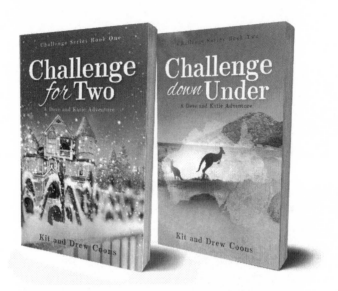

More from the Challenge Series

Challenge for Two
Challenge Series Book One

A series of difficult circumstances have forced Dave and Katie Parker into early retirement. Searching for new life and purpose, the Parkers take a wintertime job house sitting an old Victorian mansion. The picturesque river town in southeastern Minnesota is far from the climate and culture of their home near the Alabama Gulf Coast.

But dark secrets sleep in the mansion. A criminal network has ruthlessly intimidated the community since the timber baron era of the 19th century. Residents have been conditioned to look the other way.

The Parkers' questions about local history and clues they discover in the mansion bring an evil past to light and create division in the small community. While some fear the consequences of digging up the truth, others want freedom from crime and justice for victims. Faced with personal threats, the Parkers must decide how to respond for themselves and for the good of the community.

———•◦•———

Challenge Down Under
Challenge Series Book Two

Dave and Katie Parker's only son, Jeremy, is getting married in Australia. In spite of initial reservations, the Parkers discover that Denyse is perfect for Jeremy and that she's the daughter they've always wanted. But she brings with her a colorful and largely dysfunctional Aussie family. Once again Dave and Katie are fish out of water as they try to relate to a boisterous clan in a culture very different from their home in South Alabama.

After the wedding, Denyse feels heartbroken that her younger brother, Trevor, did not attend. Details emerge that lead Denyse to believe her brother may be in trouble. Impressed by his parents' sleuthing experience in Washita, Jeremy volunteers them to locate Trevor. Their search leads them on an adventure through Australia and New Zealand.

Unfortunately, others are also searching for Trevor, with far more sinister intentions. With a talent for irresponsible chicanery inherited from his family, Trevor has left a trail of trouble in his wake and has been forced into servitude. Can Dave and Katie locate him in time?

More from Kit and Drew Coons

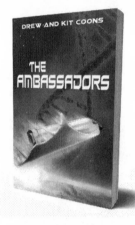

The Ambassadors

Two genetically engineered beings unexpectedly arrive on Earth. Unlike most extraterrestrials depicted in science fiction, the pair is attractive, personable, and telegenic–the perfect talk show guests. They have come to Earth as ambassadors bringing an offer of partnership in a confederation of civilizations. Technological advances are offered as part of the partnership. But humans must learn to cooperate among themselves to join.

Molly, a young reporter, and Paul, a NASA scientist, have each suffered personal tragedy and carry emotional baggage. They are asked to tutor the ambassadors in human ways and to guide them on a worldwide goodwill tour. Molly and Paul observe as the extraterrestrials commit faux pas while experiencing human culture. They struggle trying to define a romance and partnership while dealing with burdens of the past.

However, mankind finds implementing actual change difficult. Clashing value systems and conflicts among subgroups of humanity erupt. Inevitably, rather than face difficult choices, fearmongers in the media start to blame the messengers. Then an uncontrolled biological weapon previously created by a rogue country tips the world into chaos. Molly, Paul, and the others must face complex moral decisions about what being human means and the future of mankind.

What is a more than ordinary life?

Each person's life is unique and special. In that sense, there is no such thing as an ordinary life. However, many people yearn for lives more special: excitement, adventure, romance, purpose, character. Our site is dedicated to the premise that any life can be more than ordinary.

At **MoreThanOrdinaryLives.com** you will find:

- inspiring stories
- ideas and resources
- entertaining novels
- free downloads

https://morethanordinarylives.com/

more than
ORDINARY
lives
MINI SERIES

More Than Ordinary Challenges— Dealing with the Unexpected

Many heartwarming stories share about difficult situations that worked out miraculously or through iron-willed determination. The stories are useful in that they inspire hope. But sometimes life just doesn't work out the way we expected. Many people's lives will never be what they had hoped. What does a person do then? This mini book uses our personal struggle with infertility as an example.

More Than Ordinary Marriage— A Higher Level

Some might suggest that any marriage surviving in these times is more than ordinary. Unfortunately, many marriages don't last a lifetime. But by more than ordinary, we mean a marriage that goes beyond basic survival and is more than successful. This type of relationship can cause others to ask, "What makes their marriage so special?" Such marriages glorify God and represent Christ and the church well.

More Than Ordinary Faith— Why Does God Allow Suffering?

Why does God allow suffering? This is a universal question in every heart. The question is both reasonable and valid. Lack of a meaningful answer is a faith barrier for many. Shallow answers can undermine faith. Fortunately, the Bible gives clear reasons that God allows suffering. But the best time to learn about God's purposes and strengthen our faith is *before* a crisis.

More Than Ordinary Wisdom—
Stories of Faith and Folly

Jesus told story after story to communicate God's truth. Personal stories create hope and change lives by speaking to the heart. The following collection of Drew's stories is offered for your amusement and so that you can learn from his experiences. We hope these stories will motivate you to consider your own life experiences. What was God teaching you? "Let the redeemed of the Lord tell their story." (Psalm 107:2)

More Than Ordinary Abundance—
From Kit's Heart

Abundance means, "richly or plentifully supplied; ample." Kit's personal devotions in this mini book record her experiences of God's abundant goodness and offer insights into godly living. Her hope is that you will rejoice with her and marvel at God's provision in your own life. "They celebrate your abundant goodness and joyfully sing of your righteousness." (Psalm 145:7)

More Than Ordinary Choices—
Making Good Decisions

Every moment separates our lives into before and after. Some moments divide our lives into never before and always after. Many of those life-changing moments are based on the choices we make. God allows us to make choices through free will. Making good choices at those moments is for our good and ultimately reflects on God as we represent Him in this world.

Visit **https://morethanordinarylives.com/**
for more information.